THE PERILS (

Pauline bent right across the large photocopier and stretched both arms down the far side, reaching for the release lever. She didn't hear the door open behind her, nor was she aware of Jim Browne standing inside the doorway, staring in surprise at the long, golden-brown legs and the round, ripe, mini-skirted bottom that pouted up at him so invitingly.

He took a stealthy step forward. No man on earth could possibly be expected to forego such an opportunity, he assured himself as he unbuckled his belt . . .

The Perils of Pauline Peach

Alison North

Delta

First published in 1998
by HEADLINE BOOK PUBLISHING

A HEADLINE FEATURE paperback

10 9 8 7 6 5 4 3 2 1

ISBN 0 7472 5776 0

Typeset by CBS, Felixstowe, Suffolk

Printed and bound in Great Britain by
Mackays of Chatham plc, Chatham, Kent

HEADLINE BOOK PUBLISHING
A division of Hodder Headline PLC
338 Euston Road
London NW1 3BH

AUTHOR'S NOTE

Many thanks to my close friend, Pauline Peach, for her permission to relate this recent episode from her life. Girls often talk frankly to each other about this sort of thing, but I think you'll agree that Pauline has spoken even more frankly than usual.

My thanks, also, to Richard A. and Lynn for their unswerving support, Nick A. for the use of his Lambretta, and Mike B. for possessing the right sense of humour. Also to Sarah and Samantha, for looking so pretty.

Alison, 4th November 1996

Special Acknowledgment: buttocks by TT, NP and SJD.

PROLOGUE

Pauline looked absolutely stunning, a vision in virgin white, as she walked slowly down the aisle towards Michael. Her curly blonde hair was piled high on her head, with ringlets cascading over her shoulders and down her front and back. Long, golden ringlets that would have graced any fairytale princess. Undoubtedly she was one of the most gorgeous girls on earth. In addition to her expensively tailored bridal gown, which fitted snugly wherever it touched her body, and her see-through lace train, she was wearing a full-length veil and white lace gloves that ended at her elbows. Everyone in the church was thinking that she was the very epitome of beauty. The men were thinking other things as well, the cleanest of such thoughts being that Michael was an exceptionally lucky man indeed.

Pauline jerked her head back towards the front of the church and groaned inwardly. As she was halfway down the aisle, arm in arm with her father, she'd noticed Jonathon Ward sitting beside her sister's best friend, Alison. Surely Alison could have had the decency to bring along a different boyfriend today of all days! How hideously embarrassing to have him here at her wedding! It was almost two months to the day since that unfortunate episode in the beach hut. She just knew he was sitting there staring intently at her rear end as she continued along the aisle. Perhaps, after all, she should have chosen a dress that wasn't quite so tight across the hips

1

and bust? Something a little more modest might have been a bit nearer the mark. And if she were to try to control her natural wiggle, she'd probably end up tripping over the dress and falling flat on her face . . .!

She could feel herself going red as she thought about Jonathon Ward, the beach hut, and the terrible row with Michael. Nearly everyone must know all the sordid details . . . Still, now that she was finally getting married she was going to put all that sort of thing behind her once and for all. In the past she may have been rather too weak too often. But the past was most definitely the past. It wasn't going to happen again . . .

Heads were turned as virtually the whole of the male congregation gazed in approval at the spectacular swell of boobs and bottom under the taut white material of the figure-hugging gown. Necks were craned to breaking point as they followed the gracefully undulating progress of the tall, golden-haired bride towards the front of the church.

A few minutes later as Pauline was kneeling in front of the altar, she suddenly sensed that her former boyfriend, Mark Walker, was studying her closely. She could feel his eyes all over her. She'd spotted him earlier, sitting near the front of the church. And looking ever so glum, she thought to herself with a sigh. Not that he had any real reason to be, of course. He'd known all along that she wouldn't be marrying him . . . Well, not all along, she supposed, but for the last three years, at least. Even so, she was feeling really sorry for him once again – for about the hundredth time since they'd split up. Perhaps when they got to the reception, she could ask her friend Sally to cheer him up. Sally was quite good at that sort of thing, one way or another . . .

Mr Robinson had looked pretty miserable, too. She'd noticed him standing outside the church a few moments earlier. He'd promised not to come to the service, but yesterday he'd told her he wanted to catch one last glimpse before she finally tied the knot. She was feeling terribly sorry for him as well. He was taking it really badly. He'd been dreadfully depressed last night when she'd said good-bye after work. But to be truthful, he had only himself to blame. Three years ago, if he'd asked her to be his wife instead of his secretary, she'd simply have jumped at the chance. But then, of course, she'd met Michael . . . and everything had suddenly changed . . .

It was just as well she'd decided to take a different job. Now that she was getting married, there was no way that she and Mr Robinson could keep on spending their Friday afternoons as they had for the past five years or more. But she mustn't let herself think about that right now. It simply wasn't the time or the place . . .

At last the ceremony was over, the photographer was finished, and the white Rolls Royce purred smoothly to the end of its two-mile journey to the Royal Hotel, where the reception was to take place. As the Rolls came to rest outside the huge revolving doors, Pauline was surprised to notice Mark Walker's car in the hotel car park. The car that belonged to her ex-boyfriend. Why had he left the church so early, she wondered. She hoped he hadn't decided to drown his sorrows in the bar.

'I'll nip up to our room for a moment, Mikey,' she said, gazing happily into his eyes. 'Just to check on my make-up.'

'OK, Sugarpie. I'll hang on downstairs in case the first guests arrive.'

As Pauline and Michael separated in the hotel foyer, neither was aware of Mark Walker lurking in the nearby corridor, watching their movements like a hawk.

Pauline let herself into the honeymoon suite. Huge bouquets of flowers were everywhere and there was champagne in the fridge. She pulled back her veil and started dabbing carefully at her eyes in front of the dressing-table mirror, humming happily to herself. 'Mrs Pauline Peach,' she whispered aloud, trying to get used to the new name and very pleased with the way it sounded. What a lovely feeling, she thought to herself. Married and respectable at last! Married to the only man she'd ever really loved. The man who made her laugh and sing and feel just great – and incredibly turned on, too. How much she meant the wedding vows she'd just given! Every word of every one. She'd even asked the vicar to include the vow to obey, even though all her friends had told her how silly and old-fashioned it was. She was going to make Michael the best wife a man could have. She may have been just a little wayward as a fiancée, but all that sort of thing was well behind her now. And anyway, there was an enormous difference between being engaged to someone and being married to someone. A truly enormous difference . . .

Pauline heard the door click open and then shut behind her, but didn't turn round. 'I thought you were staying downstairs, Mikey,' she sang out brightly, still concentrating on her eye make-up.

'He is,' growled Mark Walker, wrapping both arms round her from behind her back and then pulling her hard against him.

'Mark!' she squealed in surprise. 'Whatever are you doing here?'

'I hope to be doing you!' he replied breathlessly, thrusting his groin firmly into the bounciness of her buttocks as he spoke. She could clearly feel the heat and urgency of his erection through the light fabric of her gown. It was like a red-hot bar of iron pressing into the cheekiest part of her bottom. Immediately she started to lubricate – an automatic reaction over which she had no control.

'Don't be silly, Mark!' she gasped, trying to wriggle free from his embrace, but only succeeding in stimulating him further. 'I'm a married woman now!'

'That's why I'm here. I asked you dozens of times to marry me, but you always said no. Then you go and get hitched to that big bugger, Michael, the first time he pops the question.'

'I love him, Mark. That's why.'

'You used to love me.'

'I used to love making love to you. There's a difference, you know.'

He ran a hand lightly over her breasts, savouring the instantaneous response of both nipples. 'Don't do that,' she whispered. Obediently, he ran the same hand down over her stomach and cupped it round her groin. 'Stop it,' she whispered again, as he started to massage her gently between the tops of her legs. She ordered her clitoris to ignore this unprovoked assault, but it positively refused to obey. She could feel the crotch of her tight little knickers becoming tighter and damper by the moment. 'Stop it, Mark,' she repeated, but all to no avail. Despite herself, she took a deep breath and closed her eyes.

'As you wouldn't marry me, Pauline, I think the least you can do is to let me be the first to have you now.'

'Of course not!' she hissed in alarm, deciding however that it was not a good idea to try to wriggle away. It seemed to add another inch to his stature each time she did so.

'Just bend over that dressing table and I'll be through with you in half a minute.'

'Don't be daft!' she squawked. 'Go away and leave me alone!'

'Not until I've done what I said. It's only right and proper.'

'It isn't at all!' she squealed indignantly. 'It's very wrong and improper, in fact.'

'It's right for me,' he insisted. 'Surely you can see my point of view? You've always been very fair like that, haven't you? Surely you can see what I mean?'

'Well . . . In a way, I suppose I can.'

'Please, Pauline!' he pleaded. 'I simply have to do it. Just bend over like I said. It won't take me very long.'

'Mark!' she panted, struggling again. 'I hope you're not really serious?' But she suspected she already knew the answer to that.

'Of course I am. Who wouldn't be with a girl like you? You said you could understand how I feel.'

'That doesn't mean I have to agree.'

'What harm could it possibly do?'

'You know perfectly well. Anyway, I've got to get back to Michael.'

'He won't miss you for another couple of minutes.'

'Mark! No! No! Let go!'

But he wasn't inclined to listen. Slowly but firmly he guided her head down towards the top of the dressing table, meeting only slightly more than half-hearted resistance. 'Stop it, Mark!' she protested, her forehead now pressed against the wooden surface and her bottom jutting up in the air. 'Supposing Michael comes in?' she gasped in alarm.

'He won't. I've turned the key in the lock. Now, just stay like that while I attend to this dress.' He stooped down to the floor behind her, intent on tackling her train and then the dress itself.

'Mark! Don't you dare! Stop that at once!!'

'Stay still, woman!' he grunted, holding out a restraining arm as she started to straighten up and brush her veil and hair away from her face. 'I told you, the door is locked.'

'But how could I explain you being in here with me?' she wailed, as her head was returned to the dressing table and her hair tumbled back in front of her eyes. She rested her forearms, gracefully encased in her elbow length gloves, on the surface as well. It was a little more comfortable that way. 'What possible excuse could I give for having you in here?'

'I'll climb out of the window,' he panted, both arms full of silk and chiffon lace, which he was desperately trying to lift above her waist. But the material in the train was so light that it kept slipping back down to the carpet whenever he reached for more.

'Mark! This is the fifth floor! And there's no fire escape!'

'I'll hide in the chimney.'

'Don't be stupid! Besides, there isn't one.'

He looked carefully round the room. 'I'll crawl under the bed,' he said at last. 'It's one of those big, old-fashioned jobs. There's plenty of room to get right underneath.'

She glanced back over her shoulder. 'I suppose that's possible,' she conceded grudgingly, after a pause.

'Great! I knew you wouldn't mind me doing what I have to do.'

'I didn't say that at all!' she yelped. 'I simply said it might be possible to hide under the bed.'

But Mark chose not to see the difference. 'This is more difficult than I thought,' he muttered, ignoring her protests as he heaped another armful of lace on to her back and held it there while he scooped up some more with his other arm. Then he repeated the process again. At last it was done and he was able to turn his attention to hauling up her tight fitting dress. 'Stop that!' she squealed, but he took no notice at all. The hem snagged round the plumpest part of her hips and he tugged at it angrily, cursing under his breath. For a moment Pauline thought that his plans might be thwarted, but suddenly he succeeded in pulling it free and she sighed in dismay. The lower half of her bridal gown was now well above her waist, and the troublesome train was piled up on her shoulders and back, leaving Pauline standing there in her stockings and skimpy silk undies. Undies of the purest white.

Still bent forward over the dressing table, but now much more exposed and vulnerable than before, Pauline closed her eyes and groaned in despair. She was being so weak. So terribly, terminally weak. She wasn't really doing anything to resist. She knew the problem, of course: the orders emanating from her heavily lubricating pussy were directly contradictory to those from her brain. And not for the first time in her life – more like the hundred and first. 'We mustn't do it, Mark!' she stammered, feeling a puff of breeze from the window wafting coolly across her near-naked, up-turned rear end.

7

But Mark was determined that they would. He took a step back to admire the breathtaking view, at the same time fumbling hurriedly with his zip in an effort to release himself into the room without any further delay. Starting from the floor, she was wearing white satin high heels and matching stockings of the sheerest silk. These stockings stretched up and up and up, almost to the tops of her long, perfectly rounded thighs. They were not held by suspenders, but by snowy-white garters comprising copious quantities of expensive handmade lace. These ultra-frilly garters, together with the white silk ribbon she'd tied round her middle, lent her the air of a fancily wrapped wedding present. A wedding present for the lucky bridegroom, consisting of that much-sought-after part of her person that lay between stocking tops and waist. A present for the bridegroom which Mark intended to prise open and plunder for himself.

The garters were, he decided, one of the most erotic sights he'd ever seen, particularly because of the pose in which they were being displayed to him. However, the most arousing sight by far was the tiniest, sauciest pair of white transparent knickers in existence, strung tightly across the prettiest pair of buttocks in the history of the female race. Big, bouncy, beautifully shaped buttocks set off so enticingly by the garters, silk knickers and ribbon that the head of his long, plum-coloured trouser snake twitched violently and turned an even deeper shade of purple as it threatened to spit its venom all over them.

Mark stared down at the seat of Pauline's superbly filled knickers. How well he knew that incredibly sexy rear end! It had been his proudest possession before Michael had appeared on the scene. The cleft between each sweetly dimpled cheek was deep and ran all the way up to her spine. The cheeks themselves resembled an inverted heart. They were plump but firm and pert, full and rounded at the bottom, then tapering upwards in perfect proportions as far as the small of her back. And he knew that the texture was impeccable, silk and cream combined. For many long seconds he gazed in awe, her scarcely knickered bottom gleaming proudly back at him as it reflected the overhead light in the centre of each pouting cheek.

So there she stood, bent right over the dressing table, the honey-sweet elixir of her loins soaking her knickers and trickling down the bare tops of her thighs. There she stood waiting for him, the fragrant perfume of a highly aroused young woman filling the air.

His penis had never been so swollen. It ached painfully as it thrust upwards from his groin, a great horn of flesh, livid red, topped with a knob so bulbous that it felt like it was about to burst. Never had he been so huge. And never could he have been more delighted that he was.

Pauline was more than ready for him. She could tell that the lips of her vagina were curled right back, spread wide in a smile of welcome, providing as wide a channel as possible for that which they knew they were about to receive.

Mark reached out at last, almost reluctantly, and slid the sopping wet panties down over her garters and all the way to her knees. There they clung to her decoratively, their duty temporarily done. Now both of them were stripped and ready . . . and Mark moved slowly in for the kill.

Pauline looked up nervously, sensing the approaching danger. Through her wedding veil she caught a glimpse of his huge, overheated cock waggling stiffly in the mirror, just inches away from her naked posterior as it pouted lewdly up at the ceiling and waited to serve its prime purpose in life. 'Oh, grief!' she gasped to herself in disbelief. 'I've only been married for about twenty minutes. Surely this can't *really* be happening to me . . .?'

But unfortunately it was, as she discovered just a few seconds later when she felt the tip of his overgrown organ starting to nose its way into her all-too-receptive quim. Further and further it crept, scalding hot and throbbing, she could tell. Pulsating with the excitement of being alive and in use. Bursting with the thrill of forcing a deeper and deeper invasion into the soft, yielding privacy of her person.

More and more he encroached, filling her and expanding her in every direction, making her gasp with his size. But still there was more to come in. Still there was more iron hard brawn for him to feed into her as he stared down at the cheeks of her bottom and forced his way home between them. She opened her mouth to groan, but found she had to struggle for breath instead. How much did he have left to provide? How much more would she be able to take? She was already full to the brim . . .!

But at last he was all the way home. Home but far from dry. At last his long, thick member was plugged into her right up to the hilt – wedged into her as far as it could go. To Pauline it seemed to have taken ages. Tears came to her eyes at the way she was being so sorely extended. Fortunately, she was as wet as ever she'd been.

She stood there, stock still and straight-legged, wincing and gasping for breath, her head and elbows resting on the dressing table, her smooth round bottom several inches higher and pressed warmly into his groin. She was no longer just Pauline Peach, she thought to herself with a sigh. More than fifty per cent of her insides must now consist of Mark . . .

She couldn't remember him ever having felt this large inside her before. In fact she couldn't remember anyone having felt this large before, not even Jonathon Ward. She supposed it was because he'd been so pent up and desperate to have her after having waited so long. In which case, he'd probably be finished quite quickly, just as he'd promised . . .?

Pauline closed her eyes as he wrapped his hands round her waist and pressed forward into the springiness of her buttocks in order to gain maximum penetration, in order to stretch her as far as he could. Already her first mini-climax was making her shiver and shake. Another one started when he began to withdraw. His end was so knobbly, she remembered. So knobbly, that when he'd been slack (which hadn't been very often) it had reminded her of a baby's arm holding an apple. The knobbliness was definitely a stimulant. It produced a sort of scouring effect inside her quim. Not that she ever needed much stimulation in there, she reflected ruefully, as he dwelt patiently just inside the point of entry, savouring the moment and making her wait for the next thrust home.

But still it didn't arrive. Still Mark was making her wait for the meat of his manhood to fill her again. At length she twisted her head and looked up at him over her shoulder. 'You said you'd be quick,' she whispered, through a faceful of hair. 'I'm supposed to be welcoming the guests . . .'

He glanced down at the shiny bare buttocks between which his penis was poised. 'Well, I'm one of the guests,' he murmured, slowly sliding his full length back inside her and making her moan with his hardness and heat. 'And I'm feeling very welcome indeed.'

Less than five minutes later Pauline heard the bedroom door bang shut behind her back. Mark was half way down the stairs, whistling tunelessly but happily to himself, whilst she remained bent right across the dressing table, red faced and bare bottomed, fighting for breath and already leaking his seed as she waited for her climax to pass. Had Michael walked into the unlocked room at that moment, he could have drawn only one conclusion.

Eventually the waves of orgasm calmed, and she straightened up slowly and gingerly. She sighed and ran her hands over her naked nether regions, as if she was trying to ascertain whether it had all been just a bad dream. She pressed the tops of her legs together . . . and instantly knew it had not.

What a fuck, Mark Walker chortled to himself. What a truly incredible fuck! He'd certainly left his mark on the blushing

11

young bride! He'd certainly given her something special with which to start off her married life. And what a poke in the eye for the groom! That so-and-so Michael! Whatever she did for him in the future, she could never undo the fact that his brand new wife had just been comprehensively dicked by somebody else. That she'd been hugely and heavily adulterated before the marriage was half an hour old . . .!

Pauline galvanised herself into action. In no time at all she was downstairs, standing beside Michael at the entrance to the ballroom and clinging to his arm as she said hello to her other guests. The hem of her wedding dress was now demurely round her feet, not lewdly round her waist, and the tiny transparent knickers were also back in place. She was trying desperately hard to hold a sensible conversation with the vicar, who kept insisting on reminding them about the sanctity of their wedding vows. But her mind was simply elsewhere. She squeezed the tops of her thighs together anxiously, and gulped. She should never have panicked, she told herself wisely. She should never have panicked after Mark Walker had come and then gone. She should definitely have spent longer in the bathroom before dashing downstairs to rejoin her husband. After all, another sixty seconds wouldn't have made any difference. Now, because of her panic, she was absolutely awash. And not only that. A huge sticky dollop of Mark Walker had just escaped the restraining influence of her knickers and was dribbling – very uncomfortably – down the inside of each thigh. It would ruin her expensive lace garters, she thought with a sigh. It was as well she'd brought some replacements . . .

'Oh, er, yes, thank you very much, vicar,' she stuttered. 'We'll certainly remember all that you've said.'

'Yes, very enlightening,' murmured Michael, staring enviously at those guests who had already made it as far as the bar.

Pauline glanced briefly to her left. Oh, no! There was still a whole row of people waiting to shake Michael's hand and kiss her on the cheek. Including Mark Walker. He must have slipped out of the back door and popped around to the front. What a terrible cheek! And how embarrassing it was going to be.

'Congratulations,' said Mark a few minutes later, shaking Michael warmly by the hand, but wishing it was by the throat. 'You look absolutely ravished!' he said as he grinned at Pauline.

'I hope you mean ravishing?' Michael asked with a laugh.

Pauline blushed and kept her legs pressed tightly together. 'He was always bottom of the class at English,' she pointed out nervously.

'Yes, that's me, Pauline,' muttered Mark, patting lightly at the rump that was still warm from his recent ministrations. 'Always at the bottom, as you know.'

'I'm sorry, Mikey!' she mumbled, blushing deeply, as Mark Walker eventually beat a path to the bar.

'Don't even think about it, Sugarpuss,' he laughed again. 'You've had lots of boyfriends and I've had lots of girls. But that's got nothing to do with the future.'

'I love you!' she cried with feeling, throwing her arms round him and kissing him hard on the lips, whilst the next guest waited patiently in line and her garters started to ruin.

CHAPTER 1

The Eternal Quadrangle

It was Wednesday morning at the office.

George Franks followed the exquisitely filled seat of her dark blue mini-skirt all the way down the corridor that led to the photocopying room, his eyes glued to the lateral swing of deliciously bouncy buttocks. Plump, pouting buttocks so pert and perfect that the merest glimpse had been known to make grown men break down and weep openly in the street. In her three-inch high heels she was exactly six feet tall. A veritable vision of blonde carnality.

'Jesus H Christ and Threequarters!' he groaned to himself. 'That husband of only a few weeks' standing is an exceptionally lucky man . . .!'

Slightly less than an hour later Pauline sat in front of her word processor in stunned disarray, staring unseeingly at the letter she'd started earlier. She groaned to herself. It had happened again! Yet another someone other than her absolute *angel* of a husband had somehow succeeded in worming his unwelcome way into her favours. And she'd only been married for just over four weeks!

How silly she'd been to go back to Jim Browne's flat last Monday! She should have known exactly what he'd be like. And how weak she'd been with him when he *had* been like she should have known he'd be like! Mind you, that didn't mean she'd had to be weak with him three more times since then! It didn't mean that just because it had happened once she'd been obliged to let it happen again the very next morning, bottoms up across his office desk. Or in the deeds depository less than three hours later. Or only a few moments ago as she'd sat on this very small, and very uncomfortable, typist's chair. It didn't mean she'd got to keep on letting him upend her whenever, wherever and howsoever he pleased. But that was the trouble when you both worked for the same firm. Try as she might, she just couldn't keep out of his way. She was always bumping into him somewhere in the building. Perhaps if she stayed in her room and kept the bolt on the door?

But Jim wasn't the sort of person to be deterred by anything like that. That was the trouble, he wouldn't take 'no' for an answer. And to be truthful, she'd never been particularly good at giving that answer. She had to admit that much to herself. It hadn't been for the want of trying, of course. It was just the way she was made. She always went out of her way not to upset other people's feelings, and often ended up regretting it later.

She'd tried explaining herself to Jim. She'd told him several times how much she loved Michael and how she wanted to stay faithful to him. But that sort of thing just didn't cut any ice with Jim Browne. He just insisted on having his way, whatever you said to him and whether you liked it or not. Really, you'd expect a little more gentility from someone who was a fully qualified solicitor and a member of such an august body as the Law Society of England and Wales! Even if he was only a junior partner in the law firm for which she worked.

Pauline stared out of the window and sighed deeply. She supposed that in the three years she'd known Michael she'd been too weak too often. She hadn't planned it that way, it had just happened. Things just seemed to have acquired the habit of getting on top of her. And those things had mostly been man-shaped . . . Now that wasn't a very nice thought

16

for a respectably married young lady. It was rather coarse and vulgar, even if she was only giggling to herself. What she'd intended to say, of course, was that unscrupulous men were always trying to take advantage of her body for their own ends . . . Well, no, she hadn't meant to put it quite that way either!

Pauline sat back in her chair. Goodness, her mind was all of a turmoil! There was no way she could get back to Mr Fennell's typing just yet. Jim Browne had simply wrecked her powers of concentration, amongst other things. Fancy that saucy so-and-so just walking into her room and demanding to see to her right there and then as she'd sat in front of her word processor! Without so much as a by-your-leave or may I? or even a thank-you afterwards. He'd just knelt down beside her, shot his hand up her short blue skirt, and taken an unshakeable grip on the side of her tiny pink frillies. Then, despite her protests and struggles, he'd drawn them right down to her knees with one long, steady tug of the arm. Well, that had really been that. There'd been only the one road to travel. Her internal juices had suddenly started to flow like a river in flood. She'd not even had time to save the file she was working on or move the huge pile of title deeds from under her desk. Now of course, those rotten deeds were spread all over the carpet and in a most awful mess. It would take her ages to put them in order again. As for herself, she was in an even worse state than the deeds. She felt just as if she'd been hit by a whirlwind, which in a way she supposed she had. Jim was such an enthusiast. Her smart blue skirt and crisp white blouse, both carefully ironed that morning, had taken a terrible pasting. Not to mention almost every conceivable part of her poor, sore person . . . Which reminded her, she'd better retrieve her knickers and pay a visit to the ladies' without further ado. Time and tide waited for no-one, as all freshly bonked young ladies were wont to discover.

After that she'd probably treat herself to a quick walk

round the block. Perhaps a little fresh air would help to restore her composure and concentration? She could always work through her lunch hour to make up for the time she'd lose. And if Jim Browne dared try to come anywhere near her, she'd hurl something really heavy right at his head . . .

Whilst Pauline was still deep in her thoughts, Tracie Trix was perched prettily on the edge of George Franks' desk, the short tight dress that she insisted on wearing, despite her husband's repeated objections, barely reaching as far as her long, nicely shaped legs. Her jet black hair was cropped short in a type of urchin cut, in spite of the fact that her husband preferred it long.

'What's the problem, George?' she asked gently. 'Why are you feeling so miserable?'

'I'm fine,' he replied unconvincingly, stirring his tea as he spoke.

'Don't give me that!' she protested hotly. 'I know you too well, remember. It's that new girl who works for Mr Fennell, isn't it? Pauline Peach?'

'I suppose it might be . . .'

'You're really smitten with her, aren't you, George? I can tell, you know. I haven't been slipping between the sheets with you for the last twelve months without learning what makes you tick.'

George sighed. 'I guess you haven't,' he mumbled apologetically.

'Don't worry about my feelings,' she giggled. 'You know what I'm like. I'll take a bit on the side whenever the opportunity arises. From you or anyone else. So you can talk about it if you want. I shan't mind.'

'You're a good girl, Tracie. A very understanding one.'

'The ideal mistress?' she giggled again.

'Yes, indeed,' he agreed, glancing at the hint of lacy black knicker material just visible below the hem of her dress.

'So what is it about this Pauline Peach?' she asked. 'Why

has she got to you like this? I mean, I know she's classically beautiful and all that. She looks like some sort of Greek goddess, I know. But you can't have them all, George. You can't have every beautiful girl in the world.'

'It's not really that . . .'

'So why are you letting her get you down? It's silly. There are plenty of other women, if she doesn't want to let you between her legs.'

'I just can't get her out of my mind, Tracie. I've tried asking her out, but she always says no. In the nicest possible way. That's part of the problem, I guess. She's such a genuinely nice sort of girl. I *like* her far too much.'

'That sounds very bad news indeed!'

'I respect her too. She says she intends to stay faithful to her husband. I think that's a wonderful thing.'

'It's certainly very unusual,' Tracie said with a knowing grin.

'I'm sure she means it,' George said defensively. 'I think that's part of the reason I find her so irresistible. I can't help admiring her for being so loyal.'

'Poor George!' she said, ruffling his hair with her hand. 'You really have got the hots for that young lady. You've got it bad.'

'I'll get over it,' he sighed.

'Have you given up on her yet?'

'Just about. If she's so fond of her husband, it wouldn't really be right for me to press the point any further.'

'How gallant!' she squealed in delight. 'But it doesn't sound much like you at all! I thought you were one of the world's worst womanisers. Or best, I suppose I ought to say.'

'I am,' he said firmly. 'It's just that this particular woman seems to have installed herself deep inside my mind. And for the moment I can't get her out. I can't think of anything else.'

'Let's drive back to your house at lunchtime,' cooed Tracie.

'That might help you feel better. You can make love to me and pretend I'm Mrs Peach.'

'Tracie! Would I do that?'

'Weren't you doing it last week?' she asked with a smirk.

'You know too much!' he muttered.

'I know a lot about men, that's certainly true.'

'Do you want a lift at lunchtime?'

'No, thanks. I'd better drive my own car. We don't want my husband wandering about the town and spotting me in yours. He's suspicious enough as it is.'

'You could always say we were going to see a client to witness his will.'

'I said that last time, if you remember. When he saw me with Jim Browne. And he wasn't overly impressed then.'

George watched Tracie skip out of the door, boobs and bottom joggling happily as she went. He sighed again. She was a very good girl indeed. Always ready to slip out of her knickers, yet never demanding or jealous. But this ravishing blonde beauty, Pauline Peach, had really got under his skin. Still, there was one consolation. At least he had the comfort of knowing that he wasn't alone in missing out on her. His wasn't the only ship foundering on that particular rock. In all honesty, that was a relief. He just couldn't bear the thought of some other bugger having her when he himself was being denied. Some bugger other than her husband, he meant to say of course. No one could reasonably object to the lucky Mr Peach exercising his conjugal rights.

George slumped back in his chair and for the hundredth time tried to visualise her lying naked in bed beside him, those long, golden ringlets spread out over her pillow, those firm, round breasts peeping out of the sheets, topped with long pointed nipples that . . .

He shook his head and reached for his cigarettes. Surely he hadn't really fallen in love with her? It was difficult to tell, because he'd never been in that unhappy state before. Girls had come and girls had gone and he'd ploughed on regardless. But there was definitely something different about the way he regarded this one. Something different and rather perplexing.

At six o'clock that evening Pauline was in the copying room, happily humming a tune to herself. The rest of the staff had gone home, but she was staying late to get up to date with her work. The large photocopier in front of her was whirring and purring contentedly as she fed page after page through its metal insides.

She gave a little skip of pleasure. She was feeling great! Really, really great! She was ever so pleased with herself. Not because she'd almost caught up with her typing, but because she'd at last shown some strength of character with Jim Browne. Halfway through the afternoon he'd come looking for his second helping of the day. Hunting her arse, he'd said. *Very* crudely indeed. But he'd been in for a big surprise, and even bigger disappointment. She'd been very firm. She'd told him in no uncertain terms that enough was more than enough and that he simply wasn't getting any more. She'd said there was no way she was going to keep on risking her marriage for the sake of letting him have his oats. What was done was done, she'd told him, and unfortunately couldn't be undone – but under no circumstances was she going to let it be done again. And that was that, she'd said. That was final and binding and all there was to it.

He hadn't been very happy, of course. But eventually he'd seen she meant business and had trooped away dejectedly, his tail between his legs and her virtue intact.

What a splendid victory it had been, she told herself proudly. She'd actually stood up to Jungle Jim and sent him packing. From now on, life at the office was going to be much easier and more comfortable. For a start, she wouldn't have to spend half her time trying to keep out of his way. She supposed she'd still find herself blushing like mad whenever she sensed him gawping at her rear end. But there was nothing she could do about that. It was just the price she'd have to pay for having let him steal a small slice . . .

Oh yes, she was really proud of the way she'd sent him off with a flea in his ear. Not to mention his penis still safely tucked away in his pants, stiff and unsatisfied. That would teach him she wasn't a piece of furniture he could manhandle whenever he chose. It was just a shame she hadn't shown such resolve from the very beginning.

For the next ten minutes Pauline's thoughts ran along these and similar lines. Then suddenly she gave a squeal of alarm and jabbed frantically at the red stop button on top of the copier. Oh rats! The rotten machine was playing up again. And this time it was the paper dispenser jamming inside. It would be ever so difficult to free it up. The release lever was almost out of reach, halfway down the side of the machine that stood against the wall.

Pauline bent right across the large photocopier and then stretched both arms down the far side, feeling blindly for the lever. She didn't hear the door open behind her, nor was she aware of Jim Browne standing inside the doorway, staring in surprise at the round, ripe, mini-skirted bottom that was pouting at him so invitingly. He took a stealthy step forward. No man on earth could possibly be expected to forego such an opportunity, he assured himself solemnly as he unbuckled his belt . . .

Five minutes later George Franks, the other junior partner in the law firm of Snayles & Co, picked up his pen and marked three pages in the law book he'd been studying carefully. He decided to visit the copying room before leaving work, in order to make the photostats he'd need at court in the morning. He'd stop at the pub on the way home, he promised himself, opening his office door. Just for a swift two pints. He'd also have a bottle of wine with his Chinese takeaway. The alcohol would help him to sleep. He was fed up with lying there, wide-awake and daydreaming about a certain young lady who insisted on staying faithful to her husband. It was lucky for her, he reflected grimly, that she had a genuine excuse. In the past, he'd been known to turn nasty with young ladies who'd thwarted his carnal desires.

George sauntered down the corridor that led to the upstairs photocopying room, a bulky volume of law reports clutched in one hand. He'd make a quick couple of copies of the case he intended to quote in court. Not that the Magistrates ever listened to legal argument, of course, but one had to be seen to be going through the motions.

He stopped in mid-stride and listened. There was a devil of a racket coming from inside the copying room. He'd thought the building was empty. After all, the office had been closed for over half an hour. Usually it was deserted within minutes. As old Fennell had once said, rather wittily, you had to be careful at 5.30 or you'd get killed in the rush to leave. So what on earth was going on? What was that hell of a din? In his new, exalted position as a partner, albeit a junior one, he supposed he ought to investigate.

Silently George slid the door back a couple of inches and peered inside. He gasped. What a sight for sore eyes! What a picture of lust! His friend and rival, lucky Jim Browne, was trouserless and mounted fido-fashion on some female, whom he was fucking for all he was worth. Some female, wearing nothing more substantial below the waist than a rather expensive-looking pair of handmade Gucci high heels. Some female who was draped, face down, across the larger of the two photocopying machines in such a way that her naked nether regions were thrust up in the air for Jim to use and abuse.

And there was certainly no lack of either. Use *or* abuse, George was thinking. Jim was giving the young lady his all. He had to admit that it was a splendid performance, even by his own high standards. And judging by her cries and gasps and groans, she would have agreed with him

23

wholeheartedly, had she been in a fit state to express an opinion.

Christ, she was exceedingly pretty in the cheekiest part of her person! Really unbelievably pretty. She had the sweetest little rear end he could ever have wished to lay eyes or hands on. He was able to ascertain that fact in the split second intervals between Jim withdrawing to his full extent and then plunging it gleefully back into her soaking wet pussy. What a glorious spectacle they made! One of sheer sexuality. And, by way of accompaniment, what music there was to his ears! The rhythmic slap, slap, slap of Jim's iron-hard stomach muscles impacting noisily on the soft bouncy cheeks of the girl's gorgeous bottom, for all the world as if the unknown recipient of his favours was being soundly spanked as well as comprehensively screwed. Which, in a way, he supposed she was.

Silently George sucked in his breath. Just who was this enthusiastic young lady who Jim was shagging so hard and fast? It was obvious that she was thoroughly enjoying herself. He'd never seen nor heard such a gratifying response. She was clearly having the time of her life. Good God! She wasn't even waiting for one orgasm to stop before she started the next! But who on earth was she? Perhaps she'd turn her face in his direction if he waited a little longer? After all, the way she was behaving there'd be no danger of her noticing him on the far side of the slightly opened door. She was far too preoccupied for that!

George blinked and grinned widely. Now here was something quite fascinating. Jim had started to torment her by drawing back past the point of entry and then loitering there, leaving her temporarily dickless and groaning with frustration. This, of course, was only serving to make her squawk even more loudly each time he deigned to shaft her again. Each fresh stroke was now being greeted with hysterical sobs of relief as she jammed her upturned rear end into his abdomen and wriggled it as hard as she could.

Ah! She'd suddenly shifted positions and turned her head towards him. Here was his chance to get a good look at her face, if he could ever see it through that tangle of hair. And if . . .

Suddenly George was an unhappy man. To put it mildly. To put it accurately, he was now seething with anger and indignation. He had finally realised that the mouth-wateringly plump bare bottom draped so obligingly over the edge of the photocopier belonged to none other than the girl who he himself had lusted after for the past three weeks. The girl, he snarled to himself, grinding his teeth, who had spurned his every attempt to get her outside her knickers. The girl who had assured him that the only reason for her persistent refusals was that she wanted to stay faithful to her husband of less than five weeks' standing. The girl who had sworn that she'd have loved to meet him one evening for a drink but for the fact that she'd married the man of her dreams. The girl who had smiled so sweetly and sincerely and told him it was nothing personal against him. Anyone else in the world would receive exactly the same response, she'd said so convincingly. The treacherous, lying little tart!

For a full two minutes George stood in the partially opened doorway, boiling with fury, mouthing obscenities to himself. His anger mounted as, with a clinical detachment, he watched his fellow junior partner porking their newest and most attractive employee with a ferocity that defied belief. And with every thrust, every gasp and squeal, every wriggle of lewd bare buttocks, George's ill humour grew more bitter. He clenched his teeth and bunched his hands into fists of rage, trembling with the sense of outrage and sheer helplessness he felt. How had he, one of the world's greatest lovers, been so duped by this two-faced little harlot? How had he allowed her to make such a fool out of him? What in God's name would Tracie make of the way he'd been taken in?

And then George was struck with a brainwave. A flash of

pure genius. Divine inspiration. An idea so simple that it took a while for him to grasp it to the full. Yes, that was clearly the answer! Yes, yes, yes indeed! That was how he could gain his revenge for the unforgivable way he'd been treated. That would certainly help to put matters right. All he had to do was nip downstairs to his office, unlock the desk, and then tiptoe back to this room armed with the means of ensuring that full retribution would be taken against this fornicating little bitch whose excuses had seemed so genuine. Against this fornicating little bitch who'd somehow managed to convince him that she'd been telling him the truth, the whole truth and nothing but the truth, when all the time she'd been letting his arch rival, Jim Browne, into her hot little hole!

But enough of that for the moment. He knew exactly how to rectify matters. He must set to work at once, without a moment's delay.

Judging her needs to perfection, Jim reduced the pace right down to a crawl, just as George Franks crept away along the corridor. Pauline turned her head and laid the side of her face on the surface of the copying machine, as if it were a pillow on which she was sleeping. Her blouse and front-fastening bra were wide open and her breasts nestled plumply in the palms of his hands. 'That's lovely!' she sighed dreamily, as he glided slowly and smoothly up the full length of her hot, soaking wet channel.

This was a beautiful bonk, she sighed to herself. A really beautiful bonk. Jim was such an expert lover. He seemed to know exactly what she wanted him to do. He seemed to know instinctively when she wanted it sharp and fast, and when she needed it long and slow. As a result, she was swooning with the pleasure of these long, slow, gentle strokes – with the way he was almost floating his penis in and out of her wide-open pussy. She could feel his hardness well enough, but it was such a sleek, slippery hardness that it made her want to cry out with delight as he slid so sweetly up to the hilt, nestled, and then eased himself all the way out. She could tell the effect it was having inside her. She was becoming wetter and more slippery by the moment. She could feel her love juices pouring out of her and running hotly down her legs.

And another thing, at this pace she could feel his dick so well. She could feel the fat, bulbous tip and the thick cord of artery that ran all the way down to his balls. It fitted her perfectly, like a hand in an elasticated glove. She could discern every ridge and wrinkle he had. Every lump and bump of his penis as it slithered lazily in and out . . .

Pauline closed her eyes and moaned softly, luxuriating in the warmth of an orgasm so slow and tender that she could scarcely believe it was true. The leisurely rhythm of the coitus had brought her to a most delightfully different form of climax. One that soothed and pampered, instead of hammering right through her. One that lasted and lasted, bringing tears of pure joy to her eyes as she squirmed her hips against him. Now Jim was motionless inside her – solid and still inside her, allowing her the freedom to work him just as she chose. 'That's unbelievable!' she gasped, as the warm waves of pleasure flowed gently up through her body. 'That's really unbelievably good!'

But soon it was time for Jim to revert to more vigorous tactics. As she continued to wriggle with satisfaction, he began to speed matters up. He looked down, watching appreciatively as his dripping wet erection slid briskly back and forth between those pouting pink cheeks. She was a truly incredible grind, he thought gleefully. And what a fantastic little honey pot! One that was as hot as Hell itself. He could feel it positively scorching the end of his prick! And it gripped him so wonderfully well! So firmly and tightly, just as if she was squeezing him in the palm of her hand. Yet it was as smooth and slick as could be. Lubricated so beautifully that it seemed to draw him in of its own accord, without any effort from him, making her impossibly easy to fuck. Making it seem that he was racing his end back and forth through hot, liquid silk. One day he really ought to get his mouth down there and taste it for himself. It was bound to be a very special treat. But at the moment it was too nice porking her like this, making her moan and groan as he watched her beautiful bare bottom joggle and bounce with every thrust of his groin.

Gently he squeezed and kneaded her breasts. The nipples were hot and sharply pointed, the breasts themselves full and firm. They were weighty in his hands, so that the nipples felt as if they were boring into his palms. Those people were wrong, he told himself wisely, who proclaimed that more than a handful was a waste. It was impossible to have too much of treasures like these. He'd never handled such magnificent boobs in his life. Last Monday, in his flat, when he'd first whipped off her front-loading bra, he'd thought he was going to ejaculate into his boxer shorts. Her breasts had sprung into the room so spectacularly. There'd been not the slightest suggestion of droop. In fact, they'd seemed to point up at him even more once he'd stripped them bare. But not only that, they were in perfect proportion to the rest of her body. They were exactly the right shape and size, with nipples that seemed to stand to permanent attention. Long, pointed nipples that cried out to be sucked, just as the girl herself absolutely screamed aloud to be fucked. Fucked in precisely this way, her bare buttocks offered up to him in total submission.

And Jim was certainly taking advantage of them. With controlled aggression he continued to slither his full length in and out of her highly receptive middle section, skating it back and forth at speed. All the way back until the knob was visible between her buttocks, then all the way forward until the root was crushed against her vaginal lips. He was producing once again the rhythmic sound of groin spanking bottom of which George Franks had earlier approved, before that gentleman had known whose bottom it was.

Once again Jim's mind wandered back to the previous Monday. What an experience it had been, he gloated dirtily. What an experience, stripping her off as she'd stood in the middle of his lounge! Pulling off her skirt and top as she'd stood there protesting that she had to go home! And yanking off her bra and goggling at those stupendous bare boobs. Those truly unbelievable bare boobs. But then, when he'd knelt on the floor in front of her and whisked down her knickers, he'd been given an even nicer surprise. The vision of her totally shaven pink pussy smiling at him in all its glory had been the most erotic sight he'd ever encountered. Completely bare and hairless it had been. Completely naked and winking at him in welcome, the pretty pink lips glistening with moisture and sweetly apart, literally right in front of his face. Apparently, she'd shaved herself as a honeymoon treat for her husband, and he'd been so smitten with it on her wedding night that she'd decided to keep herself bare. But she wasn't just bare, her plump little, pink little pussy was as smooth as a baby's bottom. It was an absolute delight to fondle and squeeze in the palm of his hand. She used some sort of special cream on it, she'd told him, after he'd finished poking it for the first time that night. Some sort of ultra-expensive cream, twice a day, which kept her not only hairless but silky smooth as well. Yes, he really must get his mouth down there and use it on her. Perhaps tomorrow, before giving her the first instalment of her daily rations?

Now bare of boobs and bottom once again, Pauline bent over the copying machine, moaning with pleasure as Jim slid in and out of her well-oiled quim. It was the second time that day he'd been inside it, but even so he was lasting longer than usual, with the result that her insides were now melting away. Melting away, yet yearning for him to implant her, for him to force feed her with Nature's own special gruel. And at long last he began to provide. She gasped with excitement as the first fierce squirt seared her insides. Once again she experienced the sensation of being a complete woman as she felt the long awaited produce of his loins gushing warmly into her womb. The delicious sensation of being a woman completely at one with the natural world as she shuddered with pleasure and submitted so willingly to the duty imposed on all womankind at the very dawn of creation. Submitting to it, subservient to it, slavishly accepting the hot male seed, whilst mounted from above and behind in the classical fashion of the animal kingdom.

A couple of minutes later Pauline bustled anxiously along the corridor that led from the ladies' toilet, hurriedly adjusting her blouse and skirt and hoping that Michael would already be preparing the dinner. He was ever so good like that, she told herself warmly. A real angel of a husband, in the kitchen as well as the bedroom. But she'd really better hurry. Once again that wretched Jim Browne had flatly refused to listen to a single solitary word of her protests and had just ploughed ahead regardless, with the result that she was now hideously late in leaving the office, as well as behind with her work. And her knickers were really uncomfortable. They were damp and the crotch was cutting right into her pussy. For obvious reasons, of course. She supposed she ought to have spent a little more time composing herself in the ladies', but time was a commodity of which she simply had none to spare. Even so, proper attention to her under-unmentionables wouldn't have taken that long.

Pauline stopped and stared into the distance. How was she ever going to be able to look her dear, sweet Michael in the eye tonight? How could she possibly face him when she'd broken her wedding vows twice in a single day? For the third day in a row? Not that it had really been her fault. Well . . . not entirely, anyway. She'd tried her best to keep Jim Browne at bay, after he'd found her alone and unprotected in the photocopying room, with the rest of the office deserted. But as she'd already found to her cost, her best was often not very good at all. But what more could she do? She couldn't alter the sort of person she was, much as she might like to do so. Neither could she help the way in which her body reacted when certain things were done to it. That was just the way she was made. She'd always been the same, ever since the very first time. It was something beyond her control. 'I undo my zip and you go off faster than a pint of shrimps in a heatwave!' Michael had once said, rather coarsely she'd thought at the time, but also rather accurately too. Oh dear! Why hadn't she been able to stay faithful to Michael? Why hadn't she been able to keep herself only unto him?

Still, that was all in the past. It would never happen again. She'd promised herself that much a few minutes ago, whilst Jim Browne had been helping her search for her knickers. How on earth they'd ended up inside that packet of deeds, she'd never begin to know. But that wasn't the point right now. She'd told herself 'never again' . . . and she'd jolly well stick to her word, even if it meant screaming for help the next time Jim tried his luck. 'Never again' was what she'd said, and never again she'd meant. *Never* again was anyone going to succeed in sliding her out of her panties – apart from her own sweet Michael, of course.

She hurried into the copying room to collect the handbag she'd left on the floor. Again she glanced at her watch. She really must get a bit of a move on. It was getting so late. Much as she'd like to nip back to the toilet, she'd simply have to wait until she got home. Then she'd be able to slip into a nice fresh pair of knickers that didn't keep reminding her of her latest fall from grace. Her latest and her last, she reminded herself severely, as she tugged at the hem of a skirt that suddenly felt rather too short.

'Good evening, Mrs Peach!' George Franks said coolly, lounging against the wall on the far side of the room.

'George!' she squealed in surprise. 'Goodness, you made me jump! I thought everyone had gone home.'

31

'I know you did,' he replied. 'I could tell that much quite easily.'

'Pardon?'

'Otherwise you'd have had the good sense to lock this door.'

'I'm sorry, I'm not with you?'

'No. That's what I'm complaining about. You were with Jim Browne, rather than me.'

'What d'you mean?' she stammered, feeling herself turning red in the face.

'Do you really need me to describe exactly what I saw happening in here only a few minutes ago?'

'Oh, no!' she groaned in dismay, holding her hands in front of her face. 'How embarrassing!'

'After all those times you assured me you only had eyes for your husband!'

'It was true . . .'

'It certainly didn't look that way while I was standing over there by the door!'

'Oh Lordy!'

'Watching you and Jim going at it like rabbits.'

'I couldn't help it, George . . .'

'Pardon?'

'It wasn't my fault.'

'Oh, I see. It was purely an accident, was it? Accidental adultery. You just happened to be bending, bare-arsed, over the photostatting machine and accidentally backed into Jim Browne? Is that how it was? What a tragic coincidence that Jim was also wandering about the office with his private parts on display!'

'There's no need to be like that.'

'But I'm angry, Mrs Peach. Very angry indeed!'

'It's nothing to do with you.'

'Oh yes it is. After all the things you said to me about wanting to stay loyal to your husband?'

'But I did want to. I mean, I do want to . . .'

'After all that,' he continued, ignoring her completely. 'After all that I walk in here and find you and Jim Browne spread out over that machine, copulating as if the world was about to end!'

'I'm sorry, George . . .'

'Yes, you certainly will be,' he said smugly, holding aloft the pride and joy of his career as an amateur photographer – his top-of-the-range Nikon Triple X camera. 'Just as soon as I develop this film!'

'Pardon?' she asked nervously, fiddling once again with the hem of her skirt.

'You remember I showed you this little beauty last week? My latest acquisition? The one which is bound to win me this year's Camera Club Premier Award? The one that can take up to fifteen shots in eight seconds, in the pitch black, soundlessly and without a flash? Each one in perfect focus?'

'Yes, I remember.'

'Well, while you and Jim were shagging each other stupid, I stood in the doorway and fired off a full thirty-six exposures of you two performing over there. The results will be fascinating for all to see, particularly for your husband. I'm sure he'll be delighted to know how his faithful little wife spends her working day!'

'George! You wouldn't! You couldn't!'

'Try me, sweetheart!' he hissed nastily. 'You'll find that I can . . . and I will.'

'But that would be an awful thing to do!'

'I'm an awful sort of person. As you're shortly going to find out.'

'Surely you don't mean it . . .?'

'I can assure you that I do.'

'But why? I've not done anything to you.'

'Have you not! How about all the garbage you've been feeding me about being in love with Michael and wanting to stay faithful to him?'

'You mean you're going to show those pictures to Michael,

33

just because I haven't let you have your way?'

'No, not just because of that. I was disappointed, of course, but I could have learned to live with it. Until I discovered it was all a tissue of lies and that Jim Browne – of all people – was being allowed the access I'd been denied.'

'Oh, crumbs!'

'I wonder what Michael will say?'

'George!' she gulped, dabbing her eyes with a hankie.

'I've got some really good shots of your face. Not that it was necessary, of course. I'm sure he knows that blushing bare bottom far too well ever to mistake it for somebody else's.'

'Please don't be so cruel!'

'And there'll be no mistaking what Jim was doing to you, either. I'm far too good a technician for that.'

'George!'

'Anyone will be able to see that it was the real thing. Anyone will be able to see how well he was giving it to you.'

'Please tell me you're only joking.'

'I'm afraid I can't,' he said quietly. 'But I suppose there could be another way out of this mess.'

'What is it?' she gasped eagerly. 'I'll do anything.'

He smiled sardonically. 'I rather thought that you might.'

'What is it, George? Tell me what you want.'

'You, of course! I want you. You and your fat little rump, sprawled right across that photocopier, exactly as you were for Jim Browne only a moment ago.'

'What!' she squawked in alarm. 'What was that you said?'

'I want you across the photocopier. I want to have you in precisely the way you've just given yourself to Jim. Every bit of you. All the way up to the top of your cunt. I want to smack my groin against that adulterous little arse exactly as he's just done!'

'Oh, no!' she groaned, refusing to believe her ears. 'Oh no, surely you can't be serious?'

'I've never been more serious in my life.'

'But it just isn't right.'

'It's no less right with me than it was with Jim.'

'Of course it is.'

'I don't see why.'

'I'm a married woman, George.'

'Are you saying that you were an unmarried woman a couple of minutes ago?'

'No.'

'So where's the difference, then?'

'It's just different, that's all.'

'I really don't see why!'

'Well, Jim and I are, I mean were, er, um . . . having a sort of a thing . . .'

'I know. That's exactly what I'm objecting to. That's exactly why I'm so peeved.'

'But there isn't any reason for you to feel that way.'

'You think not? Well, that's beside the point, because I do.'

'It's unfair,' she cried.

'Not to my mind. As far as I'm concerned, Jim has had his treat and I'm entitled to the same.'

'But no one's entitled. Except Michael . . .'

'If Jim is, I am,' he said stubbornly, refusing to so much as consider her point of view. 'And I'm bloody well going to have it! Before you're two minutes older!'

'Surely there's another way out?'

'Only one. As I've said, I can show these photos to your ever-loving Michael, first thing tomorrow morning. I know where he works. It's on my way to the office. He's bound to find them a laugh.'

'You mean it, don't you?'

'I certainly do.'

'You'd actually show those photos to Michael if I don't let you do the same as Jim?'

'Like a shot. Before you could blink your eyes.'

'That's despicable.'

35

'I agree entirely. But that's what I intend to do, if you don't come across with the goodies very quickly indeed.'

She took a deep breath and closed her eyes. 'Oh, mother!' she moaned aloud.

'I'm afraid she can't help you now. Not this time, I'm sorry to say. Now then—'

'George! There isn't time.'

But George was not disposed to listen to any further argument. Placing a hand firmly on each shoulder, he turned her round to face the copying machine. He sensed, rightly, that her initial state of outrage was gradually turning to an acceptance of her fate – a reluctant acceptance, but an acceptance nevertheless. Slowly he coaxed her forward, until she was standing directly in front of the photocopier. 'Just bend over until your head is resting on that part near the back. Just as you were for Jim. I'm sure you can remember the position you were in.'

Pauline stood stock still, staring at the top of the machine, reluctant to move a muscle, hoping it was all a bad dream. But she knew it wasn't. She knew he meant it. How she'd misjudged him! She'd always thought he was nice. Nice, and really quite fanciable. Now here he was, fully intending to take advantage of her in one of the most wicked ways she could imagine, blackmailing her into letting him have her, just minutes after Jim had done so . . .

'Bend over,' he said calmly. 'Bend forward and put your head down over there. Don't make me any angrier than I already am!'

For a while she refused to move, simply wishing that she'd be whisked away somewhere else. But then, after a pause that seemed a decade, she gave a deep sigh of resignation and placed both hands, palms down, on the work surface. 'Go on,' he ordered. 'Bend right across it just like you were before.'

Very, very slowly she began to do as he said, her long blonde hair tumbling in front of her eyes as her head moved down towards its appointed place of rest – almost the same spot it had occupied such a short while earlier. She could even see a smear of lipstick that she'd left behind. Several smears, she realised, as her face got closer and closer to the top of the machine.

'That's right!' he breathed, transferring his eyes to the delightful contours of her buttocks, now more plainly discernible than ever through the thin, tightly stretched material of her skirt. And the more she bent, the more discernible they became.

Pauline could feel his gaze all over the upturned cheeks of her bottom as she continued to bend over the top of the machine. She groaned to herself in dismay. How embarrassing! How humiliating and embarrassing! What a posture to have to achieve! Her skirt was so short she knew that the plumply filled crotch of her knickers would soon be peeping out at him. And this was all so terribly wrong. For one thing, she'd scarcely finished with Jim. She could still feel him deep inside her. In fact, come to think of it, of course, some of him *was* still deep inside her . . .

She squeezed her thighs together discreetly, and sighed. Some of him wasn't that deep at all . . .

'That's it!' George murmured appreciatively, as she rested on her elbows and then placed her forehead on the far side of the copying machine. 'That's absolutely perfect. Now stay exactly as you are, on tiptoes. I want that ruttish little rear end to be the highest part of you above the floor. You'll see why in a moment.'

He stood directly behind her, still staring at the spectacular shape of her bottom, and feeling himself growing as erect as ever he'd been. He could feel his penis forcing its way up towards his rib cage in anticipation of what lay ahead. He no longer liked this lying little trollop who'd made him look such a fool, but that didn't mean he wasn't going to fuck her every bit as well as Jim had done. Every bit, and then some more. He was going to fuck her silly. He was going to fuck her until she had no fucking left in her at all. Then he'd speed her on her way home. On her way home to hearth and hubby, wet and wiggling as she went . . . and as full of his seed as it was possible for her to be.

How much longer? Pauline asked herself. How much longer was he going to make her wait? How much longer was he going to stand there behind her, saying and doing nothing? How much longer was she going to have to suffer this very undignified pose? She supposed he was doing it deliberately. She supposed he was deliberately making her wait in order to shame and humiliate her. She could tell how angry he was. Not that he had the slightest reason, of course. But, unfortunately, he didn't seem to see it that way.

Oh, Lordy! She felt so exposed and vulnerable, bent right over this rotten machine, with her lightly clad bottom thrust up at him in such an indelicate manner. She felt rather like some naughty schoolgirl about to be caned. No respectably married young lady should have to stand like this, waiting for the dicking he had no right to insist on giving her.

How was she ever going to live with herself when it was over? How was she ever going to live with the fact that she'd let him have her so soon after Jim? And, even worse, how would she ever be able to face him in the future, armed as he'd be with the knowledge of exactly how she'd been had?

And what about her lovely Michael? Would she be able to hide her shame from him? Or would he see it in her face the moment she stepped inside the door? Oh, what a truly terrifying thought!

At last George took a step forward and cupped both hands round the cheeks of her plentiful bottom, squeezing hard and making her jump. 'It's terribly late,' she protested weakly, glancing at him over her shoulder through a tangle of curly blonde hair. 'I'm supposed to be cooking dinner for Michael and my parents.'

By way of reply George took hold of the hem of her skirt with both hands. Because of her stance, it had already ridden right up to the crease between buttocks and thighs. 'Now then, Mrs Peach!' he growled, starting to ease it even higher. 'Let me find out for myself exactly how it was for Jim. Let me join the multitude of others who've been allowed to sample these very second-hand goods.'

'George!' she made one last, desperate plea as she felt the hemline of her skirt being lifted up past the plumpest part of her bottom and exposing her to his view even more. 'It's so late! What about cooking the dinner? What about the family?'

George smiled thinly. 'Some unfeeling people might well say fuck the family!' he replied evenly, whilst at the same time gazing with approval at the flimsiest, frilliest pair of semi-transparent pink panties he'd ever had the privilege to behold. 'But not me. Oh no, I wouldn't say that. All I'd ever say,' he continued, using his right hand to take a purposeful grip on the seat of the tiny pink knickers, 'is fuck the beautiful young wife! Which is *exactly* what I intend to do now!'

And sad though it is to relate, he was entirely true to his word. No one could have complained about the exceptionally thorough and highly conscientious manner in which he kept his promise. Pauline screwed up her eyes and groaned with embarrassment as her pretty silk panties were zoomed unceremoniously down to her ankles. They were noticeably soggy from her oh-so-recent encounter with Jim Browne. A fact which did little to cool George's anger and sense of indignation. Then he stepped back and allowed himself to admire the view. To gaze long and coolly at the cheekiest little bent-over bottom he could ever have wished to see. The same little bent-over bottom from which his great friend and rival, Jim Browne, had only just disengaged.

'You lied to me!' he snarled, slapping hard at her pouting right cheek and making her shriek in protest.

'It's got nothing to do with you,' she gasped, once she'd caught her breath.

39

George glared balefully at the perfect pink hand print he'd planted across her saucily dimpled cheek. He smacked hard twice more, turning the hand print bright red and blurring the edges. The process was then repeated on her other cheek – with exactly the same result. Six more times he slapped as hard as he could across the very centre of each wildly bouncing cheek. The pain brought tears to her eyes, as well as boiling hot oil into her vagina. Now she was doubly lubricated, the residue of Jim Browne mingling with her own juices.

But still her ordeal wasn't over. *Slap! Slap! Slap!* Pauline squirmed her hips and screwed up her face in anguish. Oh! Ouch! Oww! Her poor bottom was being set alight! Why did men always want to do this to a girl? And why did it always make her quim so soaking wet? She supposed it was because she felt so utterly feminine, waiting helplessly whilst one stinging blow after another cracked down noisily across her upturned cheeks . . . Ouch! That really hurt! He'd caught her unaware, because she'd thought he'd finished.

Behind her back she could hear George unzipping his trousers, and knew that her time with him had finally arrived. It was so wrong, she said to herself once again. It was only a few short minutes ago that she'd been bending over this machine and doing it with Jim. That in itself had been wrong enough, but now, having to let in George almost immediately after . . .!

George gripped her tightly round the waist, making her wince. Then he lifted her even further forward across the photocopier, so that the top half of her body was lying on the surface, whilst her legs dangled downwards at right angles. With her toes not quite touching the floor, she lay there waiting, as open and available to him as she could possibly have been. George seemed in no hurry, so, despite herself, she darted a quick glance back, immediately glimpsing the awesome brutality of his cock as it stood stiffly up to attention just behind the cheeks of her red hot bottom. He was even bigger than Jim!

George thrust into her as roughly as he could. She was still wide open from Jim. So wide open and wet that he sank right up to the balls in less time than it takes to tell. Immediately he felt her tighten around him, gripping him greedily, almost as if she were reluctant to let him withdraw. Then she began to climax. The same climax that Jim Browne had started earlier, and which George Franks had now revived. She had no means of controlling her reactions, dearly though she would have wished to do so. With her eyes tightly shut, she wriggled her hips against his stomach and savoured his long pole of penis as it pulled her pussy from side to side. He was so rigid that she couldn't move it, however hard she tried. She was nailed to him as securely as it was possible for her to be. And, despite herself, she was loving every moment. Every moment and movement. His penis had driven everything out of her mind apart from its own bulky presence inside her.

The more Pauline wriggled, the more viciously he screwed her, making her sob and shriek, making her gasp with delight. Exactly as she'd done for Jim Browne, he reminded himself, gritting his teeth and slapping his groin into her buttocks without respite. The thought provoked him to even greater extremes, causing him to hammer into her with a brutality she found hard to abide. Another orgasm exploded inside her and she howled at the painful intensity of her spasms, bewildered as to why her body should be reacting so wantonly to such savage treatment.

One violent orgasm after another crashed through her as George continued to shaft her with all his might. She marvelled at his stamina. The minutes ticked by, yet there was no relent. In and out he thrust with a force she'd never imagined he could sustain for such a period of time. Already she'd had more cock from him than Jim Browne had given her all day. But still there was no sign of an imminent reprieve. Still yard after yard ran through her, stretching her insides

41

to capacity and ramming hard against the neck of her womb. Eventually she closed her eyes and lay still, concentrating on the way her grossly over-poked pussy was being so wonderfully misused. Worn and weary though she was becoming, the storms of orgasm continued to rage, exhausting her even more.

At last Pauline felt the first powerful ejaculation scalding her insides, and pushed back against him as hard as she could. Spurt after spurt followed at speed, flooding her in a matter of seconds, implanting just as heavily as she'd been implanted a while before. She cupped a hand over her mouth, suddenly anxious to deny him the satisfaction of hearing her squeal with pleasure.

That felt a bit better, thought George, the tip of his half erect organ still lodged inside her. But only a bit. He was still as angry as hell. So he'd fuck her again in a moment, although he had a strong suspicion that it wouldn't help all that much. Still, it would be infinitely better than not fucking her at all.

Away they went again, Pauline lying there stock still and drained of all resources, the whole of her weight born by the photocopier whilst George squelched rapidly in and out. Now she was completely passive. Now she was simply lying there semi-comatose and letting him shag her however he pleased. George stared down with interest, watching his avenging penis working back and forth between her well-spanked cheeks. The germ of an idea occurred to him. He'd think about it later, he decided. He'd think about it at home that evening, and then carefully lay his plans.

Some twenty minutes later George was finally spent, although Pauline was still draped right across the photo-copier, her nose pressed against the on/off switch on the far side, her skirt above her waist, and the frilly pink panties decorating her ankles to perfection. For the third time that evening she was brimming over with freshly shot sperm.

42

'Well, at least I've now joined the club,' he muttered, carefully wiping the tip of his slowly shrinking weapon back and forth across the middle of one highly coloured cheek. 'Although percentage-wise I don't suppose it makes much difference to the membership.'

Pauline heard the words but was far too exhausted and breathless to respond. 'You can get up now,' he told her. 'You can get up and get back into your pants.'

After quite a lengthy pause she managed to do as he'd suggested, still very short of breath, still feeling decidedly bonked. Decidedly shaky and bonked. It was an effort just to reach down for her knickers, let alone pull them up.

George leant smugly against the wall, watching her struggling with her clothes. Yes, he thought to himself vindictively, he'd certainly given the randy little wench every good reason to be so unsteady on her feet. Phase One of her rehabilitation was now complete.

CHAPTER 2

Remorse

Riddled with guilt, Pauline wrapped her arms round Michael and snuggled up closely, laying the side of her face on his shoulder. She could feel herself melting all the way into his body as he returned the embrace, but the pangs of remorse were no less. 'I'm sorry I'm late, Mikey,' she whispered. 'A couple of things, er, came up at work and I had to deal with them.'

She groaned to herself. That wasn't exactly the best way in which she could have put it! She could feel herself going red in the face once again. She must try really hard to hide how bad she felt. The very least she could do for Michael was to keep him from suspecting the truth.

'That's OK, Sugarpie,' he said cheerfully, running his hands lightly over her buttocks. 'I've got the dinner under way already.'

As he fondled her bottom with husbandly affection, she could feel George Franks' fluid spilling out of her in wave after glutinous wave. She closed her eyes and wished she could turn the clock back three days. She wished she could have Monday evening all over again. Then she'd stay at home and not go with Sally to that fashion show where they'd bumped into Jim Browne.

'I'll just have a shower,' she said after a while. 'Then I'll finish the cooking.'

'And then we can fuck,' he murmured lovingly into her ear.

She looked up, her eyes bright with the love she felt for him. 'Yes,' she said softly. 'All night long, if you like.'

Michael watched the seat of her mini-skirt swish its way sexily out of the room. He was a very lucky man, he said to himself happily. He knew it, not because everyone under the sun and their uncles had spent the last four and a half weeks telling him so until they were blue in the face, but because he'd told himself three years ago, when he'd first met her, that whoever eventually married Pauline would be the luckiest beggar ever to walk the face of the earth. He'd loved her ever since he'd first laid eyes on her at that party at Mark Walker's house. He'd promised himself faithfully that he'd do anything in his power to make her his wife, even though he'd realised at the time just how difficult that was going to be. He'd known that the competition to accompany her to the altar would be fierce.

And in the three years that had followed, his feelings towards her had grown by the minute. Of course he'd had a couple of one-night stands during that time. But that was only natural. What red-blooded man would refuse when it was offered to him on a plate? Sex was only sex, after all. It hadn't made any difference to his feelings for Pauline. There was no harm at all in a little bit on the side – provided you didn't get found out, of course.

Oh, yes. He was an extremely lucky man. He'd beaten off the challenge from the rest of the world and won the race by means that had been both fair and foul. But he could still hardly believe it. Had Pauline changed her mind at the altar, he wouldn't have been surprised. Devastated perhaps, but not particularly surprised. He'd programmed himself to acknowledge the possibility that some third party might still pip him to the post . . .

Michael sat down in front of the television and lit a

cigarette. Mind you, he continued to himself, it would be daft to think that the competition for her favours would slacken just because she was now married. If anything, it would probably increase. After all, married women were considered even fairer game than fiancées, as he himself should know. He'd had his moments, just as he was sure that Pauline had had hers. So he had to be realistic about her, and being realistic it was too much to expect that never again was anyone else going to succeed in prising her out of her panties. He knew he could trust her to do her best to stay safely inside them, but sooner or later someone was going to slip under her guard and catch her when her defences, or whatever, were down. It was a sad fact of life. If you had a really beautiful wife or girlfriend, the whole of the rest of the adult male world was continuously beating a path to her door. That was the price you had to pay. And Pauline was only human. Well, to be honest, she was very human indeed. Sometime, somehow, someone was going to get lucky. He had to accept that fact. He just hoped that when it happened he wouldn't get to know of it. That he wouldn't have to hear about it in the way that he'd learned about her and Jonathon Ward in that bloody beach hut two months ago . . .!

By God, he'd seen red after that! The knowledge that that repulsive little reptile had succeeded in getting his leg over Pauline had really made his blood boil. Laying Jonathon Ward on his back with a good right hook had made him feel fractionally better. And then spanking the blazes out of Pauline's beautiful bare bottom had helped him even more . . .

Oh, yes indeed. He was an extraordinarily lucky man. But until that bust-up two months ago over Jonathon Ward he hadn't really appreciated just how lucky he was. Then, confronted with the prospect of life without her, he'd suddenly found himself terrified beyond belief. Still, that was all in the past. They'd got over it. In fact, their relationship

47

had emerged from the trouble untarnished and stronger than ever. He just wished it had been someone other than that terminal tit, Jonathon Ward.

Pauline stood in the shower, tall and naked, enjoying the thought of the piping hot water washing away the final physical traces of Jim Browne and George Franks. A few minutes earlier she'd buried her soaking wet panties at the very bottom of the dirty linen basket, underneath a bath towel and beside two other pairs of sperm encrusted knickers – one from yesterday and the other from the day before. She groaned to herself at the further stab of guilt that raced through her as she thought of the three pairs of knickers now grouped together in the basket, a flimsy silk and nylon reminder of her three days of infidelity.

But things weren't always as bad as they seemed, she said to herself. That time eighteen months ago when she'd felt so guilty had produced a truly wonderful result in the end. It had been a couple of days before Christmas, she remembered. She'd been feeling dreadfully guilty about the ease with which that cheeky Eric Crowther had been able to slide her out of her knickers at the office party the night before. But as it had turned out it had been a blessing that she hadn't repelled his advances. If nothing untoward had happened at the party then, just possibly, she might never have married Michael. It was strange when you thought about it. Fate, and all that sort of thing. If she hadn't been feeling so guilty about Eric Crowther, she might never have said 'yes' to her lovely Michael just the very next night. 'Yes' to his proposal of marriage, she meant, not to the other kind. She'd previously said 'yes' to that more times than she could possibly recall . . .

She could remember exactly what had happened. The evening after the party she and Michael had been in the back of his car in their usual place, down the lane behind the rugby club, having just had a really nice bonk. She could remember it vividly. She'd been wearing nothing but her bra at the time, and even that she'd been struggling (and failing) to fasten at the front. It had been one of her usual 'front loaders', as Michael always called them.

'Why don't we get married, Sugarpuss?' Michael had said. All of a sudden. Just like that. Right out of the blue. Or rather, right out of the dark of the night. Anyway, rather unexpectedly.

Earlier that week both Mark Walker and Clive Calver had again been pestering her to get engaged, and of course she'd given them the usual answer, in the nicest possible way. But Michael had never even hinted that marriage might be on his mind. It had come as a complete shock to her. And added to the element of surprise had been the fact that she'd been feeling really dreadful about what had happened at the office party the night before. In fact, at the very moment that Michael had popped the question, she'd been telling herself how badly she'd behaved.

'Yes, of course, Mikey!' she'd cried, without so much as a thought. 'Of course we ought to get married!'

Well, that had simply been that. After all the proposals she'd had, and refused, she'd finally said 'yes', without pausing for even a second. She'd accepted him on the spot. Bang! Just like that.

Michael had been ecstatic. He'd fallen on her at once, even though they'd only just finished. He'd snapped open her bra the very same second she'd finally managed to fix it. He'd fallen on her and started all over again, as if his life had depended upon it. And she'd responded in exactly the same way. She could remember how blissfully happy she'd felt as he'd bounced her wildly about the back seat, his re-erected penis threatening to split her in half. She'd suddenly realised just how much she'd always wanted to marry him. It had come as a complete revelation. She'd never consciously considered the prospect until then. But all at once she'd known that marrying Michael was the only thing she'd always wanted to do.

Pauline directed the shower water over her smoothly shaven pubic area, luxuriating in the warm pleasure that it provided. That was how she'd arrived at the best decision she'd ever made in her life. So, as it had transpired, her little misadventure with Eric Crowther had resulted in something really good. She took a deep breath and sighed heavily. If only she could convince herself that her present misdemeanours would bear a similar result!

Pauline heard Michael tapping on the bathroom door. 'Do you fancy sharing that shower, Mrs Peach?' he called.

'Of course,' she replied at once.

They stood facing each other, pressed lightly together, hands on each other's buttocks as the water splashed all over them. In bare feet she was at least five inches shorter than Michael and had to stand on tiptoe to kiss him, his handsome erection nestling solidly against her stomach, her nipples poking stiffly into his chest. She sank to her knees and took him into her mouth. His cock was exactly the perfect size, she thought to herself, as she swallowed him all the way down to the hilt. Exactly long enough and thick enough to give her all the pleasure she could possibly want, but without any of the discomfort that a really overgrown weapon could cause. And it was such a lovely shape. Long and straight and precisely in proportion. Sometimes, in bed, she'd just lie there and gaze at it for ages, without so much as taking it in her hands. Then she'd lean over and spend even longer kissing and licking it with her tongue, and his heavy round testicles as well. She could make him come like that – just licking, not sucking. She could lick and lick and lick and then open her mouth and let him squirt inside. It was such a wonderful feeling, bringing him off in that way. Making him spurt with the very minimum of contact between them, and then savouring every drop of his hot salty come as she swallowed as fast as she could . . .

Michael could feel that her lovely mouth was bringing

him to the brink. He reached down and eased her back to her feet. Then he turned her away from him so that she was facing the side of the shower. Understanding precisely what he wanted, she leant forward, placing her hands on the tiled wall and poking her bottom out and up at him in a highly provocative manner. She'd already decided to blame the heat of the shower, should he notice how she'd been spanked. As he slithered smoothly inside, she was struck with yet another agonizing pang of conscience. He was the third that evening, she sighed to herself in despair. The third man that evening to enter her from behind. The third to make full use of the plumpness of her buttocks and the receptiveness of her quim. How on earth had all of this happened? How had she allowed herself to get into this situation, when she knew for certain that her lovely Michael was all she could possibly need? How was it possible for her to be standing here making love to him whilst at the same time tortured with the knowledge that less than half an hour earlier she'd been plugged full of another man? How in Heaven's name had she let it all happen?

Michael pressed forward against her luscious bare bottom and started to climax. 'That's wonderful, Mikey!' she whispered truthfully, knowing that the shower water would readily disguise the tears that had started to roll down her face.

CHAPTER 3

Mr Harris And The Smooth Machine

Pauline arrived at the office bright and early next morning, looking as gorgeous as ever. Her curly blonde hair twisted and twined almost all the way down to her waist, and her pale pink summer dress revealed acres of smooth, round thighs that had been tanned to a light golden brown during her honeymoon in Majorca. It was an all-over tan, thanks to her assiduous use of a thong and nothing else except nail polish and suntan lotion. The stretch of sandy beach outside her hotel had been noticeably less popular after she'd boarded the jet home.

She glanced at her watch as she let herself in the back door. She was nice and early. There was plenty of time to finish yesterday's photocopying work, she told herself happily. The work that had been so rudely interrupted, first by Jim Browne and then by George Franks almost immediately afterwards. And she'd even be able to type her outstanding letters, before making a start on Mr Fennell's filing.

Heavens, she was feeling better today! Much better than when she'd finally left the building yesterday evening awash with semen. She'd been able to come to terms with herself during the wee small hours of the night. First of all she'd been really passionate with Michael. Really, really passionate. It was the first time she'd ever known him beg her to let him get to sleep, so that was a bit of a record in itself. Then she'd lain awake beside him for ages, listening to the sound of his breathing and turning matters over in her mind.

Eventually she'd finally accepted that she'd had no alternative but to succumb to that awful George Franks. No other course of action had been open to her. She'd been wickedly blackmailed into letting him have her. That being so, she'd told herself carefully in bed, it could hardly be counted against her. Which of course meant, in turn, that she hadn't actually broken the earlier promise she'd made to herself. Her promise that never again would anyone other then Michael be allowed to get her outside her knickers. Since she'd been given no choice in the matter, how could anyone say she'd failed to keep faith with herself? George Franks may have breached her defences (or whatever), but he hadn't broken her spirit, or her resolve to put such matters behind her once and for all. In future, she'd turn her back on the likes of Jim and George. Well . . . not literally, of course. That could be fraught with danger, as witness yesterday's experience . . .

Pauline skipped lightly up the stairs, feeling good. She'd spent hours lying awake last night, thinking everything through. Now, as a result, she was completely at peace with herself. The photocopying room, which she was just about to enter, would hold no horrors for her now. Nor would that huge QX2DL copying machine, across which she'd been lain and then extensively laid, by two men, one after the other. There it was now, standing in the corner, just an ordinary copying machine once more, no longer a vehicle enabling Jim and then George to bonk her into oblivion.

She stopped in her tracks. What was that large red notice doing on top of the machine? 'Warning!' it said. 'Out of order. Do not use.' And then below that it continued, 'Mrs Peach, please see Mr Harris ASAP today. Signed, J Harris.'

Whatever was all that about? The machine had been working perfectly last time she'd used it. Last time she'd used it to take photocopies, she supposed she ought to say. She'd managed to press the release button and successfully free the paper the very second that Jim Browne had suddenly seized her from behind and then forced his red hot dick right between the tops of her thighs, turning her insides to water and making her wretchedly wanton pussy throb and gush with oil. Surely the copier hadn't been damaged during the course of all that had followed? She knew it was getting a bit long in the tooth, but it was still hale and hearty and robust enough to withstand that sort of thing. At least, she hoped it was . . .

So why did Mr Harris want to see her? She knew he was the partner in charge of the photocopying room, but why did he want to see *her*? She realised she'd been the last one to use the machine. She'd been copying a couple of commercial leases when Jim Browne had found her and fallen so heavily upon her. But of course Mr Harris wouldn't know about that. About the fact she'd been copying leases, that was, not about Jim Browne falling upon her – obviously he'd know nothing about that. So why had Mr Harris put this notice on the machine? It was all rather mysterious . . .

Pauline checked her hair and make-up. Not that she minded having to contact Mr Harris, she said to herself with a smile. He was ever such a nice man. And very fanciable too, in a tall, rugged sort of a way. Or perhaps she should say that she might have found him so, had she not been a respectably married young lady. He was one of the 'senior' partners in the firm. Not like those two louts, Jim and George. Mr Harris was a full equity partner, which meant he received a share of the profits, not just a salary from the firm. That's what was meant by the expression 'senior partner'. It had nothing to do with his age. In fact Mr Harris was only three or four years older than the louts, Jim and George. He was in his early thirties, she'd imagine. And ever so hunky and nice, as she'd already said to herself. A tall, broad hunk of beefcake, even taller than Michael . . .

'You wanted to see me, Mr Harris?'

'Yes, do come in Mrs Peach. I mean, Pauline. You don't mind if I call you that?'

'Of course not, Mr Harris.'

'I always think it's friendlier to call the girls by their Christian names. It creates a more relaxed atmosphere in the office.'

'Yes, I quite agree.'

'So how are you settling down after four weeks with us, Pauline?'

'I'm fine, thank you, Mr Harris.'

'Getting on well with the other secretaries, are you?'

'Oh, yes. I knew several of them before I came here. From my previous job with Mr Robinson.'

'Ah, yes. John Robinson, of course. I know him well. We often play squash together. You worked for him for quite a long while, I believe?'

'Five years, actually.'

'Was it really? I expect he was sad to see you go?'

She tried hard not to blush. 'I just felt I needed a change. Once I was married, I mean . . .'

Mr Harris knew just what she meant. Men talked amongst themselves all the time about that sort of thing. Secretary-shagging and so forth. 'Yes, quite so. You're doing the same sort of work here for Mr Fennell, are you? As you did for John, I mean?'

'Yes, Mr Harris. Domestic conveyancing and commercial leases. That was mainly Mr Robinson's workload as well.'

'So you're a highly experienced young lady?'

'Sort of, I suppose . . .'

'And I understand that quite recently you've acquired an altogether new and enthusiastic interest in certain aspects of our office equipment?'

'Pardon, Mr Harris?'

'In our photocopying equipment, to be more precise.'

'Pardon?'

'I'm given to understand that you've developed a very

56

close interest in our photocopying machines. The large QX2DL in particular.'

'I'm afraid I don't quite follow you . . .'

'I understand you've been working on it very recently, Pauline? Slaving away on it, in fact? With great energy and enthusiasm, I'm led to believe.'

She swallowed hard and stared at Mr Harris. Surely she couldn't be hearing what she thought she was hearing? Surely she couldn't? And if by some chance she could, then surely it couldn't have the meaning she thought . . .?

She smiled to herself. Yes, that was the answer, of course. Either she'd misheard or misunderstood him. After all, he was still smiling and acting in the most charming manner imaginable. So he couldn't possibly have been referring to last night's unfortunate sequence of events in the copying room. Phew, what a relief! Just for a moment she'd thought that George Franks must have been spilling the beans about yesterday's candid camera session . . .

'The problem is, Pauline,' he continued easily, 'that the old 2DL has simply conked out at long last. Just years of wear and tear, I have no doubt. It certainly doesn't owe us anything, after all. We've had far more service out of it than we could ever have reasonably expected.'

'I see, Mr Harris.'

'But be that as it may, the machine has finally gone home to meet its maker. It has ceased to be. But, as I've said, it was way past its normal lease of life. I imagine that some minor knock or mishap has finally pushed it over the brink.'

'Yes, Mr Harris . . .'

'So I was wondering whether you'd care to help me choose its successor? In view of your close involvement with the now defunct machine?'

'. . . Er, yes, of course, Mr Harris. If you think I can be of assistance.'

'I'm sure you can, Pauline. After all, you've years of experience of this sort of thing. Working for John Robinson for so long, I mean. Beavering away on this kind of machine.'

She blinked momentarily. Crikey, she hoped Mr Harris wasn't telepathic! She hoped he hadn't been able to look right into her mind and read exactly how she and Mr Robinson had spent well over an hour last Christmas! Fortunately for Mr Robinson and the profitability of his practice, his machine had continued to function normally, despite the undue stress and strain of a really energetic dicking.

'Come and have a look at these,' said Mr Harris, guiding her by the arm to a large table beside the window. 'I'm sure you'll find them interesting.'

'Goodness! she murmured, gazing at the vast array of glossy brochures, pamphlets and price sheets stacked along the far side of the table. 'I never realised there were so many different types of photocopying machines.'

'There are hundreds on the market,' he replied, taking up a position behind and to her left. 'I suggest you start with that one over there. It has so many new functions you'd hardly credit it.'

Pauline leant forward to read the brochure, which lay open at its centre pages. 'It's a colour copier, of course,' he explained. 'Very useful for plans on title deeds, I should imagine?'

'Yes, very useful,' she agreed, absorbed in her research. 'It's always difficult to colour them up properly on a black and white copy. Particularly the edging.'

'Just as I thought. Now then, perhaps you'd take a look at the one to its left. That's right, the new Philips PITS100. It's less expensive, but according to the literature it does exactly the same job.'

'I can see,' she murmured thoughtfully, leaning further forward to read the small print at the foot of the page.

'You'd find it refreshingly different, I'm sure. Working on something like that, as opposed to the old QX2DL that's now deceased.'

Pauline had been about to agree when suddenly she stiffened and closed her mouth without uttering a word in reply. Whatever was going on? What on earth was happening to her? Whilst Mr Harris was continuing to talk breezily about the PITS100, his right hand had snaked out behind her and was now fiddling absentmindedly with the zip on the back of her dress! Did he realise what his hand was doing? Or was it acting of its own accord? After all, he was still carrying on a perfectly normal conversation about the pros and cons of the new Philips machine.

Surely this couldn't have anything to do with what she'd thought he might have been implying a moment earlier? About Jim and George and last night's blatant misuse of the QX2DL? No, no. That couldn't be the case. She was certain that this was just some totally unintentional mannerism caused by the fact that he was so engrossed in the subject they were discussing. Any moment now he'd realise what he was doing and apologise profusely . . .

But maybe he wouldn't! Maybe she was wrong! Slowly but ever so surely he'd succeeded in running the zip all the way down from the nape of her neck to well below the small of her back. Lordy, how embarrassing! And he was still chatting away just as if absolutely nothing untoward had happened . . .

'So there we have it, Pauline,' he said, letting go of the zip and returning his hand to his pocket. 'Two excellent colour copiers, one considerably cheaper than the other. It makes me suspect that there must be some sort of a catch with the Philips. You only get what you pay for, after all.'

Pauline shivered. Oh dear! This wasn't very good at all. It didn't bode too well, to say the least. And it was a trifle uncomfortable too. The draught from the window was really rather chilly on her back. Perhaps she could ask him to close it? The trouble lay in the design of her light summer dress. It was one of those that fitted quite snugly all the way down to the cheeks of her bottom and then flared out in an A to finish a mere three inches below the crotch of her knickers. Consequently the zip was long and only ended when it was almost down to the cheekiest part of her bottom, which meant that she was now somewhat exposed to the unseasonably cool breeze that was billowing gently around her. Should she say something to Mr Harris? Should she ask him to close the window? Or should she try to behave as if everything was perfectly normal? Perhaps he really was unaware of what his right hand had recently undone . . .?

'Don't you agree with me there?' he asked eagerly.

'Oh, um,' she stammered, completely ignorant as to the nature of the question. 'Well . . . Yes, I suppose I do . . .'

'You don't think that the fast forward/return facility is all that important?'

'Well, probably it isn't . . .'

'Nor the twin toning feature?'

'No, not that either . . . I think . . .'

'Excellent!' he murmured, adjusting his stance so that he was able to ease the shoulders of the dress down over her arms and then allow the top half of it to slide right down to the plumpest part of her hips. 'I felt sure you'd feel that way. Now, perhaps you could run your eye over those three rather different models illustrated just there.'

'The ones at the back?' she only just managed to gulp. She glanced nervously down at her frothy black bra, and blushed. The lacy little scrap of nonsense was struggling heroically to contain all that she had to offer, but there was no mistaking the bulbous outline of nipples instantly erect. She sighed heavily. Now it was very difficult to convince herself that there was any real doubt about Mr Harris's state of awareness. 'Those ones over there?' she asked faintly.

'Yes, that's right. Just have a quick look at those.'

As Pauline leant even further forward over the table top, Mr Harris gave a deft twist and tweak to the back of her dress, with the result that it fluttered gracefully down to her ankles in sad, silent surrender. She stared after it and groaned

60

to herself in despair. She'd been right all along. George Franks was behind this for sure . . .

'Excuse me,' Mr Harris said politely, stooping to retrieve the fallen garment from the carpet.

'Oh,' she mumbled unhappily, stepping out of the dress as daintily and demurely as her scantily clad circumstances would allow.

Red-faced, she turned back to the table, studiously avoiding his eyes. It would be nice, Mr Harris reflected briefly, if tiny black knickers and matching bra, plus a pair of high heels, could become the compulsory office uniform. It would certainly brighten the working day . . . Jesus! What an incredible body! What a truly incredible body . . .!

'I'm particularly interested in that model. The one with automatic feed-in and reverse,' he continued, carefully folding the dress over the back of a nearby chair, before reaching up to shut the window. 'Do you feel it has some potential?'

'Possibly, Mr Harris,' she said weakly, closing her eyes in the hope that it was all a very bad dream. For the second time in less than twenty-four hours.

'Yet I wonder if auto reverse is really that important?'

'Maybe it isn't, Mr Harris . . .'

'You can see from the brochure to the left that the high speed auto tuning is one of the main features there?'

'Yes, Mr Harris.'

'Turn to the next page and you'll be able to read how it compares to the WW4.'

'Yes, Mr Harris,' she sighed, having to bend right across the table to do as he suggested.

'If you study those four main functions carefully, I think you'll see what I mean.'

'Yes, Mr Harris . . .'

Pauline sighed to herself once again. Oh dear! How embarrassing! How awful having to stand here in front of Mr Harris trying to make sense of literally hundreds of pages of extremely confusing diagrams and print, whilst all the time wearing nothing but the very skimpiest undies imaginable! She was blushing as bright as a beetroot at the thought of the spectacle she made. Her fully committed bra was one of her usual little half-cup extravagances. She supposed the frilly little thing just about did its job. It just about covered her nipples, but certainly no more than that. But as for her knickers, for all the good they did they might as well not exist at all! They were one of those tiny little pairs you could roll up and fit in a matchbox . . . and still have room for the matches. With the result that at least ninety-five percent of her bottom was well and truly outside them! Why, oh why, couldn't she have been wearing decent, respectable underthings, just for today?

Oh, mother! She'd suddenly been struck by a really terrible thought. The knickers in question were those naughty little black ones that that cheeky Eric Crowther had bought her for her birthday two years ago. The frothy bikini knickers with the words 'Kiss-Kiss' right across the middle of the seat. Whatever would Mr Harris be thinking of her, bent over this table and displaying such a saucy message for all the world to see? Well, for Mr Harris to see. She hoped they didn't inflame him in the same way they had that awful Tim Reynolds during her engagement party eighteen months ago!

But she'd better forget all about that and concentrate on the matter in hand. Mr Harris was still talking animatedly about all these complicated pamphlets and brochures . . .

'Now take a peek at the prize of this collection,' he urged eagerly.

'Which one is that, Mr Harris . . .?'

'There. The latest model from Tachiti. The updated version of our old photocopier. The brand new QX4DL. It's an absolute gem of a machine!'

'It does look rather interesting,' she mused, slowly turning the pages of the largest, brightest brochure on the table. 'Crumbs, look at this! Double speed auto feed-out! That's a good idea, isn't it?'

'Just read the full specification on the back, Pauline.'

She did as he advised. 'I've never seen so many extra features and functions,' she enthused, having momentarily forgotten her unhappy state of undress. 'But there must be a really long waiting list for all these new machines? Particularly the QX4DL?'

'There is. That's the trouble. And I can't even place a preliminary order until I've worked out which of all these models is best for the firm.'

'Well, you'd better get to the bottom of it right away,' she suggested over her shoulder, still absorbed in the brochure she was studying.

Mr Harris gazed down at the highly erotic sight of her not quite naked cheeks. 'I believe you're probably right,' he breathed slowly, staring intently at the seat of the filmy black panties. Carefully he hooked one large thumb right round each frilly piece of side elastic. 'I have to admit that the thought had already occurred to me. To the bottom it shall be!'

'Mr Harris!' she squeaked nervously. 'I meant—'

'I'm glad you understand my point of view.'

Oh dear! She wasn't too sure about that. But she certainly understood all about the *view* he had at that precise moment in time. She understood it only too well. Not to mention the even fuller view he seemed intent on achieving any second now . . .

Slowly Mr Harris slid the palms of his hands down the outside of silky hips and thighs, until the skimpy little garment was drawn, inexorably, several inches in the direction of the floor. She screwed up her eyes and tried to think about something else. Anything else at all, apart from the spectacle of her totally bare bottom pouting up at him so cheekily.

Thrusting both hands deep into his trouser pockets, Mr Harris allowed himself to admire the way in which he'd left the lacy black knickers clinging prettily across the tops of her thighs, just an inch or so below the most delightfully dimpled pair of buttocks he could ever have wished to unveil. Buttocks so slippery smooth and immaculate that in the glare of light from the window they glistened and shone like highly polished porcelain. Big, bare buttocks so excruciatingly impudent in their sheer and utter perfection that they sucked his breath away.

Mr Harris stood stock still, his head cocked to one side as he absorbed the vision of carnal beauty that shimmered before his eyes. Never in his wettest dreams had he encountered such a beautiful bottom. Never had he encountered buttocks of such quality and calibre. Buttocks, he pondered thoughtfully, that must have afforded her lucky husband untold pleasures and delights ever since the day he'd first unwrapped them and taken possession. Buttocks that had since been sampled and enjoyed by others as well. Others such as Jim Browne and George Franks, for instance. Both had taken their fill. Both had gorged greedily upon them just a few short hours ago . . .

Big, bouncy buttocks, Mr Harris gloated silently. Big, beautifully shaped buttocks into which you could ram your groin with all your force and experience the ultimate in sexual luxury as they squashed around and about you.

Big, bouncy, beautifully ripe buttocks that squashed and squelched delectably around your stomach and groin, whilst you jammed yourself into the tight little pussy nestling between them and stretched it as far as it would go. Buttocks so steeped in recent adultery that its stigma was almost a physical thing . . .

Pauline could feel his eyes on her as surely as if he'd been running his hands back and forth over the cheeks of her bottom. Suddenly a nasty thought flitted into her mind. How embarrassing if he were standing there staring at her bare bottom and trying to visualise just how it had been mounted in the copying room last night! Mounted by two men, one almost directly after the other. What a truly awful thought! She'd better try very hard to persuade herself that Mr Harris simply wasn't that sort of a man . . .

But nearly all men were like that, she argued silently with herself. Nearly all men would look at a girl and wonder what it would be like to have her, or how it had been when they knew that someone else had recently done so. That was just how they were made. Girls, on the other hand, were so much more refined in their thoughts. They wondered about such things as what sort of a car a man drove, or what he did for a living, and waited until they found out for themselves what he was like when he'd discarded his boxers . . .

Mr Harris continued to stare at Pauline's plump, pouting cheeks. And he continued to speculate. Had anyone ever shagged that incredibly beautiful bottom? It was such an inviting shape that he wouldn't be at all surprised to learn that someone had insisted on fucking her in there. He had no way of knowing that the very pair of knickers he'd just lowered had provoked such a demand from Tim Reynolds almost a year and a half before.

After a pause of at least another two minutes, Mr Harris coughed discreetly into his hand and decided he could trust to the semi-normality of his voice. 'Yes, well, er, that's certainly one feature that, um, appears to be entirely satisfactory,' he mumbled rather thickly, his eyes still riveted to the smooth, oval cheeks. 'The triple-speed feedout, I mean, of course.'

'Of course,' she said to herself somewhat ruefully.

He tapped the brochure that lay open in front of her with a long, thick forefinger. 'The question is whether or not the firm ought to be looking at this sort of extra expense. That's what I have to decide. What are your views on that?'

Pauline took a deep breath and counted slowly to three. After all, she told herself bravely, she had nothing at all to be ashamed about. She was aware that her bottom was quite pretty, and it most certainly wasn't her fault that it was now so bare. 'Well . . . er . . . I suppose you've got to make up your mind whether the machine is value for money . . .?'

'That's it, Pauline!' he cried loudly. 'Thank you! Thank you indeed!'

'Oh . . .?'

'The QX4DL,' he informed her, leaning over her shoulder and tapping the glossy illustration of that particular model. 'It's very pricey, but that machine represents remarkably good value for money. There is no doubt in my mind about that.'

'Oh, good,' she murmured rather half-heartedly.

'And, as you say, value for money is what matters. Value for money, that's the bottom line . . . And so is this, of course. And an exceptionally pretty one it is too.'

'Thank you, Mr Harris . . .'

'It seems to go on for miles,' he breathed, poking a fingertip gently into the ample cleft. 'I just love the way it runs from here all the way up to here. And then, of course, all the way back down to here again.'

'Oow! *Mister* Harris!'

'But enough of that for the moment. It's decision time at last. And thanks to you I think I know what my decision will be.'

'Oh, yes . . .?'

He moved to his left, so that he was standing beside but still behind her. 'The QX4DL,' he said happily.

'Yes, Mr Harris,' she sighed, before realising that she must have sounded more than a little uninterested. 'That's nice,' she added politely.

'The QX4DL. You've all but convinced me that it's the one for us.'

'Oh, good . . .'

'Yes, here is a very smooth machine,' he enthused, once again tapping the brochure with his large left hand, but at the same time no longer able to resist the temptation of using his right hand, none too gently, to seize a handful of her bare, blushing and cruelly over-exposed nether regions. As he did so, one giant fingertip pushed a good inch or so into her bottom, inadvertently or otherwise.

'OH!!' she squawked loudly, taken completely unawares.

'Ye gods!' Mr Harris murmured in surprise and delight. 'Unbelievably smooth, in fact!' He started to squeeze rather firmly. 'Exceptionally smooth,' he purred. 'Very, very exceptionally so! The smoothest machine in the land, without a shadow of a doubt.'

Mr Harris drew a deep breath and closed his eyes, feeling his penis stretching itself even further as he continued to knead both buttery smooth cheeks together in the same gargantuan grip, vigorously and with ever-increasing enthusiasm. As he did so, his fingertip encroached even further.

'Ow! Ouch!' she gasped, as Mr Harris' right hand persisted with the extensive exploration of her bottom and the other tapped away at a photograph of the QX4DL.

'Indeed, the smoothest machine in the history of creation!'

Pauline squawked and then grimaced. Oh, mother! What a meal he was making of her poor, unprotected posterior! She'd be black and blue if this continued much longer. This slow, deep, rhythmic massage of both cheeks in one huge, very hard hand. Not to mention the trespassing finger that was starting to make her insides melt away . . .

'Far, far smoother,' he wheezed hoarsely, 'than I'd ever imagined possible. So wonderfully, perfectly, idyllically smooth that I've decided I've simply got to possess it.'

'The QX4DL?' she asked hopefully, trying not to wince.

'Yes, probably that as well,' he breathed, slowly stepping back and removing his hands from brochure and bottom alike. 'I think you must have persuaded me,' he croaked, unable to transfer his gaze from the rapidly darkening patches his right hand had imprinted on the twin globes of her gorgeous bare bottom. On the smoothest of the two very smooth machines.

She waited anxiously, wondering precisely what she was meant to do next. Now that Mr Harris had made up his mind about the new copying machine, surely she would be justified in forgetting about this brochure and slipping back into her dress, and then returning, at last, to Mr Fennell's typing? Should she start to ease her knickers into position in readiness for her departure? That would certainly be a very welcome manoeuvre. Tiny though they were, she'd already decided that they were infinitely better than not wearing them at all. Or wearing them strung uselessly across her thighs, she supposed she ought to say. Heavens, her poor rear end must be blushing furiously from the recent manhandling! The sooner she could give it some cover, the better she . . .

Oh dear! She shouldn't have been quite so optimistic about replacing her panties! That sound behind her back was definitely the noise made by a zip fastener urgently parting company with itself. And that was the unmistakable chink of keys and loose change as a pair of men's trousers hurriedly hit the deck . . . and other equally ominous sounds were now emanating from behind her. The outlook was beginning to look somewhat less than rosy. The odds on her escaping with her virtue completely intact seemed to be lengthening by the second, particularly now that a pair of bright red briefs had just landed, rather indecently, on the table right in front of her . . .

'Now then, Mrs Peach!' growled Mr Harris, slowly turning her round to face him and then reaching forward with both hands for the clip at the front of her bra.

'Yes, Mr Harris?' she stammered, as two firm, friendly new arrivals bounced happily into play, at the same time nosing themselves upwards and outwards with the pleasure of their release.

'Now we have to deal with one final matter arising. One of fairly major proportions.'

She stared down at him and swallowed hard. He could certainly say that again! 'Mammoth proportions' would have been a little nearer the mark. Yet another truly upstanding member of the British legal profession! Lordy! Wherever was all this going to end up? Oh dear! She rather suspected that she already knew the answer to that . . .

And indeed she did. Her suspicions were extremely well founded, as she was shortly to learn. Very gently Mr Harris eased her backwards until her naked rear end was reposing gracefully on the edge of the table. Then he lowered his gaze. He stared, mesmerised, at the sight of her lovely bare groin. At the way that the total absence of pubic hair displayed her pretty little female parts to perfection, emphasising them and making them seem larger than normal. Larger and even more ready for taking. Vulnerable in the extreme.

Pauline looked up and blushed fiercely. There was no mistaking the nature and extent of his interest as he continued to stare unashamedly down. How embarrassing, she groaned to herself. But rather arousing as well, she had to admit. It was obvious that he was fascinated by what he could see, and that in turn was having its effect on her. A very familiar effect. Below the waist, both of them were now as ready for each other as they could possibly have been . . .

At last Mr Harris was able to drag his eyes away from the pretty pink plumpness. 'You're beautiful!' he murmured with feeling, leaning forward and beginning to nibble at the nearest bulging nipple.

'Ohhh!' she gasped at the first sharp stab of pleasure. 'Ohhh! Ooow!' she gasped again, as he transferred his mouth to the equally pouting twin.

A few seconds later she was surprised to find that, without any conscious effort on her part, she'd reached out and was now cradling his scalding-hot erection in the palm of her hand. So massive was it that she could only encircle it by little more than half. 'Crumbs!' she was unable to prevent herself murmuring aloud. He was even longer than that awful Slim Trelawny . . . !

'Pardon?' he mumbled, his mouth still full of boob.

'Er, nothing, Mr Harris . . .'

She swallowed hard once more and wondered, in all seriousness, whether she'd be able to take him in. It was the largest organ she'd ever encountered both in length and girth. A great tower of hot, iron-hard flesh that stretched and strained all the way up to his rib cage . . .

Mr Harris straightened up and smiled nicely. 'You're not worried, are you?' he asked, having for the moment finished his feast of firm, plentiful breasts and bursting nipples.

'Well . . . just a little,' she admitted slowly. 'I've never seen anyone as big . . .'

'Most women seem to appreciate it,' he chuckled, slipping a hand between the tops of her legs and starting to stroke the warm, wet, velvety lips that dwelt so delightfully within. 'I'm sure that you will, too.'

'You'll have to put it in very slowly . . .'

'Don't worry. I'll be as gentle as a lamb. Really I will. As gentle as the proverbial lamb.'

She was inclined to believe him. After all, she told herself reassuringly, he'd been very tender with her of late. First with his mouth round her boobs, and now with his fingers inside her quim. Very tender indeed. True, he'd gripped her bottom rather ferociously when she'd been leaning forward across the table a few minutes earlier. But, then again, men were always taking the most terrible liberties with that particular part of the female anatomy. Especially with hers, it seemed. She'd lost track of the number of times she'd ended up across somebody's knee for totally trivial reasons. It was really jolly unfair. Just because a girl happened to be quite nicely shaped in her posterior region, there was no reason why she should find it the subject of constant abuse. Even Michael, who was always so kind and considerate in bed, was ever so cruel to her poor, long-suffering rear end . . .

'You don't look very lamblike to me,' she mused at length, still staring intently at his groin. 'Not very lamblike at all . . .'

'Ba-aa-aa-aa!' Mr Harris bleated meekly, making her giggle, as well as wriggle against his deeply probing fingers.

70

She squeezed the huge, swollen head of the object under debate. 'I hope this isn't what they mean when they talk about "one of the Law Society's practising members"?'

'You should know, Pauline. After all, you've spent the last five years working in the law!'

'Eight, actually. Ever since I left school.'

'So you must have practised on a member or two before?'

'Well, yes, one or two, I have to admit . . .'

'John Robinson, for instance?'

'Yes, I had a great deal of practise with Mr Robinson . . .'

Slowly he removed his dripping wet fingers, feeling her insides sucking hungrily at them as they withdrew from the fiery furnace she harboured permanently within her loins. 'I think it's time to practise on this one now.'

He helped to swing her legs up onto the table. She lay back, her beautiful breasts pointing proudly up at the ceiling, as he slid a cushion from a nearby chair under her head. 'Thank you,' she smiled. 'Don't forget your promise to be gentle . . .'

Slowly he removed the scrap of frilly black knicker material that had remained strung across her uppermost thighs. 'Kiss-Kiss,' he said with a grin, holding up the panties as he clambered onto the table beside her.

She turned her face towards his. 'Yes, please,' she whispered softly. He was more than happy to oblige.

Very carefully he mounted her in the good old fashioned missionary position, still kissing her as he did so. She spread her legs as wide as she could and prayed that she was large enough to accommodate him. 'Let me guide you in,' she suggested, reaching down and taking hold of his enormity once again.

'Don't you trust me?'

'Yes, of course I do. But I think it might be easier for me if I can help to point you in the right direction.'

Slowly, very very slowly, he bore down on her with his groin. 'Oh, no!' she gasped to herself, starting to panic as

71

she felt him against her. 'He's far too thick to get inside me. There simply isn't room. There simply isn't the width . . .'

But she was wrong. Centimetre by painful centimetre she began to receive the end of his monstrous member, groaning with a mixture of discomfort and delight as he opened her wider and wider. And even wider still. She could feel her oil gushing out and running down the cheeks of her bottom. Thank heavens her pussy was being such a good little girl . . .!

Now she knew she had sufficient stretch, although only just, and without a micro-millimetre to spare. Now her one concern was whether she had the depth to accept him to the full. She wanted that so much. She wanted all of him inside her. She wanted yards of him inside her. Yards and yards and yards. She yearned and burned for her quim to house every inch that he possessed.

And eventually her wish came true. Eventually the entire length of his colossal column of cock was buried deep inside. Deep, deep, deep inside. So deep that she was convinced he must be protruding from her mouth. He'd been patient and careful, with the result that it had taken him ages, but at long last his giant pole of penis was now immersed right up to the root. 'Don't start to move yet,' she moaned fearfully. Never had she felt so excruciatingly extended. She needed time to readjust.

Suddenly, against his rock-hard intrusion into her person, he could feel her starting to orgasm. He could feel her sorely overstretched insides contracting in a series of violent convulsions against him. She goggled wide-eyed at the ceiling, helpless and unseeing, her face flushed, teardrops running slowly down both cheeks and beads of perspiration standing out on her forehead. Her mouth was wide open in an O, as if she was about to scream, but the only sound to emerge was that of her heavily laboured breathing. Her climax went on and on, silent yet so intense that he actually began to worry.

At last she started to groan. A long, low groan of contentment and relief. Then visibly she began to relax. 'Welcome back to the land of the living,' he said, when he gauged that she could hear him.

She giggled sexily and began to gyrate her hips slowly underneath him. 'You can screw me now,' she whispered breathlessly. 'You can screw me as hard as you like.'

Mr Harris didn't take her at her word to begin with. He did however start to move back, very slowly and gently, because over the years he'd learned to become a considerate lover. He'd had little alternative, endowed as he was.

Pauline gasped in amazement as he began to withdraw. It felt as if the huge knobbly end of his enormous erection was turning her inside out. It felt as if it was drawing her insides out with it, leaving her empty in its wake. Empty and disembowelled. The process of this first withdrawal seemed endless, so much brawn was there for him to remove. She couldn't believe how long he was. She couldn't believe that she was capable of harbouring something that size, nor that there was still more for him to withdraw. The process had started at a point that had seemed somewhere high in her chest, and she could still feel him retreating, despite the bulk that he'd already pulled out. How on earth had she managed to take him? A vast amount of cock had already slithered out of her, yet he was still powerfully present inside. They were still fully coupled, even though he was now over half way out.

Further and further he drew back, continuing to suck out her insides as he went, leaving a throbbing empty void where his oversized organ had been. It was a completely unique experience for her. Never had she been so filled and then so emptied. Suddenly Mr Harris felt her climax return. Her vagina began tugging and squeezing hard at the ample portion of penis that still remained within. But this time she was far more relaxed and in control. He looked into her face and smiled. She was very flushed and her eyes were sparkling with the heat of her passion. She stared back at him and managed a watery smile of her own. She was glad he was aware of the effect his exiting prick was having on her.

At long last only the massive knob was left. It rested just inside her, stretching her wide apart. Thank heavens Michael wasn't hung like this, she gulped to herself. She'd never be able to put up with this sort of stretching day after day after day. And she'd never be able to go down on him, taking him deep into her throat. All she'd be able to do was suck at the end. And how disappointing that would be! She loved using her mouth on Michael. She did it at least once a day. It was so satisfying doing that to a man, swallowing him right up to the hilt and then making him squirt down your throat . . .

After a short pause, Mr Harris eventually voided her completely, making her groan with frustration. She'd never felt so deserted. So empty and alone. So drained of all resources.

But she wasn't left in that unhappy plight for long. For the second time that morning Mr Harris sank into her hot wet pussy. Not too hurriedly, but much, much faster than when he'd made his first incursion. Pauline moaned with pleasure as she felt him opening her all the way up to the top of her channel. She opened her mouth wide and sucked in her breath with delight. It was a truly wonderful sensation, being so filled and expanded in just a couple of seconds or so. She could feel herself straining to accommodate him. And as he'd slid into her, she'd been able to hear her own juices squelching inside her. Squelching against the monstrous shaft that was now stretching her painfully but deliciously in every direction.

Leaving himself crammed into her right up to his testicles, he lowered his head and kissed her again with his tongue. Hungrily she sucked him into her mouth, at the same time pushing up with her breasts and forcing her hard, burning hot nipples into his chest. Then she began to wriggle her bottom up and down, sliding him several inches back and forth as fast as she could. Almost at once another orgasm exploded inside her and she lay back on the table, closing her eyes and fighting for breath. He slid his hands under the silky smooth cheeks of her bottom. They were slippery and wet with the oil that was gushing out of her. Steadily and evenly he began to pole her, using strokes of awesome length and weight. He listened with fascination to the slurping sound of his penis working away inside her. Working away in the tightly confined space – the oh-so-tightly confined space – of her piping-hot little hole. Pauline sighed to herself. He was wedged into her so solidly she felt sure that something must give. Not that she was concerned. She was loving every moment, even the pain and discomfort he caused. In fact, particularly the pain and discomfort he caused. It was making her squeal and spasm almost all of the time, now that he'd picked up speed.

She shut her eyes even tighter and concentrated every cell in her body on the way she was being so fearsomely fucked. What would it be like when he eventually climaxed? Surely he'd absolutely flood her, bearing in mind the size of his tackle? She really loved the sensation of being heavily spunked. It always brought her off all over again. There was nothing to better the thrill of one long, fierce squirt after another splashing and splattering her insides, coating her womb within seconds, and scalding her with its heat. It made her just want to die . . .

'Are you all right?' he asked, shagging her forcefully but with control.

'Mmmmm!' she sighed happily.

'Am I hurting you?'

'Yes. It's lovely . . .!'

'Would you like a little more pace?'

'Oh, yes please!'

'Hold on to your hat then, Mrs Peach! I'm going to open the throttle wide!'

'Not as wide as you're opening me!' she giggled wickedly.

Twenty minutes later Mr harris watched as Pauline stood beside the table, wriggling herself back into her knickers as carefully as she could. The crotch bit into her much more fiercely than usual, but of course she knew the reason why. 'Ouch!' she mouthed silently. Seconds later the knickers were soaked with his seed. A thick, sticky reminder of the way he'd just pumped stream after boiling hot stream straight into her womb.

She caught his eye as she reached down for her bra. 'I told you you'd appreciate it,' he said with a grin, zipping himself up as he spoke.

'I still can't believe it,' she murmured. 'I never dreamt I could be so full!'

She fastened her bra at the front and picked up her dress. 'How on earth does your wife cope with you?' she asked.

'I'm not married,' he replied, sounding pleased. 'So you can have a repeat performance whenever you like.'

'I'm afraid I *am* married.'

'So it's thanks but no thanks?'

'I'm afraid so.'

He squeezed her nicely knickered behind as she started to drop the dress down over her head. 'That's a pity,' he said softly. He removed his hands from the warmth of her bottom so that the dress could fall over her hips.

'If I wasn't married to Michael . . .'

'But you are,' he protested mildly.

She folded her arms round his neck and then melted her body into his. 'Well, at least you've had me,' she whispered, before pressing her tongue into his mouth. There was absolutely no reason in the world for her to feel sorry for him, she reminded herself, gently licking his tongue with hers. But she never had been very good at controlling how she felt about a man when she was still awash with his sperm. She knew, however, from past experience, that her emotions would grow more sensible once she'd started the process of shedding it . . .

Mr Harris stared at the cheeks of her bottom as it wiggled its way out of his office, respectably clad once again in the short pink dress and filmy black knickers. She was a lovely girl, he reflected, in every sense of the word. And she was right about one thing too. At least he'd had her. That was the thing about fucking a woman, particularly somebody else's wife. There was something very permanent about it. Once fucked, there was no way in the world she could get herself unfucked. Once you'd had her, she was obliged to spend the rest of her life having been had. Three, five, or however many years later, you could see her in the street with her husband and children and say to yourself that you'd been there, where only poor hubby was supposed to tread. You'd say to yourself that you'd had a slice of the action, a slice of her smooth little bum. A slice that had belonged to somebody else. And however hard she might try, there was no possibility of her returning it to its rightful owner. It had gone from him once and for all, poor chap! You'd know it, she'd know it, and both of you'd know that the other one knew it . . .

Oh, yes. She could smile at you sweetly in the street, but you'd know that she knew exactly what you were thinking. You'd know that she knew you were recalling that earlier occasion when she'd let you all the way up her cunt. You'd see her blush, ever so slightly, as she walked past, arm in arm with her husband . . .

Pauline could sense his eyes all over her as she left the room. Oh dear! Another one had 'joined the club' . . . as that awful George Franks had so rottenly put it. Joined in a very big way. And what a terrible state he'd left her in! She must head straight for the ladies' loo. Fortunately there was a hairdryer on the wall which she could use on her knickers, just as she'd done yesterday morning after Jim Browne had emptied himself into her . . .

It was just as well that she'd arrived early at work. If she could be quick and efficient, there was still time to catch up with the typing before Mr Fennell sent her any more tapes . . .

What a mess she was in! She could feel Mr Harris gushing out of her and straight through her saturated knickers as if they simply didn't exist. His hot, sticky juices were now almost halfway down to her knees. It was a lovely sensation, apart from the fact that this was slap bang in the middle of the working day, and the further fact that her short summer dress was no longer able to conceal her plight!

Oh, panic! It was that not-very-nice Mr Davis-Davies, the partner in charge of the secretarial staff.

'Not working, Mrs Peach?' he asked coldly.

'Mr Harris wanted to see me, sir,' she replied, her legs pressed firmly together.

'Does Mr Fennell know?'

'Yes, sir. Of course.'

Mr Davis-Davies strutted away down the corridor, leaving Pauline to dash the final few yards to the sanctuary of the ladies' cloakroom, the tops of her thighs wet and slippery against each other as she ran.

CHAPTER 4

George And Jim At Work

Whilst Pauline was still on her back on Mr Harris' table, being stretched much further than she'd comfortably go, Jim Browne was an extremely distracted man. For the past sixty minutes or so he'd searched high and low for her, but with a conspicuous lack of success. 'Your worships,' he said, standing at the front of the court and addressing the three magistrates who sat, rather wearily, in front of and above him.

'Yes, Mr Browne?' the chairman asked patiently.

'Your worships,' he began again, wishing he'd spent just a little longer clearing the morning's post from his desk, instead of hunting the building for a piece of that lovely young lady.

'Yes, Mr Browne?'

'Your worships, I appear for the defendant in this case.'

Jim sighed inwardly. Damn it to hell! He had appointments for the rest of the day. He simply couldn't leave the office that evening without doing something about his outstanding paperwork. He'd just have to stay late and deal with it . . .

'We realise that, Mr Browne. Otherwise you wouldn't be standing there addressing us, would you?'

'I'm sorry, your worships. But this is a rather difficult matter. There is considerable mitigation, despite my client's plea of guilty.'

Jesus Christ! How horny she'd looked when he'd caught a glimpse of her in that short summer dress that fitted so sweetly around her hips and boobs . . .!

'Yes, Mr Browne?'

'I'm sorry, your worships?'

'Your mitigation, Mr Browne?'

'I beg your pardon, your worships?'

'What is this mitigation of yours, Mr Browne? What is its nature?'

'Oh, I do apologise, your worships. Where was I?'

'The mitigation, Mr Browne.'

'Of course, the mitigation. I'm sorry.'

But where the hell had she been? He'd checked the copying room and her own room several times, as well as cashiers and the two interview rooms . . .

'Mr Browne! We're still waiting!'

'Yes, of course, your worships. Is there anything else I can say that may assist you?'

'Quite a lot, I should imagine, Mr Browne.'

'I'm sorry, your worships?'

'I said, I imagine there's quite a lot you can say – since you've not said anything at all so far.'

'Haven't I really? Didn't I explain how good he is to his poor old mother?'

'No, Mr Browne. You didn't.'

'Well, he is, your worships. Very good to her indeed. Every Sunday he takes her for a walk in the park. And then he pushes her wheelchair down to the beach for an ice cream – for which he always pays out of his own money.'

Why the devil hadn't she been in her room or taking dictation from Mr Fennell? He must have checked at least six times . . .

'Is that all, Mr Browne?'

'Eh? I'm sorry? All what, your worships?'

'All the considerable mitigation to which you referred earlier?'

'Er, no. Not quite, your worships . . .'

Jim glanced down at his file. Oh Christ! What had he

80

done? What had he just said to the Bench? He'd just trotted out part of tomorrow morning's case! It had been nothing at all to do with the present defendant, whose rather attractive young mother was sitting anxiously at the back of the court listening intently to Jim's plea in mitigation. She must be rather bewildered by the proceedings so far, to say the very least . . .!

'Well, may we hear the rest, Mr Browne? If you don't mind too much?'

'Of course, your worships. Of course . . . Er, um, the defendant was drunk at the time, your worships. Otherwise he'd never have done it. Never in a thousand years, your worships. It's just not in his character. Not at all. He was drunk . . . And that's all there is to be said about it.'

'It's hardly surprising, Mr Browne.'

'Your worships?'

'It's hardly earth-shattering news to hear that he was drunk, Mr Browne. We're not at all surprised to hear you say that he wouldn't have done it if he'd been sober. Particularly as the charge to which your client has pleaded guilty is one of driving whilst under the influence of alcohol!'

Jim Browne sagged visibly. Oh, bugger it! Sod it sideways and backwards! What a cock-up! . . . That last statement he'd made had been part of yesterday's case. What the hell was up with him? Was he totally unhinged? Could he think of nothing in the world apart from the delectable Mrs Peach and her hot little fanny . . .?

As Jim was floundering in the well of the Juvenile Court, George Franks was at his desk, a cigarette in one hand and a paperback in the other. The book was an erotic novel entitled *Jillie Jackson, the Very Bottom Line*. It was written by someone with the unlikely name of José Felattio. George had purchased it from W.H.Smith's that morning. The write-up on the back cover had appealed to him. 'A fantasy with several parts,' it said, 'set in the permissive society of the

1960s. Escape from the guilt-ridden nineties. Escape from the decade of safe sex, surrogate smoking and sensible eating. Escape back in time to the swinging sixties. To the golden age of free love, flower power, flared jeans and micro miniskirts. Return, alas briefly, to the time when everyone bonked everyone else and no one really minded that much.'

George put the book in his desk. It was really rather tame, he thought to himself. If that was the great sexual revolution of the sixties, then someone must have caught the ringleaders very quickly and had them shot . . .

The telephone rang and he picked it up. 'Mrs Mason on the outside line, Mr Franks,' said the attractive young receptionist with the superb bust and one of the most up-and-down pairs of knickers in the world.

'Put her through, Janet,' George sang out.

'Mr Franks?'

'What can I do for you, Mrs Mason?'

'I came to see you last month – about my matrimonial problems.'

'Yes, of course,' he replied smoothly, without a clue as to her identity. 'It's nice to speak to you again. How are you?'

'Fine, thank you. At least I will be after a few days' rest. But that's nothing to do with you. I'm phoning to say that my husband is still refusing to give me a divorce, so I've taken the advice you gave me last time.'

'Oh, that's good,' George murmured. He scratched his head. What the hell had he advised her to do? He could now vaguely remember the young lady concerned. She was about thirty and extremely fanciable. But as to the nature of her problems and the advice he'd given, he really had no idea . . .

'So how soon can I start the divorce proceedings, Mr Franks?'

'Well, that depends, Mrs Mason. How long have you and your husband been separated?'

'Just over two months. Didn't I tell you that before?'

'Of course. It just slipped my mind, that's all.'

'I'm really very anxious to get the divorce underway, Mr Franks, as soon as I possibly can. Very anxious indeed.'

'I see. Well, I'm sure I explained to you last time that unless you've been separated for two years you have to have grounds for the divorce.'

'Yes, you did. You explained that very carefully. You said there were only two grounds, either adultery or unreasonable behaviour. Is that right?'

'Quite right, Mrs Mason. Adultery or unreasonable behaviour. Cruelty as it used to be called in the bad old days.'

'Well, there's no cruelty or unreasonable behaviour or anything like that. We just didn't get on together and we split up.'

'So you want to start divorce proceedings based on adultery, Mrs Mason?'

'Yes, that's right.'

'Fine. It's usually the quickest and cleanest way to proceed. I shall need the marriage certificate in order to file the petition. And also your husband's address.'

'That's not a problem.'

'Excellent. Now, what about the woman concerned? Do you know who she is?'

'I beg your pardon?'

'The woman concerned. Do you know her identity?'

'I'm afraid I don't follow you, Mr Franks.'

'The woman with whom your husband has committed adultery. Do you know her name and address?'

'But he hasn't committed adultery. I don't think he's got it in him, personally.'

'I'm sorry, I'm getting confused . . .'

'So am I, Mr Franks.'

'I thought you said you wanted to take proceedings for divorce based on adultery?'

'That's right. I do.'

'But how can you do that if he hasn't committed adultery, Mrs Mason?'

'*He* hasn't committed adultery . . . I have. Lots of times since I last saw you. Just to be on the safe side.'

'You have?'

'That's right. Nearly a hundred times, in total. Just to be sure.'

'But you can't divorce him on those grounds!' George managed to say politely, without guffawing down the phone.

'Why not?'

'Because you just can't. No one can divorce someone on the grounds of their *own* adultery, Mrs Mason.'

'Say that again, Mr Franks?'

'You can't divorce your husband on the grounds of your own adultery. It has to be on the grounds of *his*.'

'*What?*' she screamed down the phone. 'What are you saying? Do you mean to tell me that I've been jumping into bed with every available male under the age of eighty-five, all to no avail?'

'I'm afraid so, Mrs Mason.'

'I'll sue you, you bastard! I'll ruin you!'

'What?'

'I said I'll sue you. You told me last time I could take divorce proceedings straight away on the grounds of adultery.'

'Yes, of course. But not your own adultery. It has to be your husband's.'

'You didn't tell me that!' she howled at the top of her voice. 'You just said adultery! Oh, my God! To think of all I've been through! All those awful men! Oh God, I'm going to be sick!'

'Now steady on, Mrs Mason,' George said with alarm. 'Steady on.'

'Oh, Jesus Christ! The ordeal I've been through! All on your advice. On your professional, legal advice for which I paid you. I've hardly been in a vertical position for the past four weeks. I'll sue you for every penny you've got! And for

84

every stinking penny you haven't! I'll see you in the Bankruptcy Court, if it's the last thing I do. Oh my God!'

Bang! Dialling tone . . . Silence . . .

'Fuck it!' groaned George, reaching for his personal telephone directory. He must phone his insurers at once. He hoped and prayed the firm had paid the last premium on the negligence policy . . .!

Jim Browne decided to slide into the Volunteer Arms for a quick pint to celebrate his narrow escape. He could hardly believe his luck. The bloody magistrates had actually listened sympathetically to his hastily rearranged argument that if his client hadn't been so rotten, stinking drunk, he'd never have dreamt of driving home in that condition. It just showed how it paid to be quick at thinking on your feet. Mind you, the client's rather personable young mother had given him a very old-fashioned look afterwards . . .

Jim poured half the contents of his pint pot down his throat in one gulp and glanced at the TV set in the corner. It was broadcasting the local news. 'The inquest heard that the body was bound hand and foot and in chains,' said the newsreader. 'It was also lashed securely to a heavy steel girder. The dead woman had been strangled, stabbed repeatedly with a knife and then shot through the head and chest. The body had then been extensively burnt. Concluding the inquest, the Coroner pronounced a verdict of unlawful killing.'

'Jesus Christ!' Jim Browne gasped to the landlord behind the bar. 'Where can I get a fucking job like his?'

CHAPTER 5

Mr James And The Swivel Armchair

Half an hour later, George Franks leant back in his chair and plonked his feet on the desk. He was more than satisfied with his morning's work. His negligence insurance was in place after all. And on the Pauline Peach front, all was going according to plan. Not that he was feeling any better disposed towards her, of course. Not after the way she'd lied to him and made him look such an idiot. But at least she'd got her come-uppance, in several more ways than one. The horny little bitch was certainly getting her just deserts! She must already have begun to realise that she couldn't tangle with George Franks and come off best. Imagine her thinking that she could get away with feeding him all that rubbish about loving her husband, whilst all the time she was pulling her knickers up and down like a yoyo for that bloody Jim Browne! What a fool Tracie must have thought him, after he'd spent half an hour yesterday telling her his feelings about Pauline. After he'd bared his soul explaining just why she'd got so deeply under his skin.

At that precise moment Tracie Trix, Mr Davis-Davies' slim, raven-haired secretary and George's part-time lover, leapt to her feet in front of her word processor and cried 'Eureka!' to the empty room. She'd finally cracked it, she told herself happily. She'd finally solved the problem that had been grating on her all morning. Inspiration had come out of the blue, right in the middle of tapping this long, hugely boring contract into the word processor. The answer was so simple. All she'd have to do was to make one short phone call, then she'd be home and dry. Well, not so dry, if she managed to have her wicked way, which she was confident she would . . .

Her husband, Peter, had been a pig towards her earlier that morning. A real pig, and as stubborn as a mule, despite the fact that she'd done her best to put him in a good frame of mind. She'd made love to him before getting up, lying on top so he could watch her bottom in the wardrobe mirror, as he always liked to do. Not that she blamed him for that, as she was only too well aware of the way men regarded her randy little rear end. Then she'd started to get dressed in front of him, very slowly and slinkily, whilst he'd been sprawled out on the bed studying her every move . . .

Wearing nothing but a frothy, plumply filled bra, she'd looked back at him over her shoulder and asked, very sweetly and innocently, about the dates of the Torquay conference the following week.

'Why do you want to know?' he'd asked, staring suspiciously at her bottom as she'd wriggled it sexily into a pair of G-string knickers.

'I'd just like to make some plans, that's all.'

'Who with, exactly? One of those horny buggers from the office who're always trying to get between your legs?'

Tracie looked back at the screen of the word processor. Of course Mr Jealousy Bollocks had been absolutely one hundred and ten per cent correct! She was certainly hoping to make some plans, either with George Franks or Jim Browne, or preferably with both, since the course would take Peter away from home for two nights. Two whole, wonderful nights of glorious sexual freedom!

But which two nights would they be? That had been her problem. Without that knowledge there was no way she could make any arrangements at all. And if she left it too late, both George and Jim might make other plans. Mind you, that would still leave Young Harry, Mr James' trainee. There were many worse ways of spending a night than curled up in bed beside him. Or rather, underneath him. The only slight drawback there was that it would have to be her place, as Harry still lived with his parents. It was never quite as relaxing, rutting and raving in the matrimonial bed, with the half thought at the back of your mind that you might hear the latch key turn in the front door just as you were about to be shot full of lovely hot spunk . . .

Peter had remained extremely dogged and unhelpful, so after the expert blow job she'd given him by way of reassurance, she'd slipped downstairs in her undies whilst he'd still been in bed and hunted high and low for his diary, without reward. Obviously the ultra-suspicious so-and-so had hidden it somewhere . . .

She supposed she knew why poor Peter was so untrusting. It was a result of that bad business last year. What a crying shame that he'd decided to take a walk round the block at just the wrong moment. At precisely the moment that Martin, or Raymond, or David, or whatever his name had been, had just started to shag her silly on the front seat of his car. Peter had strolled past, tickled pink to observe that some couple was having it off nineteen to the dozen inside. He'd been less tickled twenty minutes or so later, however, when on his way back he'd recognised his own wife clambering out of the passenger door and tugging down the hem of her mini-skirt.

Yes, Tracie thought ruefully, that had been a very bad business indeed. Peter had been far from the most trusting of souls beforehand, but he'd been considerably worse ever since. Not to mention the painful fact that every night for the next week he'd put her across his knee and painted her bottom bright red, as well as the backs of her thighs. He'd flatly refused to believe her (rather feeble) excuse that she'd simply been giving the driver directions. Anyway, to cut a long story short, he'd become so unbearably jealous and inquisitive that she'd often had to go as long as three or four weeks without getting her end away elsewhere. And with a tail such as hers that needed constant variety, three or four weeks was an intolerable length of time . . .

But now she had the solution to the problem of the Torquay conference. It had turned out to be quite simple in the end. All she had to do was to ring Peter's company and say that she was from the central clearing agency for Trust House something-or-other, and then ask them to confirm the details of their bookings for the conference because her computer had gone a bit wobbly.

It was a great shame that this year they'd cut the conference from three nights to two. Obviously George and Jim had to be given the first option as they had prior claim by dint of precedence. Both of them had fucked her before she'd been with the firm a week. But it would have been nice if she'd been able to accommodate Young Harry as well. After all, they could easily have booked into a small hotel somewhere, rather than sleep at her house. Well, she'd make him first reserve, as it was always possible that one of the others might have another commitment. She knew George wouldn't object . . .

As Tracie reached for the telephone, Kevin, the office boy, was busy in the stockroom moving huge cartons of headed notepaper from one end to the other. His objective was to clear sufficient floor space to enable two people to stretch out in comfort.

He was feeling lucky, he told himself, as much in hope as expectation. After all, it was about time it happened to him. Hell, he'd be seventeen next week! He didn't want to end yet another year without having lost his virginity.

At least he felt that he had some sort of a chance with that slinky Mrs Tracie Trix, old Davis-Davies' sexy, long-legged secretary. Everyone at the office knew that she put it about a bit. It was common knowledge that Mr Franks and

Mr Browne had been getting their share of her. There were rumours about most of the other men, too. Certainly Harry Hotspur, Mr James' trainee, had come close at the office disco last week. Harry had told him that she'd sat on his lap for almost an hour, wriggling her plump little bum and letting him finger her as hard as he'd pleased. And Harry wasn't the sort of guy to make that up. Apparently, when he'd asked her if he could take her home, she'd told him she'd love to say yes, but her husband was so suspicious of her that he'd be meeting her off the mini-bus. There'd be hell to pay, she'd told him, if she wasn't on board. Then she'd furtively slid her hand down the front of his trousers, squeezed his overstretched cock, and told him with a giggle that he'd simply have to be patient. After that she'd closed her eyes and allowed Harry's fingers to bring her off, even though several of the other secretaries had been sitting nearby and must have been able to guess what he was doing to her under cover of the table top.

Carefully Kevin inspected the bolt he'd recently fixed inside the stockroom door. So Harry was confident about Mrs Trix, he pointed out to himself. Harry was sure he'd have his leg over there. And if Harry could score, then why couldn't he? OK, Harry was twenty-one and had already screwed half a dozen girls or more, but everyone had to start somewhere . . .

Kevin thrust his hands into his pockets and thought deeply about his wretched state of celibacy. Surely Tracie was just the right type to give him his start in life. And she'd been very amenable towards him of late. In the last few days he'd taken to patting her bottom whenever the opportunity arose and there'd been no protest from her, just knowing grins of reproach and vaguely suggestive remarks. Indeed, once or twice she'd even patted him back . . .

So that was it, Kevin decided at last. Next time he was alone with Tracie he'd definitely press the point and see what she did. After all, she could only say 'no'. That would be disappointing, of course, but it wouldn't be the end of the world. It wouldn't make him any more of a virgin than he already was. And if by some chance she said 'yes' . . .!

Of course, the girl over whom *everyone* really creamed their jeans was that new blonde beauty who worked for old Mr Fennell. But she was a different proposition, to say the very least. He couldn't in his wildest dreams, convince himself that he had any chance there. Friendly and pleasant though she was, she was altogether too classy to drop her knickers for someone like him. Even Harry had admitted that the incredibly fuckable Mrs Peach was totally out of his league. Mind you, Harry had said wisely, that didn't mean that you couldn't follow the example set by all the rest of the men in the world. It didn't mean you couldn't goggle at the front of her tight-fitting blouse, or the seat of her mini-skirt, and daydream about just how it would be . . .

Gingerly Pauline lowered herself onto her meagrely upholstered typist's chair, holding her breath as she did so. Crumbs, Mr Harris had made her ever so tender! Perhaps she should have asked him to lend her that cushion she'd had under her head. Right now it would have been even more welcome elsewhere . . .

She stared forlornly at the screen of her word processor. How on earth was she expected to keep up to date with Mr Fennell's work? How on earth was she expected to settle down to work after all she'd been through? And after all that had been through her? Oh dear! That wasn't a very nice thing to say, even if she was only talking to herself. It was decidedly smutty and unladylike. But it was true, nonetheless, that it was going to be rather difficult to concentrate on her typing. It was all right for men. They seemed able to zip up their trousers and then bustle straight back to whatever they were doing beforehand. But girls were very different. Once bonked, they stayed bonked for ages. And she didn't just mean in the sticky, physical sense. It could take hours to get your mind back into gear, particularly after the kind of comprehensive sorting out she'd just received from Mr Harris. You just sat there like a zombie, all wet and throbbing, and thinking all sorts of unrelated thoughts. Thoughts like why did you enjoy it so much when you knew it was so wrong? Or would you go red in the face when your husband asked what you'd been up to all day? Or how on earth could you have one orgasm after another with that awful George Franks, whom you despised so greatly? Or why did it always seem that big men like Mr Harris were even bigger down there than they should be?

The telephone rang and she lifted the receiver. 'Hello, Pauline,' said the voice at the other end.

Oh, how nice! It was Mr Fennell, her boss. The most senior of the senior partners – although only in his early forties or so. He was a real sweetheart into the bargain. She was very fond of him. He was such an easy person to work for . . .

'Mr James would like to have a word with you,' Mr Fennell explained down the phone. 'I'm not sure what it's about, but if he wants you to put any of his private mortgages on the word processor, just tell him you haven't got time.'

'Well, that would certainly be true, Mr Fennell,' she replied, glancing anxiously at the half typed letter on the screen of her machine. 'I haven't been doing too well this morning . . .'

'Never mind. I'm sure you'll catch up soon. You're a good girl, Pauline. I'm very pleased with your work.'

She replaced the receiver and stood up. How nice of Mr Fennell to say that! He really was a treasure. He was ever so pleasant and polite, and he never chased her for her typing, even on urgent matters. He was almost too good to be true.

Hey ho! She'd better nip up to Mr James' room straight away. And tell him, very politely, that she couldn't spare him any of her time because she was up to her ears in Mr Fennell's work. It was nothing but the truth, anyway. And respectably married young ladies always told the truth. Except, she supposed, when they didn't . . .

Why was Mr James always so busy? Why did he generate so much typing? She knew he had loads of clients, but then again so did Mr Fennell. So why was Mr James always trying to offload his typing onto the other secretaries. After all, Julie, his own secretary, was very competent and had been with him for years . . .

Mr James was about five years older than Mr Harris, she'd imagine, but much brisker and more businesslike. She supposed it was his military training. He'd been a major in the Army, or something like that. She expected it was just his manner because, after all, he'd always been perfectly pleasant whenever he'd spoken to her, although that hadn't been very often.

There was one very definite plus about going to see Mr James. His personal assistant, Harry, would be there. 'Young Harry,' as Mr James always called him. Now there was a lovely young lad that all the secretaries fancied like mad. That Tracie someone or other, Mr Davis-Davies' secretary, was always hanging round him. But then again, she was always hanging round most of the men at work. Anyway, Pauline could easily understand exactly what the other office girls saw in Young Harry. But she'd better not let herself dwell on that sort of thing right now, because respectably married young ladies simply did *not* allow themselves to fantasise about handsome, hunky trainees.

She'd have to pay yet another visit to the ladies' cloakroom on her way upstairs to Mr James' office. Mr Harris was proving extremely difficult to shift, due of course to the phenomenal size of the equipment with which he'd implanted her. He reminded her of that very coarse song she'd once heard at Michael's rugby club about an Italian with balls like a bloody stallion. Oh dear! Another smutty thought . . .

'Come in!' Mr James cried briskly. 'Ah! Mrs Peach, my dear

young lady. Do come in and close the door.'

'Mr Fennell said you wanted to see me, Mr James?'

'Quite right, dear girl. I have a little assignment that might interest you.'

Pauline sighed to herself. It was just as she'd thought, engrossing horrible mortgages. But this time it sounded like engrossing a horrible assignment of a horrible mortgage. She'd have to remember what Mr Fennell had told her to say.

She glanced around the room and was instantly impressed. Crumbs, it was ever so nice! A large, comfortable office that overlooked the main shopping centre, and with a number of huge potted plants scattered here and there, which always helped to make such a place more interesting. The walls were panelled in oak and held a number of good quality paintings. They were originals, not prints, she noted with approval. In the corner there was a colourful fish tank, full of exotic-looking tropical fish and burbling away to itself like mad. It was a much smarter room than any of the other partners had. Mr Fennell's was a real tip in comparison. She supposed that as Mr James was in charge of ordering office furniture and equipment, he made certain he got the best. She wondered what his partners felt about that. Well, it was their concern, not hers. But she was rather fond of Mr Fennell, and it was a shame that he had to put up with such inferior fittings and decoration. After all, he was supposed to be the most senior senior partner. However, there was nothing she could do about that . . .

'No need to hover about the door, dear lady. I don't bite! Ha, ha.'

'I'm sorry, Mr James. I was just admiring your room.'

Crikey, she'd just noticed a huge armchair in the middle of the carpet. It looked hideously expensive, real calf leather she was sure . . .

'Yes, it is quite pleasant. I do my best to make it attractive. The clients seem to like that sort of thing. It doesn't bother me, of course.'

'Of course,' she agreed, not exactly certain what it was she was agreeing with.

'You know Young Harry?' he asked, waving a hand towards the handsome young man who sat at the desk in the corner.

'Oh yes,' she replied brightly, flashing a smile in that direction. 'Hello, Harry.'

'Yes, of course you do. I'd forgotten you've been here several weeks now. Harry is my conveyancing assistant, which means I assist him to learn how to handle conveyancing so that he can trot off later and get a better job down the road.'

'Oh,' she said unsurely. 'Really?'

'No, not really, Mrs Peach. That's just my little joke. Sorry, Harry, no offence intended.'

Pauline glanced quickly at Young Harry. He was really ever so sweet. Every time he saw her he started to blush like mad, just as he was doing now. It was obvious how much he fancied her. She felt quite motherly towards him, bless his nice, crisp little cotton underthings! Not that he was quite as innocent as he looked. She'd seen him at the office disco, sitting there for ages with his hand thrust right up Tracie's skirt. And when she'd smooched with him on the dance floor later, she'd been able to feel his dick, hot and hard and wriggling like a snake against her. How wet it had made her knickers, the gentle pressure of his hand across her bottom and his groin against her own . . .!

'Right, then, Harry,' Mr James continued with brisk efficiency. 'Eyes down and carry on with drafting that conveyance while I talk to Mrs Peach.'

'Yes, Mr James,' murmured Harry, trying desperately to tear his gaze away from the spectacular swell of her breasts.

'Now then, my dear,' Mr James said decisively. 'I'll come straight to the point, as I usually do. It's probably my years in the Service, I expect. My military training. That sort of thing, anyway. The point is this, I'm sure you'll be pleased to know that I hear very good things about you.'

'Oh! Thank you, Mr James. That's nice.'

'Yes indeed. Very nice indeed. Yes indeed. I hear what an excellent worker you are. All that sort of stuff.'

'Thank you, Mr James.'

'But in particular I hear you've developed an in-depth new interest.'

'Pardon, Mr James?'

'An in-depth new interest, dear lady. Not only in photography and in the photocopying machines, but in our office equipment too. Yes, particularly in our equipment here at the office. A very in-depth interest, so I'm led to believe.'

She stared at Mr James and groaned. Oh no! *Not* again!

'I believe that you're also extremely photogenic, my dear. That's a very valuable asset, I must say.'

This was the end! Those rotten photographs would be the ruin of her, she just knew it. She had a really, really bad feeling about them.

'I've seen one or two examples myself, dear lady. I must say they were highly unusual.'

Pauline seethed with anger. If that sod George Franks had been standing there in front of her she'd have murdered him on the spot. Laughing as he died horribly before her eyes . . . Oh, how horrendously embarrassing!!

'And I must say they were of exceptionally high quality,' Mr James continued in the same brisk but friendly manner. 'The photographs, I mean to say.'

She wouldn't have killed him instantly. She'd have poisoned him first, and then stabbed him in all the non-vital places, before crushing his arms and legs, as well as his genital organs. Then she'd . . .

'Personally I think photography is a marvellous hobby,' he enthused. 'I know very little about it myself, but I understand that some of the new cameras can do quite incredible things. As indeed I've seen for myself this very morning.'

Pauline winced. So that bastard George Franks had shown Mr James the photographs of her and Jim Browne! What a fiendish thing to do! But why was Mr James telling her? Unless, of course . . .

'The photographs showed such artistry, young lady. Not only on the part of the photographer, but the model as well. How difficult it must have been for you to have remained so natural and unaffected! But then, you'd know all about such things, of course!

'Oh yes. It's always a pleasure to have a young lady in our midst who's interested in internal matters. Someone who isn't content just to be here from nine till five and collect her salary cheque at the end of the month. Someone who's prepared to put her back into whatever comes up . . . after office hours if necessary. Things that can prove to be very hard indeed. Stiff assignments, often long and drawn out. Yes, it does you great credit, Mrs Peach. I can always admire a young lady who has acquired a deep interest in office affairs. Particularly in office equipment.

'Now then, Mrs Peach. To business. To my reason for calling you up here. It's that chair there in the middle of the floor. A very fine-looking piece, isn't it? And very expensive too. Unbelievably so, in fact . . . You see, it's just a demonstration model. I'm hoping that I will decide to buy it. For myself, of course. For this room, I suppose I should say. It's really very comfortable, as well as attractive to look at. I'm extremely keen on it, I must say. But as you would expect, it's horribly pricey. I have to know that it's worth the money before I can decide whether to buy it. It's rather an important decision, in view of the price. Indeed, it's a very important decision. You see, if I decide to buy it and then find it's not up to the job . . . well, I can't in all honesty splash out on another one, can I? You understand my predicament? So, knowing your deep-seated interest in our equipment, I thought I'd ask you to assist me. To try it out, I mean to say . . . You see, I must have all the available data to enable me to arrive at an informed opinion. You do see my point, don't you Mrs Peach? You can see that, I'm sure?'

Despite herself, Pauline lowered her gaze and stared at the bulge in the front of his trousers. 'Er, well, yes Mr James,' she gulped.

'So if you'd care to take a closer look. It's a truly splendid specimen, is it not? It costs the earth, but I have this feeling that it may be worth the money. I often have such feelings, my dear. And usually they are right. Now then . . . see how it swivels and rocks at one and the same time, in any direction. In any direction at all. Incredible, isn't it? Unbelievable. And look at the covering. Touch it as well, feel free. It's the very finest and softest calf leather, isn't it? You can feel the quality with the lightest of touches. Marvellous, isn't it? The whole creation, I mean. But I must be certain that it's the right buy for me. I must know that for sure. Before I commit myself, you see. And the firm's money, of course. I must be completely satisfied about it, you understand? I know I can bank on your full co-operation, my dear Mrs Peach. I'm totally convinced of that fact, after all I've heard about you I mean. And seen, I suppose I ought to add.

'Now then, Mrs Peach. If you could just spread yourself out on the chair as comfortably as possible. Really stretch out and make yourself feel completely at home. Lean right back and recline it as far as you can.'

Gracefully Pauline lowered her bottom onto the chair, wincing slightly at the pressure on that very private part of her person to which Mr Harris had so recently been attending. Then she sat back in the chair and reclined it to an angle of approximately thirty degrees from the horizontal.

'That's fine,' enthused Mr James, as she tugged down on the hem of her dress and pressed her thighs together as firmly as she could. 'Is the chair comfortable, my dear lady?'

'Yes, Mr James,' she replied truthfully. 'Very comfortable in fact.'

He stared hard at her satin-smooth thighs, bare because the summer day was far too hot for stockings. Standing as he was to one side, her dress was just long enough to hide the nicely filled crotch of her panties. 'Well, then, my dear Mrs Peach, make yourself comfortable too.'

'Pardon?'

'Make yourself comfortable, if you please. Lift your dress a little higher, why don't you. Just so you're completely comfortable and unfettered. Just for your own comfort and convenience, and freedom of movement too. At the moment you're looking a trifle tense.'

'I'm quite OK, Mr James.'

'But you'll be even more so if you do as I suggest. Just lift it a little higher . . . and then stretch right back and relax. Stretch out those lovely long legs of yours and relax.'

Pauline edged the hem of her dress half an inch upwards. Then she looked up at Mr James, who smiled wanly and shook his head. 'Much more than that,' he laughed, thereby confirming her fears. 'Much, much more, in fact. Up past your waist, if you please. We must have you totally free and unfettered, and fully at ease.'

She blushed fiercely and dropped her gaze. 'Mr James,' she began.

'Well past your waist,' he continued smoothly, as if she hadn't spoken. 'This is a very important assignment, after all. As I've already explained. I need you to feel perfectly free and unrestricted. It's vital that you do.'

She looked at him again. His smile was still perfectly friendly and normal and gave not a hint that anything was amiss or that anything remotely unconventional might be afoot. His tone of voice was the same, as natural as could be. She glanced quickly at Young Harry and was glad to see that he was studiously engrossed in his paperwork. With a sigh of resignation she lifted her bottom and slowly eased up her dress.

'Just a little higher, young lady. Just a shade higher, please.'

'Yes, Mr James,' she said weakly.

'And a little bit more, as well.'

Now knickers and navel were exposed to him, and also

the micro-thin silver chain she wore round the very slimmest part of her waist. Despite herself, she darted a peek at Harry and caught his eye. Both of them blushed and looked quickly away. But even so, she felt a very definite stab of pleasure at the knowledge that he was there and aware of her – aware of the way she was sitting so scantily clad, just a few feet in front of his desk. She could feel herself starting to lubricate at the thought that he'd been staring at her in her tiny knickers. Somehow she just knew that he was fiercely erect.

Mr James continued to gaze at the lacy black undies. 'What a charming little pair!' he purred, completely entranced. 'So small but so frothy and frilly as well. In all honesty, I can't say that I've ever seen their like before. Where do they come from?'

'I'm not really sure,' she stammered. 'Someone bought them for me . . .'

'A girlfriend, I trust?' He laughed pleasantly.

'Not exactly.'

'Your husband, then?'

'Not as such . . .'

'Well, never mind. However, they do look to be rather on the tight side.'

'Oh, no, Mr James,' she replied quickly. 'They're fine. Very comfortable indeed. Really they are. They're not at all tight.'

'No, no, my dear young lady. I can see quite clearly that they are restricting you badly and preventing you from being totally relaxed and at ease. It's obvious. Just slip them off and hand them to me. You'll feel far freer if you do. I can assure you of that. I understand these things, you see. I understand them far better than you imagine. Just take them off and see if I'm not right.'

She swallowed hard and looked down at the tiny black triangle of semi-transparent knicker material. The knickers were minuscule, but they were knickers nevertheless. At least they covered the essentials, even though only just.

Mr James held out his hand and waited, smiling patiently but with a certain degree of determination. A fact that was not lost on Pauline. There wasn't really any point in arguing further, she said to herself with a sigh. Clearly he was intent on having her knickers off her, and one way or another he was going to succeed, whatever she said or did.

Blushing more brightly than ever, she slid the skimpy black panties down her legs and off over her feet. 'Thank you,' Mr James said politely, as she handed them to him. 'And now another burden has been lifted from you. Well, not exactly lifted I suppose. But you know what I mean.' He held the minute garment up to the light and smiled again. 'Good heavens, they are tiny, aren't they! What an incredibly saucy little pair! And what a wicked little message too! Has anyone ever taken you up on it?'

'Well, um . . .'

'But you still look so tense, my dear young lady, sitting there with your legs pressed so tightly together. Won't you ease them apart just a little? I'm sure it will help you to feel more calm and comfortable . . . Yes, that's fine. That's much better for you, I'm sure. But on second thoughts, just a tiny bit wider . . . And just a tiny bit wider than that.'

Mr James gazed unashamedly at the prettily shaven pink pussy. And Pauline knew for certain that Young Harry was staring too. She could just sense that fact, and it made her insides churn. She looked up at him and caught his eye once again. But this time neither of them hurried to look away. For several long seconds they looked steadily into each other's eyes, then quite openly he lowered his gaze back to her crotch, showing no signs of embarrassment now, just a highly aroused interest instead.

She flushed and looked away. She felt another surge of excitement, her heart starting to beat faster and her breathing growing more shallow. She was only too well aware of the fact that her vaginal lips were glistening wet and wide apart, presenting both men with a perfect view of that greatly-sought-after part of her person. The knowledge made her lubricate even more freely. It was very disreputable, she thought to herself, but she had to admit that it felt rather nice sitting here in front of Harry, so naked and open before him. In fact, she could almost say that it seemed to feel right. Which was rather peculiar, because she knew beyond a shadow of a doubt that it was very wrong indeed.

Did he know about Mr Harris? she wondered. Did he and Mr James know what Mr Harris had been doing to her such a short while before? The office intelligence service seemed so good that she rather suspected they might. And she couldn't deny that for some reason she liked the idea. She felt more than a bit sexy at the thought of sitting here, knickerless and bonked, with Harry and Mr James gazing at her open, bare pussy and knowing that it had so recently been reamed out by somebody else. Knowing that it was still all stretched and throbbing from the way she'd just been fucked. It was very embarrassing, of course, yet strangely arousing, nevertheless. Much as she loved her husband and wanted to stay faithful to him, she could definitely feel her insides starting a mini-orgasm at the prospect of these two men staring down at her wide open quim and contemplating the fact that only a short while earlier it had been in the process of being misused.

Pauline groaned to herself. She could feel her vaginal oils pouring out of her and down onto the chair. This was not the way she was supposed to react. Not the way at all. And she was quite certain that the men could see her plight. But that wasn't really the point. She ought to be feeling so horribly humiliated and embarrassed by her situation that she was shut as tight as a clam. No married woman who loved and respected her husband should be gushing in this way. No respectably married young lady should be turned on by the thought of sitting here whilst two men goggled at her lewdly displayed pussy and pondered on how it had just been so thoroughly screwed.

But turned on she certainly was. Her nipples were rock hard and bursting with life, and her clitoris was standing rigidly to attention as well. She longed to reach down and touch it, knowing that the delicious thrill inside her would suddenly burst into orgasm.

She groaned inwardly once again. The more the men stared at her, the wider and wetter she became. Her clit was now so stretched and strained that she was by no means certain she could continue to refrain from stroking it. She knew the men could see it poking up at them, pert and proud and swollen and waiting to be used. Indeed, aching to be used.

At last Mr James began to speak, his voice betraying just the faintest tremor. A fault which he promptly corrected. 'Now then, Mrs Peach,' he began again. 'I do fear that I may have been wrong. That I may have made a mistake. About your dress, I mean. It does look rather bunched up like that, does it not? Bunched up and uncomfortable around your middle. I feel, on reflection, that we'd be far better off if you simply removed it altogether. Surely you agree?'

'Yes, Mr James,' she sighed, unzipping the dress at the back without further discussion and then lifting it carefully over her head.

'Thank you so much, dear lady,' he said, placing it on the nearby chair. 'I feel sure I've made the right decision this time. Absolutely so, I'm sure you'll be pleased to hear.'

Pauline leant back in the chair once again. Now she was wearing nothing but her black half-cup bra and high heels. And she rather imagined that the first of those garments would very soon be gone. Not that it would make much difference, she thought to herself. The bra was so small and transparent and overburdened that the men could already see almost everything she owned up there. And it would be even nicer to have Young Harry staring at bare boobs as well as bare pussy – even more right, despite the fact that it was so very wrong . . .

Mr James' attention had now shifted to the top half of her body. 'Oh, I say again! What an attractive little number! Very cute indeed. All those frilly bits, I mean. And exactly matching the little black knickers . . . How odd! Oh, I see. The clasp's at the front, is it? How novel! But rather handy I should imagine? But I do think that some more liberation is called for, don't you? The pressure in there does look rather intense. Especially as you're stretching back so nicely. We don't want anything to give way, after all. Perhaps you'd care to unhook? I can assure you it won't give offence.'

She slipped out of the bra and handed it to Mr James. Now she was proudly naked from head to foot. The men noticed at once that her lovely breasts were positioned exactly as they had been when encased in the bra. They were uplifted to exactly the same extent, without any suggestion of droop. Two beautifully extended nipples pointed upwards and slightly outwards, just as they'd done before. Two firm, perfectly rounded breasts, topped with hard, strawberry coloured nipples, were exposed to the light of the working day. Mr James bent forward until his face was directly over them. 'Good heavens! They *do* seem pleased to be free, don't they? Very perky indeed. Positively brimming with delight, in fact. Just excuse me while I introduce myself to them, if you don't mind.'

His tongue began to lap each excruciatingly suffused nipple in turn, causing them to stretch even more, until they felt they were about to burst. 'They certainly respond to a little kindness!' he breathed. 'That's always most gratifying, I can assure you. I'll just attend to them a little further before it's time to proceed with the important work of the day.'

Pauline moaned aloud as he swallowed one breast after the other as far into his mouth as he could. Firmly she pressed both hands under the cheeks of her bottom in order to prevent herself from fondling her tortured quim. For at least another sixty seconds Mr James continued to lick and lap, turning the moans to groans of delight.

At length he straightened up and reached for the buckle on his belt. Within seconds his trousers and pants were round his ankles and Pauline's eyes were glued to his more than adequate penis as it pointed stiffly up at his chin. 'Now then, Mrs Peach,' he said softly. 'If I were to kneel down here . . . Fortunately the carpet is of a very high standard, so you needn't be concerned as to my personal comfort . . . Perhaps you could move that leg a fraction to one side?' . . . Now then, now that I've slipped out of these I think it's time for me to slip into something more comfortable. Purely and simply so that we can give the chair an exceptionally thorough going-over. A really good workout, in fact. We'll put it through its paces, I'm sure. Just see if we don't.'

Having dropped to his knees in front of her, Mr James carefully positioned himself between her long, outstretched legs, glancing again at the visibly moistened target of his ambitions, so openly in view, so ready to be taken. He judged his aim to perfection, leaning forward without any guidance of hands and slowly starting to sink himself into the hot little honeypot that was entirely at his command. As he started to penetrate her, she looked up over his shoulder at Harry and smiled shyly but sexily, her face now flushed with arousal rather than embarrassment. Much to her delight, Harry returned exactly the same smile. They held each other's eyes as Mr James eased himself into her up to the hilt.

No sooner had Mr James entered her than he felt her starting to climax. She stared into Harry's face, delighted that he was able to see for himself the effect that Mr James was having on her. Without breaking the eye contact, Pauline began to roll her head from side to side, moaning softly to herself as she massaged each throbbing, overwrought nipple between forefinger and thumb. She knew that Harry wished he was the one between her legs, and she also knew that he knew she wished the same. Nevertheless, there was something extremely exhilarating about him sitting over there watching her being had by someone else.

After a while Mr James inched backwards by degrees, very slowly, taking his time and savouring every second, just as he had when he'd sunk into her a short time before. Eventually he withdrew himself all together. 'Suppose I said you weren't getting any more?' he murmured teasingly. 'Would you be very disappointed?'

She groaned and thrust forward with her groin, as if she hoped to snare him unawares. 'Not quite so fast,' he laughed quietly, pulling back another inch or two, so that his long damp member was tantalisingly just out of reach. 'Everything comes to she who waits.'

She slid her hand down to her quim and encircled her clitoris, gasping with relief. 'That's not allowed either,' he chuckled, guiding her hand back to her nipple. 'I've told you already, you've simply got to wait. You'll enjoy it all the more.' To her dismay, be backed even further away, making her fear she was being deserted. Her worries were groundless, however. He lowered his face and kissed her lightly between the tops of her legs, before using the tip of his tongue to sample her fruitiness. He was far from disappointed. She was as juicy as a honeydew melon, and as far as he was concerned, every bit as sweet. Again she groaned with frustration.

He pushed his tongue further inside her. Pauline felt herself fainting away with desire as he proceeded to eat her alive. She was yearning for the comfort of his penis, the comfort of the strength and stiffness of his elongated male organ. But it was not to be. Not for a while, at least. For the moment she was obliged to suffer the delicious torment of his lips and tongue as he worked on her with devilish expertise. She stared at Harry, wide-eyed and imploring. But there was nothing he could do to help, much as he would have liked to provide her with the comfort she craved. All he could do was watch as she thrashed her head wildly from side to side and groaned loudly. 'Please!' she gasped breathlessly. 'Please let me have it now!'

But Mr James was not inclined to ease her plight. He gobbled her more, making her shriek and cry real tears. Yet again she stared at Harry, her eyes begging for help. If only she could have his dick, she thought to herself. Young Harry's. Right now. Stuck right up inside her. How wonderful that would be!

Mr James' mouth was making her climax, but it was not the sort that satisfied. Much the opposite, in fact. It simply heightened the intense longing she felt. It made her yearn even more to be filled to the brim. To be full of hot male flesh. It made her long to be shafted as stiffly as Mr James could manage, whilst Harry sat at his desk and watched. That would be really exciting, Harry watching intently whilst she was being stuffed with length after length of another man's steaming hot cock.

Just when the torture was becoming intolerable, Mr James at last finished his meal and lifted his head. He was a very sloppy eater, she thought to herself, staring at his glistening lips and chin. Then he moved forward to his former position at the apex of her thighs. There he paused, coiled like a cobra about to strike. She took a deep breath and prayed that relief was close at hand. Or at pussy, she supposed she really ought to say.

She felt the tip of his ample erection brushing her lower lips, and looked knowingly across at Harry. He returned her stare and she fully understood that he wished he was there himself. But did he realise just how much she was going to enjoy having him watch?

Suddenly Mr James arched his back and then drove himself forward and into her with all the power he could muster. 'Now to test our office equipment!' he growled. But his words were drowned completely as she screamed with the ecstasy of sudden, uncontrollable orgasm.

* * *

There is very little left to add, except to record for posterity that the chair performed with the utmost credibility, taking into account the extensive battering to which it was subjected. The rocking and swivelling movements showed no signs of instability, the rollers remained locked, even under the most extreme pressure, and so did the reclining mechanism. The springing proved itself firm, yet buoyant and comfortable, and gave no indication of being anywhere near breaking point. The chair did not squeak or creak or complain in any manner whatsoever. It did all that it should and nothing it should not have done. In short, it behaved impeccably. Which is more than can be said for its occupant, who gave her normal post-penetration performance. The sort of exhibition, from the very moment she was speared, that had once prompted a boyfriend to remark, rather cheekily she'd thought at the time, that if only she could orgasm for England we'd be assured of at least one Olympic Gold.

Because the chair had proved itself so worthy, Mr James was an extremely happy man as he struggled to regain his feet as well as his Y-fronts, his trousers and his composure. 'Yes . . . Thank you . . . Mrs Peach . . . Thank you so much . . . That was a most, er, exhaustive and, um, satisfying experience . . . Excuse me whilst I catch my breath . . . Her-Hum . . . Ah, that's better . . . As I was saying, a most pleasing experiment . . . One can't research these matters too thoroughly, you know . . . Good Lord, I'm more tired than I thought . . . Excuse me again. A few deep breaths should do the trick . . . Ah yes! Now I'm OK . . . Yes. Well, that was a comprehensive testing, don't you think? We really put that demonstration model through the mill, didn't we? I can't imagine that it will have to put up with any greater wear and tear than that. Unless of course . . .?

'Now that's a point I hadn't entirely considered. Perhaps I shouldn't be quite so hasty in my judgement. After all, the price is astronomic. Perhaps I am being a little premature?

It's just possible that I'm wrong – about the stress and strain factor I mean. It *is* conceivable that it might, at some stage in its life, be subjected to an even greater burden. Unlikely, but conceivable, nevertheless.

'Harry! Harry, put down that draft conveyance for a moment, will you. And come over here, if you please. Good grief! No need to rush, my lad. We've got all day. You nearly knocked your desk over in your haste . . . Now then, Harry. Pay attention, please. This is very important indeed. Mrs Peach here is helping me to decide on the suitability of this new armchair. For my office, of course. And I'm finding it a rather difficult decision to make, bearing in mind the huge cost of the article in question. Not to say astronomic. Now then, I must say that I am minded to buy it. It has just performed exceptionally well, as you may have noticed. But I don't want to be accused of extravagance or lack of research. My partners can be rather parsimonious. So before I finally make a decision, I am anxious to know whether it is liable to face an even more strenuous assault in the future. And if so, whether it's entirely up to the job. In short, Harry, I feel I should seek a second opinion.

'Harry, old chap. I know it's asking a lot of you, and that it's outside the terms of your contract of employment, but I was just wondering – would you be prepared to help?'

Pauline snuggled comfortably back in the chair and watched Harry start to disrobe. As she did so, she could feel Mr James' fluid beginning to ooze out of her. She sighed happily to herself. What a glorious feeling! What a glorious feeling, lying back here, porked purple and prodigiously spunked . . . and eagerly waiting for a second man's cock to do it to her all over again! And this time it would be Young Harry on the end of that cock! What a disgraceful but truly glorious sensation! She knew it was wrong, of course, but she could do nothing to alter her feelings. Her one consolation was that this was none of her seeking. She had no say in the

110

matter. All she could do was open her legs and oblige.

She gazed at the handsome penis that Harry had just revealed. It was almost exactly like Michael's. Long and thick and as straight as a die. Even his balls reminded her strongly of Michael. They were weighty and nicely rounded, and hung high, just as every girl preferred. She was in no doubt that she was going to enjoy him. And she was sure that he felt the same about her. She could see that his long, smooth cock was incredibly swollen and rigid. What a shame that it was impossible to have it in her mouth at the same time as it was pleasuring her down below!

Mr James moved to one side, allowing Harry access to the beautiful girl on the chair. Access which that young man wasted no time at all in taking. 'Ohhhh!' she gasped, as he speared her with an alacrity that took her by surprise. Then he started to pump, forcefully and hard, displaying an urgency that made her squeal with delight.

'I'm sorry,' he murmured, after kissing her with his tongue. 'I ought to be much more gentle than this. But I just can't help myself. You're far too gorgeous.'

She smiled at him. 'It doesn't matter,' she giggled, one violent thrust following another and bouncing her up and down on the chair. 'But you'll never make it last.'

'You might be surprised,' he panted, bouncing her more than ever.

'That's the ticket!' enthused Mr James. 'That's the sort of really comprehensive workout we need. Give it all you've got, young man! It's absolutely vital that you do. Spare it nothing, dear boy. Show it no mercy at all. I said I needed a second opinion and by jove you're giving it to me! A second opinion, I mean, of course.'

On and on raced Harry, seeming never to tire. On and on he thrust, pounding her and bouncing her wildly up and down whilst she squeaked and squirmed and squawked. He was voiding her completely at the end of each withdrawal, then lifting his buttocks high in the air before plunging down

111

and back into her with a splat. The pace was quite phenomenal, and the degree of athleticism required was exceptionally high. Nonetheless, he continued to pound with all his might, thrusting his penis into her up to the hilt, and then out and back again at electrifying speed. He knew he ought to be providing her with a far more varied and sophisticated service, but he just couldn't slow down. All he wanted was to pump her as hard as he could.

But Pauline had no objections. He was driving her into a delightful state of oblivion with the speed and strength of the coupling.

'Good grief!' Mr James breathed softly. 'That's really what I call putting your back into it!'

Harry was in no need of encouragement. He continued to plough into her with gusto, ramming one stroke after another into her from a considerable height, using his feet, knees and back to provide the power he needed. Mr James watched in admiration as he hammered her from one orgasm to the next.

Pauline goggled up at the ceiling in disbelief. His stamina was even greater than George's, she gasped to herself, as time sped happily by.

Still Harry showed no sign of tiring. With his face buried in acres of fine firm breasts, he shagged on and on and on, quite unable to get anything like enough of the piping hot little pussy he was stretching as tight as a drum.

An eternity, and a second tidal wave of sperm later, Pauline at last opened her eyes and blinked slowly. Where on earth was she? Had she been dreaming or something? Where were her clothes? Why did she ache all over? Why couldn't she move a muscle to save her life? Had she fallen into some sort of coma? And why was her poor pussy absolutely burning alive?

Then the memory of Mr James and Young Harry, and the testing time they'd given to the new armchair, came flooding back to her. There was no doubt that the chair had stood up extremely well to the ordeal, but there was considerably more doubt about her. She could see quite clearly, but when she tried to speak nothing seemed to happen. Perhaps she could signal to Mr James that she was in need of assistance? An ambulance and a stretcher would do for a start . . .

Why was she stuck so fast to this chair? Why on earth was that? Ah! Perhaps it wasn't due to any physical deficiency on her part? Perhaps the chair was stuck to her? If so, she sincerely trusted the covers were washable. Would it ever be the same again? Would she, for that matter? Crumbs, that Young Harry had legs and other appendages like steel tree trunks! What a pounding he'd been able to give her!

'Can you . . . give me . . . a hand up . . . please, Mr James?' she was able to croak fairly clearly.

'Of course, my dear young lady. Of course. It's the least I can do after all the help you've given. I'm deeply grateful to you. Deeply grateful.'

'Thank you, Mr James,' she gasped as she came unsteadily to her feet.

'My pleasure, my dear. My pleasure entirely.'

'Have you seen my knickers anywhere?' she wheezed, tottering a few paces to her left as she spoke. 'And my bra?'

Mr James smiled patiently and nodded to where Harry was standing directly behind her. 'I think that might be a trifle premature,' he murmured. 'If you see what I mean, Mrs Peach?'

Pauline turned her head and peered back over her shoulder at Harry. Crikey, that was incredibly quick! As he leant against a filing cabinet, naked and short of breath, she could see that his dripping wet tool was already halfway hard. It was poking out at her, horizontally, in a rather appealing manner. In fact, in a very appealing manner, if the whole sordid truth had to be told. And it was stiffening by the second. It was raising its head and gaining in height as she watched. Very soon it would be as tall and as proud as ever.

Oh dear! There was no mistaking the nature nor the urgency of his desire. There was no mistaking what he was after as he continued to stare avidly at the cheeks of her pouting bare bottom and grow in size. He was wanting a second helping. Even though he'd only finished his first course less than a minute ago!

'Sorry, Harry!' she giggled, immediately settling herself back on the armchair and then holding her arms out towards him. 'I hadn't realized . . .'

Pauline closed her eyes and groaned with pleasure as, once again, she felt the long thick shaft of Young Harry's young manhood slithering all the way up to the top of her quim. It had lost none of its size and strength, she reflected briefly, as the first delightful sparks of orgasm began to fan upwards from her groin. 'Ohhhhh!' she sighed breathlessly, clamping her thighs round his waist and pushing hard against the power of his erection until he was embedded in her as far as he could possibly go. She wrapped her arms round his neck and hungrily sucked his tongue into her mouth. Harry remained motionless, allowing her to massage him with her vaginal muscles and work her tongue against his. Then he slid his hands underneath her bottom and wrapped one round each damp, slippery cheek. Crammed as he was into every last available millimetre of pussy space, he squeezed hard with both hands and held in his mind the memory of those same big, beautiful buttocks that he'd seen wiggling their way across the room some sixty seconds beforehand. Big and beautiful and bouncy they'd been, and as naked as nature intended. And, to add just that touch of piquancy, liberally daubed with streaks of freshly shot semen. Thick, white streaks smeared decoratively across the glossy pink cheeks of a posterior so perfectly moulded and formed that he'd feared he might shoot his lot there and then. There and then as he'd stood watching it wiggle and jiggle and wink at him from six feet or so away.

With that portrait of carnality firmly framed in his head, Harry began to thrust harder and harder and harder into the tightness of her overflowing vagina. Pauline, in response, groaned louder and longer and wriggled her hips in delight. His fingers were now buried deep into the cheeks of her bottom, but the discomfort only added to the pleasure she felt. Suddenly he pushed a finger into her anal opening, and she screamed at the intensity of the climax this provoked. He lowered his mouth to her bulging nipples, causing her to scream even more.

As for Mr James, he stood immediately to one side of the wildly bucking armchair, surveying the repeat performance with fascination and listening to the rather satisfying squidge, squelch, squidge of second – and third-hand sperm. Then, noticing that her top half was temporarily unattended, he leant forward to apply his hands where Harry's mouth had been. His kindly act was instantly rewarded as Pauline reached eagerly for his zip and plucked him out, one handed, in the twinkling of an eye. 'Thank you,' he gasped, as she closed her lips round his bloated member and pushed slowly forward with her head until it was lost from sight. Then she drew back to the very tip, before repeating the exercise again. Mr James stared down at the wondrous sight of her mouth engorging and disgorging his overwrought penis. 'You'll excuse us, I hope, Young Harry?' he gurgled, gritting his teeth and clenching his fists.

But Harry was too busy even to hear him, let alone complain about interference. Still fixed on the mental image of those spectacular, sperm-laced buttocks, he gasped, then moaned, then groaned, and then burst forth in a further flood of seed. As if by mutual agreement, Mr James did exactly the same, squirting hotly into her face, mouth and throat, whilst below her waist Harry continued to pump vast quantities of himself into her . . . and whilst Pauline continued to wriggle and writhe in one long orgy of over-indulgence, basking in the luxury of being swamped from two different sources at once.

Pauline swallowed with evident relish, carefully gleaning every last savoury drop before handing a gradually contracting Mr James back to himself. Then she set about cleaning her face like a cat, delicately licking her fingers as she did so. Mr James had erupted so violently that both sides were streaked from chin to hairline. Yet that was only a small percentage of the amount he'd vented, such was the ferocity of the passion aroused by her beautiful mouth.

To her surprise, she suddenly realised that Young Harry was still very much alive and on board and rutting away as before – as rigid and rampant as ever, even though she knew he'd only just shed his second load. Crumbs, she thought to herself, he was truly amazing! He hadn't slackened in size or speed, or anything, despite the fact that he'd made it for the second time just a few moments ago! That was ever so rare. Carrying on without any pause, she meant. Michael had managed it a couple of times, but that was all. Once when he'd been very worked up after smacking her bottom in anger over her little misadventure with Jonathon Ward. And David had done it to her at least three times non-stop on that deserted beach in Majorca. But he'd been drinking brandy and smoking grass, which had probably helped to keep him so stiff . . .

She glanced to one side and noticed that Mr James had flopped down on his desk, looking decidedly the worse for wear. Oh well, if he was out of play she was sure he wouldn't mind if she gave all her attention to Harry. After all, he certainly deserved it. It was a really stunning performance, in every sense of the word. And once again, that old familiar fire was welling up inside her. It had been there all the time since he'd started, of course. Mind you, it was always there in some way, shape or form. Her pussy never really left her alone for a moment. Oh Lordy, he was making her come once again!

Pauline opened her eyes as the anguish began to recede.

Slowly she turned her head and blinked. Good heavens, she'd spoken too soon! Mr James was up on his feet – and that wasn't all that was up! His recovery rate was almost as good as Young Harry's. And there was no mistaking his purpose as he advanced on the chair, menacingly erect yet again. Clearly he was intending to take over from Harry, even though the latter was still in mid-stride . . . and now Harry was clearly intending to assume Mr James' earlier role in her mouth. Crikey, that would be nice! She'd really *love* to do that to him. She just knew he'd taste really special.

The men wasted no time in re-ensconcing themselves deep in her favours. She was double-dicked in a trice. Hooked high and low before she had time to blink. Whilst Mr James beavered away between her legs, making her squirm her hips with pleasure, she swallowed and sucked greedily at Harry, delighting in the added intimacy of having him in her mouth, as well as his tight, swollen testicles in the palm of her hand. Slowly and sweetly she began to fellate him in time with the long, steady push and pull of Mr James inside her. She closed her eyes, savouring the rhythm she'd established between the two rampant male organs she was accommodating. Once again she wriggled her hips. What a lovely sensation! What a delicious sensation, sitting here, doubly plugged, in a pool of thick, sticky come! And how lovely to be using her mouth on Young Harry! He reminded her so much of Michael. How lovely to be able to do this to him!

Wasn't it strange, she reflected thoughtfully, pushing down with her head until Harry was deep in her throat. Wasn't it strange how men always tasted quite different? Always nice, but never the same. All men seemed to possess their own distinctive flavour. They differed from each other both in the hot hard flesh on which she sucked and the fluid on which she subsequently feasted. And just as she'd anticipated, Harry had a *very* appetizing flavour all his own. She couldn't wait to sample what she knew was to come . . .

Pauline moaned and closed her eyes at a series of

particularly sharp thrusts from Mr James. He seemed to be gaining size inside her . . . and he'd been far from small up to now! Yet with every push he seemed to fit tighter and tighter, and she was sure he probed deeper each time.

It was true! It wasn't her imagination! He really was growing in stature. Not only was he poking her where he hadn't poked her before, but he was taking noticeably longer to withdraw. Perhaps it had something to do with him having enjoyed watching Young Harry bonk her till she was blue? Had that inspired him to greater heights? Or lengths, she supposed she ought to say. Or was it the current stimulus of seeing Harry's huge weapon slithering in and out of her mouth at the same time as his own was servicing her elsewhere? Whatever the reason, it was a very welcome turn of events. Those girls who claimed that size didn't matter were talking a load of hooey. Perhaps she could extend him even further if she wriggled her hips even more? And if she guided his face back to her painfully aching nipples?

Oh, dear! For a respectably married young lady, she wasn't exactly behaving just as she should. But what else could she do? As long as George Franks had those photographs she had no option but to submit. It wasn't her fault that her body responded in the way that it did. That was simply how she'd been put together. It was simply how she was made. She was just as powerless to prevent herself enjoying the liberties that were being taken with her as she was to prevent the liberties themselves. And at least she had the comfort of knowing that she would have prevented them had she been able. She wasn't the very best wife in the whole wide world, but she was convinced she wasn't the worst. For the time being, all she could do was to ensure that poor Michael never got to know . . .

Oh, Mother! Mr James was making her erupt all over again! Really violently, too. She'd just have to hang on to Young Harry with both hands until she was done. When she was finished, she'd concentrate on making him spout like a fountain. She hoped he still had plenty to yield. She was feeling decidedly greedy. Using your mouth on a man was always bound to stimulate your sexual appetite. But when you were also receiving a very respectable pussy-pummelling at one and the same time . . .!

For the second time that morning Mr James implanted her below the waist, spilling semen into her tight little passage to mingle and mix with the copious quantities she'd already received. Nevertheless, the long hot bursts provoked the usual response and she started to climax again.

At last she was through and was able to devote all her attention to Harry. Holding him with both hands, she slowly drew back her head until the knob of his steaming erection was lightly touching her lips. 'Where would you like to be?' she whispered. 'In here or down below?'

'Your mouth is just great,' he croaked.

She kissed the overstrained tip and then ran her tongue all around it. 'You're beautiful!' she said softly, licking him all the way down to the root, and then all the way back. Slowly and lovingly she rubbed every inch of the hard, scalding-hot cock back and forth over every inch of her face. Then, as Mr James watched in admiration, she opened her mouth wide and swallowed him all the way down to his balls.

'You're beautiful too!' he only just managed to gasp.

Skilfully she gave him head, feeling him respond more and more with every stroke. She reached out and ran a hand over his firm male buttocks. He was so like Michael, she said to herself once again. Then she cupped her hand under his testicles, admiring their size and weight. Very gently she began to squeeze in time with the rise and fall of her head. Harry goggled down in disbelief. This was a fantastic experience – a blow job from a really pretty girl. He could tell that it was going to bring him off with one hell of a bang . . . even if he had already come twice in her sweet little cunt . . .

Suddenly Harry threw back his head and let fly, straight down her throat. She pulled back quickly, allowing his hot creamy juices to splatter her face. She always loved to do that. Then she returned him to her mouth in order to savour the taste. Greedily though she gobbled and guzzled, she was simply unable to keep up with him. Stream after stream jetted into her, most of which she was able to swallow, though some she was obliged to let dribble out of her mouth and down her chin.

It was just as she'd expected. He had a lovely fresh flavour. She wished she could stay like this forever, gulping down mouthful after mouthful of Harry and enjoying the way in which the surplus was now dripping onto her bare boobs. He was certainly providing her with the bounty she'd earlier craved. She was rather glad she'd read somewhere in one of her magazines that there were absolutely no calories whatsoever in the produce of a man's loins . . .

CHAPTER 6

Tracie's Turn

Mr James and Young Harry were exhausted as they clambered into their clothes, their limp, lifeless tackle a testimony to Pauline's achievements. As for Pauline herself, she was absolutely awash with her favourite substance. As she stood up from the chair she could feel it flowing out of her and running down both legs. The cheeks of her bottom were thickly coated, as was her chin, and her face and magnificent breasts were generously streaked as well. Fond as she was of the stuff, she knew she was in a bit of a mess.

'Goodness!' she gasped, having glanced at her watch as she bent to retrieve her frothy black undies from the carpet. 'Just look at the time! And I've hardly done any work!'

'I don't know about that,' Mr James muttered wearily, his trousers and pants round his knees and his sated, shrunken dick drooping lazily north to south. 'But you've certainly done an excellent job of work on me . . .!'

Ten minutes later Pauline slipped out the ladies' cloakroom and headed briskly to her own small office on the same floor. It was just as well that the firm had an ample supply of paper towels, she thought to herself, as she opened the door and hurried inside.

'Ah, there you are, Pauline!' cried the very attractive raven-haired girl who was lounging on Pauline's chair and displaying several yards of shapely, sun-tanned legs below the hem of her micro mini-skirt. 'I thought you must have got lost.'

'Oh, er, hello, Tracie,' she mumbled, trying to collect her thoughts. It was Tracie someone or other. She couldn't quite remember the surname. Tracie, who was Mr Davis-Davies' secretary. The dreaded Mr Davis-Davies. The partner in charge of all matters appertaining to the secretarial staff. Pauline wasn't sure why, but none of the other girls seemed to like him at all. On occasions she'd caught them whispering secretly about him amongst themselves. But she'd not been let into their confidence. She supposed she would be when she'd been with the firm a while longer.

'Mr Davis-Davies has been looking for you,' said Tracie. 'He sent me to find you.'

'What's it about?'

'I'm not exactly sure,' she lied.

Pauline straightened her dress and patted her hair to check that all was in order. 'I'd better go at once,' she murmured. 'I hear he's got a bit of a temper.'

'He can wait for a while,' Tracie replied casually. 'There's something I want to show you first.'

'Oh. What is it?'

Tracie held up a square brown envelope, smiling to herself as she spoke. 'A gift from my friend George. Because I liked it so much.'

'George?'

'George Franks, of course. I expect you've heard rumours about the two of us?'

'Er, not really.'

'I'm sure you have. It's no great secret, anyway. Secretaries are always having it off with the men at the office, aren't they, Pauline?'

'Er, well . . .'

'It's only natural. In fact, it's the best part of the job. If it wasn't for that little perk, the salary would be ridiculous.'

'I suppose it isn't very good.'

'Come and have a look at this,' Tracie giggled naughtily, standing up and dropping the envelope on the desk beside

Pauline's keyboard. 'I think it's great! But tell me what you think.'

'What is it?' Pauline asked nervously, feeling a strange sense of foreboding as she moved up to the desk.

Tracie pulled a large colour print out of the envelope. 'You and Jim Browne!' she giggled again, obviously highly amused. 'Compliments of George's new camera. Taken last night, I'm told. Whilst you and Jim were occupied with other matters.'

'Oh, no!' she gasped in dismay. 'Surely it isn't?'

'Have a good look for yourself. George is very pleased with it from an artistic point of view. He thinks the composition is perfect. See how the side view of your face is clearly in focus, despite the fact that seventy-five percent of the picture consists of a close up of your big bare bottom bent over the photo-copier, and Jim's dick right on the point of entry.'

'Oh, mother! I simply can't bear to look!'

'That's just how my husband likes to do it to me,' sniggered Tracie. 'From behind, I mean. But I guess any girl with a nice plump bum mostly gets it that way. I'm sure you do, Pauline.'

'Oh, grief!' she groaned, goggling at the obscene photograph. 'How hideously embarrassing! You can see every tiny detail!'

'I think it's fantastic!' enthused Tracie. 'I'd be proud of it if it were me. And I've never seen such a pretty rear end. No wonder Jim's cock looks so swollen!'

'Tracie! It's dreadful!'

'He screwed me like that last week. Bottoms up over my dining room table. I wish George had been there to take photographs.'

Pauline turned away in despair, feeling she'd die of shame, unless the floor opened up and swallowed her first. How could George be so awful?

'Don't go yet!' Tracie said softly.

'But Mr Davis-Davies.'

'He can wait. This photo has really stirred me up, Pauline.'

'Pardon?'

'I don't see why the men should have all the fun,' laughed Tracie, moving to the door and sliding the bolt shut. 'It simply isn't fair.'

'You don't mean—'

'I certainly do,' Tracie replied eagerly, tugging once at her wraparound top and then dropping it on the desk by way of confirmation. Her button-up mini-skirt followed suit within seconds, leaving her standing directly in front of Pauline, tall and proudly naked except for her high-heeled shoes. 'You can see I came prepared,' she breathed, gesturing down at her firm bare breasts and dark triangle of pubic hair. She reached out for the well-filled top of Pauline's dress with the lightest of touches. 'Don't you like me enough?'

'Tracie, I . . .'

'Don't you fancy me at all?'

'It's not that . . .'

Slowly and lovingly, Tracie ran a finger through Pauline's long blonde ringlets. 'You're so beautiful,' she whispered, leaning a fraction forward and kissing her, fleetingly, on the lips. 'So incredibly beautiful.'

The shape of Pauline's nipples was now clearly visible through the lightweight fabric of her summer dress. Tracie continued fondling the ringlets, but at the same time she began brushing the back of her other hand against the tip of each thrusting breast in turn. Brushing so lightly that Pauline almost cried out at the sudden spark of electricity created by the other girl's touch. Tracie smiled into her eyes and then kissed her gently on the lips once more. This time she lingered several seconds longer than before, each girl savouring the sweetness of the other. Pauline stood stock still, trying not to give away any indication of the intense sensuality that was beginning to stir inside her. Tracie ended the kiss and began using her fingertips to trace the outline

124

of both nipples, very delicately, making them so hard that they felt as if they'd soon break into fragments.

Tracie smiled again. 'I bet you've made love to a girl before.'

'Not very often,' she stammered.

'Do you enjoy it?'

'Well, er, in a sort of a way, I suppose . . .'

Tracie began stroking and squeezing Pauline's breasts, so tenderly that Pauline felt that she was going to swoon away. 'You're so fuckable!' Tracie breathed hotly, feeling her own vaginal juices starting to run down both thighs. 'So soft and blonde and fluffy. So hot and moist and sexy, and unable to say no.'

'Tracie . . .'

Tracie kissed her again, this time using her tongue, briefly but oh-so-lovingly. 'You've been spanked by a girl, haven't you? I bet you loved every moment, didn't you?'

'Oh, well, er . . .'

Tracie reached behind Pauline with both hands and started to unzip her dress. Pauline raised a hand to stop her, but it was guided gently back to her side. 'The men don't deserve to have you all to themselves,' said Tracie, before kissing her again. 'You're far too gorgeous for that,' she added when she was through.

Thirty seconds later Pauline's clothes were on the floor around her feet, leaving her as naked as Tracie. 'Oh, I love that shaven pussy!' enthused Tracie. 'How long have you had it bare?'

'Since I got married . . .'

'It's lovely!' cooed Tracie, running a fingertip over the outer lips. 'So plump and pretty. And so incredibly smooth.'

'I use a special cream on it . . .'

Pauline closed her eyes as Tracie wrapped her arms around her and began to slide a hot, hard little tongue deeper and deeper into her mouth. Involuntarily she slipped both hands round Tracie's bare bottom, reflecting momentarily on the stark contrast between those smooth round cheeks and the usual hard male haunches. In their high heels, the girls were almost exactly the same height. Whilst Tracie's tongue pushed even deeper, Pauline sighed with pleasure as she felt a pair of hard pointed nipples begin gently teasing her own. The effect on Pauline was instantaneous. She could feel herself melting into her companion's soft, satin-like body, as they tightened their embrace. Then a bush of springy pubic hair was pressed firmly into her groin. Expertly her clitoris was located and worked upon by Tracie's pubic mound. 'Ohhh!' groaned Pauline, squeezing the firm, creamy-smooth cheeks she held in her hands and starting to orgasm at once. The sort of soft, slow, dreamy orgasm she could never have had with a man.

Slowly Tracie withdrew from the wet warmth of Pauline's mouth. 'You're incredible!' she whispered in admiration, as Pauline continued the long, gentle climax, completely oblivious to her surroundings. 'Utterly incredible!' she added, sliding both hands down around Pauline's bottom. 'And what a silky bum! It must drive your husband wild.'

But Pauline was unable to reply, because she was quite unable to hear or comprehend. She was in a world entirely of her own. A world of pleasure and peace, through which she floated on a cloud of silver dreams.

Tracie kissed her again, even deeper and more passionately than before. 'How can anyone come so easily?' she wondered enviously. 'And how much longer can it last?'

She decided to wait and see for herself. So there they stood together. There they stood locked tightly together, mouth to mouth, nipples to nipples, groin to groin, and hands cupped lovingly round each other's buttocks. Why did another girl's bottom always feel so nice? Tracie wondered to herself. She couldn't explain it, but she knew that most girls felt the same. Most girls found themselves turned on by the sight or feel of a shapely female bottom. And there was none shapelier than the one she was presently fondling with both hands. Those spectacular cheeks of Pauline's appealed to Tracie as much as they did to any man. If only she had a dick! She'd simply have loved to be able to fuck that beautiful bottom, as well as Pauline's slick little quim.

The two girls stood there for several more minutes, kissing passionately, whilst Pauline quivered and quaked in the throes of the most sustained and deliciously delicate orgasm she'd ever known in her life.

But at length it was over, and Pauline sighed with regret when Tracie gently drew back her head. 'That was lovely!' she groaned, still blissfully savouring the succulence of the other girl's mouth. 'Really, really lovely!'

'Yes, it was,' breathed Tracie, taking half a step back and tenderly squeezing the plumpness of Pauline's warm, wide open pussy in the palm of her hand. Then she slid two fingers inside, very slowly, gasping in surprise at the wetness and heat she encountered.

Pauline laid her head forward on Tracie's shoulder and immediately started to spasm again, slightly more sharply than before.

It *was* true what they said, Tracie thought to herself. This unbelievably fuckable blonde girl had more orgasm in her than a harem of houris. And nearly as much spunk as well, she thought as she glanced down at the dripping wet palm of the hand that had begun working away at the junction of Pauline's legs.

Mr Davis-Davies, small, dark and furtively Welsh, and known unaffectionately to his partners and employees as the 'Welsh Wizard', sat bolt upright at his desk, staring thoughtfully at the XT3 that stood in the corner beside him. The XT3 he had purchased some months beforehand for just this sort of occasion. Undoubtedly he'd been visited with a premonition, he decided. A premonition that it would be needed for some vitally important task. Being Celtic, he was prone to that sort of thing. His whole family was the same. His mother in particular had possessed incredible powers of second sight, he reminded himself proudly.

So there in the corner the XT3 had stood for more than three months, quietly awaiting its destiny. There it had stood untouched, untried and unloved. His mother would have been pleased with the vision he'd shown in acquiring it so far in advance of requirements. As far as his mother had ever been pleased with anything connected with her first-born son . . .

Mr David Davis-Davies was suddenly tempted to reach out for the XT3. But he resisted the temptation, as he'd resisted it for the last several months. Its time was drawing close, he told himself reverently. The hour of its ultimate glory was almost at hand . . .

Pauline sank to her knees in front of Tracie. 'Would you like me to make you come?' she asked, smiling up into her face.

'Oh, yes, please!' groaned Tracie, adjusting her stance as Pauline's face slid between her long, silky-smooth thighs.

Delicately, Pauline dipped the tip of her tongue into the wet, warm succulence that awaited her. 'You taste beautiful!' she murmured as Tracie's juices ran into her mouth.

Tracie cupped her hands round the top of Pauline's head and closed her eyes, sighing happily as Pauline's tongue flicked lightly in all directions. 'That's good!' she murmured quietly. 'I think you've surely done it more than a few times before . . .'

Pauline worked on her with all the expertise she'd gained over the years, darting the tip of her tongue in and out and then running it back and forth along the wide-apart labia. Running it so lightly back and forth that Tracie wanted to scream with joy. Eventually the licking ceased and Pauline pushed her mouth and tongue right inside and started to chew, relishing the sweet syrup of Tracie's loins as it trickled delightfully into her mouth and down both sides of her chin.

Tracie writhed her bottom slowly from side to side,

gasping with delight at the way Pauline's lips and tongue were devouring the inside of her pussy. She petted Pauline's head. 'That's good!' she groaned. 'That's wonderful!'

And still the delicate nibbling continued, even deeper inside than before. 'Jesus, you're good at it!' croaked Tracie, swooning with pleasure at the way she was being eaten alive.

Deeper and deeper went Pauline, licking and then sucking the delicious flesh into her mouth. The flavour was quite exquisite. And Tracie was so aroused that her internal oil flowed thickly and sweetly over Pauline's tongue and down her throat in a constant stream. Never had either girl experienced a more delightful sensation.

Tracie's breath was becoming increasingly more laboured, and Pauline knew that she could now bring her to a climax whenever she chose. She ran her hands up the back of Tracie's legs and wrapped them round the cheeks of her bottom, enjoying the lovely young flesh.

'Don't finish me off just yet!' pleaded Tracie, eyes tightly closed.

Pauline was happy to wait. Happy to leave Tracie teetering on the edge of her orgasm. For two or three long minutes she waited, her mouth as far inside Tracie as it could be, whilst she continued to suck and drink. She was enjoying the feeling of power, of being in command. Tracie had made love to her and now she was the one in charge. Now she was the one in control of how the love should be made. And she knew just how to prolong that lovemaking until such time as she chose to conclude it by drawing back her head and sucking hard on Tracie's sweet little clit.

A few minutes later both girls were dressed, but in each other's arms once again. As they kissed, Tracie could taste her own juices on Pauline's lips and tongue. 'You were fantastic!' breathed Tracie, when Pauline finally withdrew from her mouth.

'So were you,' Pauline replied with affection.

'You'd better hurry. That weird Mr Davis-Davies will be getting impatient. You'd better not keep him waiting any longer.'

'Oh, Lordy!' groaned Pauline. 'What on earth could he want to see me for? Surely it can't be . . .?'

To look at, Tracie was very much like Nancy, Pauline thought to herself, as she headed upstairs towards Mr Davis-Davies' room. Tall, slim, jet-black hair, impishly pretty features and lovely long legs, topped with a really cheeky little bum. Nancy Nicholson, her best friend, whom she'd known as long as she could remember. The only difference between them was that Nancy had now grown her hair right down to her waist, whilst Tracie's was cropped close to her head. Apart from that they were very, very similar looking girls . . .

Pauline supposed she hadn't been entirely honest and straightforward when Tracie had asked her about making love to other girls. But on the other hand, it wasn't really any of her business. There really hadn't been any reason why she should have told Tracie the truth. The truth about herself and Nancy. About the way they'd been looking after each other's pussies almost every week for years and years. It wasn't really anything to do with Tracie. After all, she hadn't even told Michael about that. Not that it was really sex, what she and Nancy did to each other. It was just an expression of the love they felt for each other. The strong, sisterly love. And your pussy felt like such a good little girl once it was over – once your best friend had finished loving her with her lips and tongue. She felt so peaceful and content for ages afterwards. She didn't try to boss you about and make all sorts of demands. She didn't scream out to be plugged full of hard male flesh. She just nestled there sweetly between the tops of your legs, very happy and content with life as it was . . .

Oh crumbs! Mr Davis-Davies! She was now standing right outside his door . . .

Kevin, the office boy, stopped in the corridor outside the kitchen, listening intently. There was the unmistakable sound of somebody washing up. As Tracie Trix was on tea duty that day, it could only be her, he told himself gleefully. Well, at least it was very likely to be her. If it was, and if she was alone, he'd make his move here and now . . .

Kevin felt nervous at the prospect. But then who wouldn't be, he asked himself wisely. And if he ventured nothing, nothing would surely be gained. At the very worst Tracie would make some joke about his age. Not that she'd done that for over a week now. Her favourite remark had been that he was hardly old enough to go to school. But recently she'd been much kinder, and had looked at him in quite a different way – a knowing, sexy sort of way. If she turned him down now, it wasn't the end of the world. Just a bit of a body blow. Just a bit of a pisser. But if she said yes, then indeed it would make his world. He would really and truly have arrived on the scene . . .

Oh God, please let her say yes! For years he'd thought of this moment. Of the opportunity to have his first woman. If it was Tracie in the kitchen, please let her say yes! He couldn't wait to get his hands on her, to run his hands all over her body and wrap them round that trim, sexy little bottom that moved so provocatively underneath her short, tight skirt. Oh Mary, his old man was threatening to burst open at the seams at the thought! There was a huge lump in the front of his trousers that no-one could fail to notice . . .

Just imagine if she said yes! He'd have done it at last! And not only would he have done it, but he'd have done it with an attractive married woman at least six years older than himself. None of his friends had been able to boast of that . . .

Silently Kevin peered round the half-opened kitchen door. He'd been right. Tracie was drying the cups and saucers, rather noisily, and she was on her own. As she leant forward across the draining board, her tiny mini-skirt was no more than a pelmet round the cheeks of her delightful little rear end. Indeed it was scarcely a pelmet, the hem having ridden up to a point where it displayed the crease between buttocks and upper thighs. For several seconds Kevin stared at the hint of cheeky bare bottom, feeling his penis swell even more.

He took a hesitant step forward, his heart beating faster and his hands beginning to sweat at the thought of what he was going to force himself to do. But there was no reason for him to react in that way, he told himself reassuringly. At the very worst she'd just laugh and tell him to behave like a good little boy . . .

'Hello, Tracie,' he said through a somewhat dry throat. 'It's nice to see you working. Can I give you a hand?'

'Of course,' she replied at once. 'How kind!'

'How's that?' he gulped, slipping his right hand under the seat of her skirt and taking a generous handful of bottom, very bare to his touch, due to the fact that she was wearing G-string knickers. 'Is that any help at all?'

'Yes, fine,' she said brightly, wriggling her hips provocatively against his hand. 'Let me finish drying this cup and I'll give you a hand as well.'

'Oh, my God,' he croaked, closing his eyes as he felt her long, slim fingers settling coolly round his throbbing erection. It was the first time he'd ever been held in that way.

'I think you were expecting me,' giggled Tracie, running the palm of her hand up and down the length of his shaft. 'I used to think you were rather too young, Kevin. But I can tell that you're a very big boy indeed!'

'I've been clearing the stockroom,' he only just managed to mumble, trying desperately to concentrate on what he had to say.

'Really?' she said with a smile. 'That sounds interesting.'

'I've cleared a space on the floor . . . big enough for two people to lie down . . .'

'Fascinating!'

'And I've put a bolt on the inside of the door,' he gurgled, as she continued to pet him inside his knickers.

'How incredible!'

'Would you like to see?'

'I'd love to, Kevin. What a good idea!'

'Great! Fantastic! Come on then. Let's hurry.'

'We can't go like this,' she laughed, indicating the position of their hands. 'We'll have to let go of each other first. Just temporarily.'

As Kevin fastened the bolt on the inside of the door, Tracie pulled her skirt up to her waist and stepped nimbly out of her tiny knickers. Kevin gazed in awe at her luxuriant bush of jet-black pubic hair. His penis seemed to stretch even further, causing it to ache with genuine pain. 'We'll have to be quick,' she whispered, unzipping him and taking his oh-so-urgent erection in both hands. She lay down on the floor, drawing him down between her legs, then slid him inside with practised ease.

Kevin gasped in wonder at the incredible sensation. A sensation that was entirely novel to him. He simply couldn't believe how good it felt. He'd often tried to imagine how it would be, but the reality far outweighed anything he'd ever expected. The glorious wet warmth and pliable tightness of her quim were a marvel to him.

'You don't have to be that quick!' she panted, as he flew in and out of her at speed. 'You can make it last a bit longer, if you want.'

Kevin slowed down. 'Sorry,' he muttered breathlessly. 'It felt so nice, I just got carried away. I just couldn't get enough . . .'

'You youngsters are all the same!' she giggled. 'Wham! Bam! Thank you ma'am!'

Kevin concentrated on keeping the pace as slow and easy as his over-excited tackle would permit. 'That's much better,' she sighed happily, as he slithered and slid back and forth

133

along the full length of her vagina. 'Now you're starting to make me come!'

Kevin was not exactly sure what she meant, but he was enjoying it, whatever it was. And he could see from the look on her face that Tracie felt exactly the same. Instinctively he began prodding her more sharply, and was delighted with the effect produced. So he kept on doing it, making her squeal with pleasure and wriggle her hips underneath him as hard as she could. But now he found he was unable to revert to a slower speed. He was unable to prevent himself poking her harder and faster with every thrust of his groin. He tried to reduce the pace, but he couldn't. He couldn't control the manner in which he was stoking her with all his strength. The delicious sensation in his loins was becoming more and more delicious with every stroke. Harder and harder he poled her, until his seed suddenly exploded into her with a velocity that neither of them could believe. 'Geronimo!' she gasped, wrapping her legs round him and then thrusting up with her bottom in order to force him as far inside as he'd go.

'You certainly seemed to enjoy that!' she laughed, when he'd finally finished emptying himself into her womb. When at last he'd concluded the very important business of shedding his wretched virginity.

'It was my first time,' he groaned, trying desperately to recover his breath as he lay beside her.

'Well, it certainly won't be your last. I shall see to that. Right now, in fact!'

So saying, Tracie lowered her mouth to his groin and sucked in the whole of his wet half-hard cock. The effect was immediate. Instantly he started to expand in her mouth. So quickly that she gasped in admiration. She lay back and in a flash he was between her legs and solidly inside her again. He could feel much of his own recently sown seed being forced out of her as he pushed all the way up to the top of her tight little passage. 'Kevin!' she gasped happily. 'I'm as full as I've ever been! And it must be years since I was gorged with virgin meat . . .'

He slid a hand underneath her bottom, relishing the silky texture. 'I'm not a virgin now,' he muttered, pumping her with all his might.

'I suppose not,' she puffed, thrusting her groin up to meet him.

He pulled her top open and was delighted to find that she wasn't wearing a bra. Clamping both hands back round the cheeks of her bottom, he sucked greedily at one erect nipple after the other, making her squirm and groan. This was the life, she told herself. This was what it was all about. How could anyone in their right mind expect you to stay faithful to one man when there was all this fresh, young meat to be had? All this prime, but not at all tender young pork . . .

As the waves of pleasure pushed her inexorably towards another climax, Tracie reminded herself to telephone her husband's company after lunch. She must ascertain the dates of that conference as soon as possible, in order to ensure a continuing supply of her favourite form of protein . . .

Kevin gazed with pleasure at Tracie's blushing bare bottom as she wriggled it into the G-string knickers. 'They're really sexy, aren't they?' he murmured appreciatively. 'The knickers, I mean. The way they cover you, but still leave almost everything on view.'

'Thank you, kind sir!' she said, wriggling her bottom at him in a highly sensual manner. 'But do you know why I always buy knickers in twos? In identical pairs, I mean? Can you guess why I never have just one pair of any particular colour or style?'

'Not really, Tracie,' he replied, deciding it was time to attend to his own garments, which were still round his ankles.

'For days like today,' she giggled again. 'Whenever I go out of the house I take an identical pair of knickers in my handbag. Identical to the ones I'm wearing. Then if anything nice happens, like it has just now, I can go home with a spotlessly clean pair that won't arouse suspicion.'

'That's called forward planning,' he said.

'But why do they have to be identical, Kevin? Can you tell me that?'

'Not really.'

'They have to be identical because my dear husband is *so* suspicious of me that he always makes sure he knows which knickers I'm wearing whenever I leave home. If I were to come back wearing a different pair, there'd be hell to pay.'

'You're joking!' he gasped.

Carefully she adjusted her ultra-short blue skirt. 'I wish I was, but it's true. I'd be over his knee in a flash. So I take the precaution of always having a spare pair of matching panties in my handbag. Just as I have right now. I'll slip into them before I leave work and put these ones into the washing machine as soon as I get home. That's the moment of maximum danger, of course. If he caught me red handed with a pair of spunk-encrusted knickers, that would be my lot. You wouldn't see me again.'

'I wouldn't want that to happen, Tracie. I want to see a lot more of you.'

'Don't worry, Kevin, you will. Hey! I've just had a really good idea. Instead of taking this pair home to wash, I'll give them to you. You can keep them as a memento of your very first time. They'll even bear your own personal hallmark. For a while, at least. How does that sound?'

'Fantastic! I'll treasure them forever.'

'I doubt that,' she laughed, pulling her top together and then pecking him lightly on the cheek. 'I always intended to keep the ones I wore when I first had it. But that was so many years ago that they've long since been mislaid. They were little virgin white ones. Quite appropriate at the time.'

She kissed him goodbye at the stockroom door and then stepped happily back to her room, feeling on top of the world.

There was nothing on earth to equal a really stiff shag from someone who wasn't your husband. Kevin was so young and keen and rigid it was a shame she couldn't put him in a bottle and take a swig whenever she chose. And if she could only bottle Pauline Peach as well . . .

CHAPTER 7

Pauline Bends The Rules

Mr Davis-Davies glanced at his watch and ground his teeth impatiently. Where the devil was Mrs Peach? She should have been here thirty minutes ago, he thought. Ah! The sound of footsteps approaching from the far end of the corridor. High heels, in fact. He glanced at the XT3 beside his desk. The hour of its coming was nigh . . .

Pauline stood outside the door, trying to steady her nerves. Oh gosh! That strange Mr Davis-Davies! He was really ever so odd. She had the very definite impression that even George and Jim were slightly afraid of him and kept out of his way as much as possible. Then there were all those rumours about him that the other girls hadn't yet repeated to her. Oh dear! She was all of a shiver . . .

Surely this interview wasn't going to follow the pattern of the morning so far? Surely there wasn't going to be some obscure reference to photographs or photocopiers or office equipment, quickly followed by the whoosh of her dress, the zoom of her knickers and the OOMPH of the commencement of the important work of the day? Surely, surely there wasn't . . .?

'Come in!' was the sharp response to her rather timid knock.

Mr Davis-Davies sat behind his desk, short, slight, dark, and definitely from beyond the border. He didn't speak. He didn't move. He simply stared icily at her as she stood nervously just inside the door. She found it impossible to hold his gaze. There was such a weird gleam in his eyes. What a cold fish, she thought to herself. Would she ever be able to find her voice to speak, assuming that he ever stopped staring at her and actually said something?

'Shut the door,' he said at last. 'And come forward so I can see you.'

Mr Davis-Davies didn't ask her to sit down, but then that would have been difficult as there was no chair on Pauline's side of the desk. 'Well?' he asked frostily.

'Sorry, sir. What was that?'

'Why are you so late?'

'Um, I'm sorry,' she stammered. 'Actually I was, er, helping Mr James in his room. In fact . . .'

'I can't accept that for a minute,' he snapped angrily. 'You work for Mr Fennell, not for Mr James. Isn't that correct?'

'Yes sir, but . . .'

'Do you consider you can absent yourself from your desk whenever you choose?'

'Mr James asked to see me . . .'

'That hardly explains such a delay in answering my summons. I'm not at all convinced that you're telling the truth.'

Pauline winced. Crumbs! She hadn't got off to a very good start at all. Mr Davis-Davies was definitely hostile towards her . . .

'I'm sorry to be so late, sir,' she murmured, staring at the floor as she spoke. 'It won't happen again.'

'I don't expect it will, Mrs Peach,' he said bleakly. 'It won't have an opportunity to happen again. Here is your P45 and your notice of dismissal,' he added, tapping a buff-coloured envelope that lay on the desk in front of him.

Pauline blinked in surprise. This was not at all what she'd expected. Much the opposite, in fact. And there was a very definite problem as well. Suppose Michael came to the office and made a fuss? Suppose he came and demanded to know why she'd been given the sack? Suppose he came into contact with George Franks and George told him about Jim Browne and the dirty photos?

And what about the money? They desperately needed her salary now that they had a mortgage to pay. And she needed that new dress for the cocktail party next week. And they were hoping to change cars later in the year. And they'd already started planning their next Spanish holiday. And there was that expensive tennis racket she'd already bought for Michael's birthday. And that video recorder they'd just bought on credit. And . . .

Oh dear! The list was endless. She earned nearly as much as Michael. They'd be stony broke without her wages. If she was dismissed by Snayles & Co so soon after joining them, she might have terrible trouble finding another job. Other firms might think there was something wrong with her . . .

She groaned to herself. It would almost have been better had her interview with Mr Davis-Davies gone along the lines she'd originally anticipated. At least there wouldn't have been all these added complications . . .

'Oh dear, Mr Davis-Davies. I mean, sir. And I thought I was doing so well here,' she whispered, with all the sorrowful sincerity she could muster. 'Mr Harris and Mr James both seem to think so. They said they were very satisfied with my, er, work . . .'

'It's nothing to do with them!' he barked loudly, banging the desk top with his fist. 'I'm in charge of the female staff. And I say who is to be hired and who is to be fired. Not Mr Harris and not Mr James. Not even the senior partner, Mr Fennell.'

Lordy! She must have said the wrong thing again. He did look ever so put out. She wasn't doing very well at all . . .

'I'm ever so sorry, sir. I didn't mean to sound rude. It's just that I thought everyone was pleased with my work. Can I ask why I'm being dismissed, sir?'

141

'You can certainly ask!' he snarled bitterly. 'But I don't have to tell you. You haven't been here long enough to gain any rights at all under the employment protection legislation. Legislation, I might add, with which I totally disagree. I can dismiss you on one month's notice without giving you any reason at all.'

'I know, sir. I realise that.'

'However, as everyone here knows well, I'm a fair-minded and reasonable man. Therefore I'm prepared to discuss these matters briefly.'

'Thank you, sir. Thank you very much.'

Pauline ran a hand through her hair. Crikey, you had to be careful what you said to him! She'd just creep round him and hope for the best . . .

'In the first place, I'm extremely cross at having been kept waiting for thirty-one and a half minutes.'

'I'm really sorry to be so late, sir. Really sorry.'

'But that's not the point at all,' he continued, as if she'd never spoken. 'I have compiled a list of your shortcomings,' he added coolly, taking a sheet of paper from his desk drawer. 'It makes very sad reading indeed.'

'I'm sorry . . .'

Sternly she told herself not to keep fidgeting from one foot to the other and to make a supreme effort to stop her hands fiddling with her knicker elastic through her dress. It just looked so bad when she did that . . .

'Item one,' he began angrily. 'It seems certain that yesterday evening you were personally responsible for the demolition of our photocopying machine, the long-serving QX2DL. A machine, I might add, of which I was personally very fond.' His voice quivered with indignation as he finished speaking.

'Perhaps something could be stopped out of my wages . . .?'

'Item two,' he continued as if he'd not heard. 'You have incited Mr Harris to order a replacement machine which is

142

prohibitively costly. Hideously expensive, in fact. Such extravagance I've never had the misfortune to encounter before.'

'I'm sorry.'

'Item three,' he almost choked on his words. 'By means of what I can only describe as malicious criminal damage, you have ruined a very valuable armchair that was on loan to Mr James. Of course the firm will have to pay for your wanton destruction. It will cost us a small fortune.'

Oh no! How embarrassing! So she'd been right when she'd thought the chair had looked rather the worse for wear . . .

'God only knows where this horrendous trail of damage would end,' he screeched, 'were we to continue your employment here!'

'Oh dear . . .!'

'Item four,' he said more calmly, fighting to gain control of himself. 'Item four. Apart from wreaking havoc with our equipment, you appear to have spent a great deal of the morning away from your room. I believe you've typed just half a letter so far. Half a letter out of thirty-three on tape!'

Pauline sighed heavily. That was also very true . . .

'And you have urgent photocopying to be done,' he continued. 'Urgent work to which you cannot attend, because of your earlier abuse of the machine.'

She hung her head and tried to mumble an apology, but the words just wouldn't come out.

'Item five. And this is by far the most serious charge of all. You have been guilty of conduct likely to bring the firm into disrepute. You have posed for what the law can only describe as obscene and indecent photographs, thereby rendering yourself and possibly this firm liable to criminal prosecution.'

'On no!' she cried. 'Surely not? Criminal prosecution? Me?'

'Yes, indeed. You. And maybe us as well, since it's clear that the photographs were taken on the firm's premises. The law takes a very dim view of this type of pornography. A very dim view indeed. I shall have to consider reporting the facts to the police without delay. That may be the only way to save the firm from prosecution.'

'Surely you wouldn't tell them? Surely you wouldn't report me?'

'I may well decide that I have no alternative. There could be thousands of these prints all over town.'

'But Mr Franks . . .'

'Mr Franks knows nothing of this matter. And the identity of the man in the photographs is also unknown.'

'But . . .'

'But nothing, Mrs Peach! But absolutely nothing at all!'

Pauline swallowed hard. This was terrible news. In fact, it was just about the worst it could possibly be. The shame and the disgrace! How weak and foolish she'd been! All this had stemmed from that fit of weakness at Jim Browne's flat last Monday. If only she'd been a bit stronger, she wouldn't now be facing the prospect of scandal and maybe even divorce . . .

'So what have you got to say for yourself?' he demanded sharply, making her jump. 'Is there any reason why I should not go straight to the police?'

Pauline swallowed hard. She'd better think jolly fast. She felt more like crying, but that wouldn't do any good at all. She must be positive and constructive. She must try to extricate herself from this ghastly situation. And the only way to do so was to win Mr Davis-Davies over . . .

Yes, she must concentrate all her efforts on Mr Davis-Davies. After all, he was only human. Well, she sincerely hoped he was. She must try to befriend him, even though that was a mind-boggling thought. He reminded her of a psychopathic rattle snake suffering from a peptic ulcer. Still, she had to try her best . . .

'Surely there must be a redeeming feature somewhere, sir?' she asked shyly, fluttering her eyelashes like mad. 'My productivity has been very good until this morning. Mr Fennell would confirm that, I'm certain.'

'Go on,' he said frigidly.

'Well sir, my work has been up to date every single day. Until last night, that is, when I rather got waylaid. You can ask Mr Fennell if you don't believe me. He's ever so pleased with me, sir. He's said so several times. You can check with him.'

'I shall have to. I can hardly regard as truthful someone who has acted as outrageously as you have.'

'I'm sorry, sir,' she said meekly, blushing and staring at her feet. 'I wish you would speak to Mr Fennell though. He'll tell you that I'm not as bad as you think.'

'I suppose it's possible that I may have misjudged you,' he said slowly.

Pauline smiled inwardly. That was better! He was beginning to defrost at last. Perhaps she should fold her arms behind her back so that her boobs were even more prominent? Perhaps she should also begin to fiddle absentmindedly with the hem of her dress . . .?

'Perhaps there is one redeeming feature, as you put it?' he mused thoughtfully.

'That's good to hear, sir,' she said, smiling as warmly as she could.

'Yes, I imagine it is, young lady. If it wasn't for this one saving grace, we wouldn't still be discussing the matter. You'd already be on your way home.'

Mr David Davis-Davies began to drum his fingers pensively on the desk, staring over the top of her head into space. He certainly looked a lot friendlier than a few moments earlier, she decided. But which way would he jump? Would he take her side and help her out of this muddle? Or would he really go to the police with the photographs? And what was this one saving grace that he said she possessed? Would it be enough to save her skin? She supposed she'd soon find out . . .

'I appreciate that a person's morals are her own affair,' he began again. 'Except, of course, when they bring the firm into disrepute. As they do here.'

She hung her head and crossed her fingers behind her back. He certainly wasn't as angry as he'd been a little earlier. Perhaps everything was going to be all right, after all? She could only hope and pray . . .

'As I have said, I consider there is – just possibly – a redeeming feature in your case. Maybe you're not completely beyond salvation.'

'I'm sure I'm not, sir. I can learn a lesson very quickly when I have to, sir.'

Mr Davis-Davies smiled thinly. 'I'm glad to hear that, Mrs Peach. Very glad indeed. For both our sakes. So are you now able to hazard a guess as to the nature of that one redeeming feature?'

Lordy, she rather thought she could! Was there nothing new in this life after all?

'Not really, sir,' she replied untruthfully. 'But I hope that whatever it is, it will encourage you to put a fresh complexion on certain matters, sir.'

'Yes, so do I, Mrs Peach. That thought has been uppermost in my mind for a while, I can assure you of that. A fresh complexion, yes.'

Mr Davis-Davies stood up from his desk and began pacing the carpet behind her. She told herself that she must stand still and say nothing. She mustn't even glance back at him over her shoulder. Appeasement was all-important. She must remain meek and mild and just stand here facing the desk, waiting to see what he decided . . .

'Yes, possibly,' he said after a minute or so. 'Possibly I could put a fresh complexion on certain matters and overlook what has happened so far. I am, in all honesty, very anxious to do that . . .'

Pauline decided that he was talking to himself rather than to her and that she'd say nothing until he had addressed her directly.

'Yes, indeed. A fresh complexion.' He moved close behind her and placed a hand lightly over the swell of each buttock. 'Yes,' he said again, as his hands began an extremely close examination of her pouting, lightly clad cheeks. 'Yes, these are certainly very delicate matters that I have here. Very delicate matters that I have in hand . . .'

This was much more like it, thought Pauline. In fact it was much as she'd originally expected. Fortunately he seemed absolutely fascinated by her rear end. She'd never been so thoroughly explored. Not roughly, but with a meticulous attention to every detail of every hollow and curve. Almost like a medical examination . . .

'Very well,' he said, dropping his hands to his side at last and striding purposefully back to his chair. 'I think I have reached a decision.'

'Yes, sir?' she asked anxiously.

'I have decided not to take the action I indicated earlier. I shall not dismiss you, nor report the matter of the obscene photographs to the authorities. Instead, I shall do as you suggest. I shall take heed of that one redeeming feature and put a fresh complexion on certain delicate matters.'

'Oh, thank you, sir!' she cried with relief. 'I'm so pleased! I'm really so ever so pleased!'

Mr Davis-Davies looked up at her, his face betraying more than just a hint of Celtic cunning. 'Maybe you will be, Mrs Peach,' he said slowly and deliberately, at the same time holding up an enormous plastic ruler, architect's XT3 variety, three feet in length and over half a pound in weight. 'On the other hand, maybe you won't. I think you can judge for yourself just how fresh that complexion will be.'

Pauline's stomach performed a somersault as she stared in horror at the huge, heavy ruler he was brandishing so triumphantly. Oh Mary, Mother and Father! Had she ever been in such desperate trouble as this?

Pauline was guided across the room towards her appointed place of torture, the evil-looking ruler held menacingly across the plump, pouting cheeks of her one redeeming feature – across the very centre of those oh-so-delicate matters upon which Mr Davis-Davies was fully intent on putting a fresh complexion. An exceptionally fresh complexion indeed.

At that very moment, Young Harry Hotspur closed the door of Mr James' room with a sigh. Pauline Peach! She was a princess! A real royal princess! Perhaps even a magical princess from one of those fairy stories his mother used to tell him when he was small. Actually, come to think of it, those long blonde ringlets made her look just like that picture of Sleeping Beauty he'd had on his bedroom wall . . .

Harry sighed again. Bloody hell! At long last he understood the *true* meaning of being in love. He'd often wondered, but now he knew for sure. It meant that when she was in view your eyes never for a moment left the object of your heart's desire. It meant that at all times you thought of no-one and nothing but her. It meant that you would willingly lay down your life for her sake. It meant all sorts of other things as well. But above everything else, it meant that you shuffled awkwardly around the office nursing a bulging, burning, permanent erection . . .

Pauline stopped in front of a chair and mahogany writing table, the XT3 ruler still pressed purposefully across the cheekiest part of her bottom. She was facing the back of the chair, which in turn was pushed right up to the edge of the table. The large bay window to her right shed its light directly onto her back. Pauline thought she understood the reason for the position of the furniture. She thought she understood it only too well.

'Bend over, Mrs Peach!' Mr Davis-Davies said coldly.

'Over the back of the chair?' she gulped.

'Of course. Over the back of the chair. And then place your forehead and forearms on the writing desk beyond.'

Pauline swallowed nervously, failing to move. 'Come on!' he snapped angrily.

'The chair seems a little bit high . . .'

'You can manage to bend over it, I assure you. Even if it means standing on tiptoes.'

'I'm not so sure.'

'Come now, Mrs Peach. I advise you not to provoke me any further.'

With a sigh of reluctance she leant forward slowly over the back of the chair and placed the palms of her hands on the table. Perhaps he'd settle for that?

'I said to rest your head and your elbows on the table. Not simply your hands.'

Pauline groaned inwardly. It meant that her rear end would be jutting way up in the air. But she supposed she had no alternative. She had to obey.

She began to bend forward from the waist. Very, very slowly and unhappily. The top of the chair cut into her midriff as her hair tumbled in front of her eyes. Further and further she bent, wincing at the pressure of the chair against her stomach. It was a good thing that she was wearing high heels, she thought to herself. Otherwise she'd never have been able to manage. But even so, she'd have to get right up on her toes to do as he asked. It was lucky she was quite an athletic girl who played squash three or four times a week.

Mr Davis-Davies stared at the nicely toned muscles in her calves and thighs. And the more she bent, the more perfectly toned they became, as did her buttocks. He gripped the ruler even more tightly and told himself to be calm. Time was on his side, not hers. The longer he made her wait, the more nervous she'd become. At last Pauline's forehead and elbows were resting on the surface of the writing desk, alleviating the pressure of the chair on her stomach as she took her weight elsewhere.

Mr Davis-Davies gazed in approval at the backs of her lovely thighs. They seemed to stretch upwards forever, from her nicely rounded knees up to the hem of her dress – which was now only a fraction below the swell of her buttocks. He longed to see more, but counselled himself to be patient. He balanced the ruler in his hand, savouring its length and weight and the power he could feel it possessed. Pauline could sense what he was doing, and tried to put it out of her mind. She'd been spanked in anger before, but never with anything remotely as vicious as that ruler. It would inflict untold agonies on the soft, bouncy cheeks of her bottom, just as a thick leather strap had once done to her sister, Pennie. Surely she was quite wrong in thinking that her wretched pussy was warming to the idea? The rest of her certainly wasn't.

Mr Davis-Davies could wait no longer. He reached out with the tip of the XT3 and lifted the hem of her dress, only a couple of inches, but enough to allow him his first tantalising glimpse of dimpled bare cheeks and tiny knickers. Honey-smooth cheeks and filmy black knickers that covered the merest fraction of that which had hitherto been hidden from view. The merest, merest of fractions.

Pauline could feel herself being exposed more and more to his gaze, and closed her eyes in shame. This nasty little Welshman was goggling at her all-but-bare behind! And she could just tell the effect it was having on him. She could just sense his gruesome little erection pushing its way upwards.

Skilfully, Mr Davis-Davies used the ruler to turn the seat of the dress inside out, so that the hem was more than halfway up her back, leaving her naked below the base of her spine apart from her almost non-existent knickers. Even higher he lifted the dress with the ruler, displaying the silver chain round her waist, before securing it in a double tuck so that there was no danger of it becoming displaced.

For a full five minutes he stood there, gripping the XT3 tightly in his right hand and relishing the moment – relishing also the way the sunlight was playing so intriguingly on upturned cheeks. He reached out playfully with the tip of the XT3 and pinged her knicker elastic, making her jump and squeal in fright.

It was at that exact second that Tracie was downstairs in the kitchen, her hand deep inside Kevin's boxer shorts. As Mr Davis-Davies studied the delightful contours, peaks and valleys of the spectacular scenery he'd unveiled with such expertise, Tracie squeezed hard and thrilled at the thought of what lay in store.

Pauline, on the other hand, was exactly at the opposite end of the pleasure spectrum. She was at full stretch, bent over the back of the chair, straight-legged and on tiptoes, her elbows and forehead resting on the highly polished writing table, the scantily clad cheeks of her bottom on prominent display several inches above the level of her head. The submissionary position, it might well be called. Whilst her buttocks trembled in terror, Mr Davis-Davies stared down at the tiny scrap of lacy black knicker material that was now stretched so tightly across the very plumpest part of the plumpest part of her bottom. Again he flexed his right wrist, reminding himself of the power of the wicked instrument of torture he held in his hand.

'Kiss-Kiss!' he chuckled, almost goodnaturedly, noting with approval how those near-naked cheeks quivered and quaked under his scrutiny. Those plump, pretty cheeks, the creamy-smooth pinkness of which contrasted so delightfully with the miniscule black knickers. 'Kiss-Kiss!' he mused thoughtfully, cocking his head to one side and scratching his chin as he spoke.

Pauline groaned to herself. Those wretched little knickers! They'd been nothing but trouble. Look what had happened the first time she'd worn them! Look what had happened at her engagement party, when that awful Tim Reynolds had found her alone and unprotected during that game of Hide Yourself In Your Undies! One of these days she really must pluck up courage to ask Michael to do it to her in there . . .

'Kiss-Kiss!' repeated Mr Davis-Davies, interrupting her thoughts. 'Kiss-Kiss!' he murmured again, his voice betraying just a hint of sardonic humour as he gazed at the perfectly sculpted cheeks that reared up right in front of him. Cheeks that felt so exposed and vulnerable as he stood there behind them, ruler in hand.

'Kiss-Kiss!' Mr Davis-Davies repeated, rather sharply. 'What an exceptionally saucy little garment to wear in a professional office!'

'Kiss-Kiss indeed!' he added angrily, slapping the ruler noisily against the palm of his hand.

Pauline gasped to herself. Oh, Lordy! She was all of a tremble . . .

'Kiss-Kiss!' barked Mr Davis-Davies. 'This is a positive disgrace!'

'I'm sorry!' she gasped in despair.

'Silence!' he yelped, smacking the XT3 down on the table top a few inches to her right.

'Eeek!' She was unable to stop herself squealing in alarm.

'Kiss-Kiss!' snarled Mr Davis-Davies, after a pause of thirty seconds. 'Well, if that's what you want, then I'm sure this XT3 ruler can oblige.'

Pauline was sure of it, too. She'd never seen a more vicious-looking thing, nor anyone so obviously intent on using it to its full potential.

'Kiss-Kiss!' he bellowed, glaring down in disgust at the words emblazoned on the tiny black triangle of over-stretched knicker material that was enraging him so greatly. 'Never in my life have I felt such a sense of outrage! But justice will be done!' Once again he slapped the ruler noisily onto the table.

Panic! The more she thought about the size and weight of that ruler, the more she continued to dread that which she was undoubtedly about to receive. And she knew that her knickers weren't going to offer her any form of protection at all. They were far too small and flimsy. At their very widest they were still less than the width of the ruler. It would bite straight through those little semi-transparent skimpies just as if they didn't exist at all . . .

'Kiss-Kiss!' ranted Mr Davis-Davies, swelling with fury

at the sheer impudence of those big, juicy ripe buttocks that shivered and shook in fear.

Pauline held her breath and tried to think about something else. Anything else, apart from the spectacle of a huge plastic ruler and her almost bare bottom thrust up towards it in abject surrender. Thrust way up into the air like some sort of sacrificial offering.

'Kiss-Kiss!' raged a furious Mr Davis-Davies, raising the XT3 ruler on high. 'So then, let's see how well my flexible friend can provide!'

'Help!' she squeaked in panic, but knowing full well that there was no hope of salvation.

'Kiss-Kiss!' roared a demented Mr Davis-Davies, bringing the ruler down in a huge hissing arc and cracking it across the offending words with all the power he could muster.

THWACK! the XT3 cried triumphantly.

A great flash of white-hot pain streaked right across both cheeks, at the same time seeming to burn deep down into them. Pain such as Pauline had never really been able to envisage. She jerked back her head and howled up at the ceiling like a woman possessed.

'That's much better!' breathed a suddenly relieved Mr Davis-Davies, taking a step back as he spoke. 'Much, much better indeed.'

'OOOHHHHHHHH!' shrieked Pauline, wriggling and writhing her buttocks from side to side as fast as she could, as if she hoped to cool them. 'OOOHHHHHHHH! THAT HURT!! THAT *REALLY, REALLY* HURT!'

'I'm so glad,' Mr Davis-Davies purred smoothly, clearly in excellent spirits now that the XT3 had finally proved its worth. 'Just take your time, Mrs Peach. Weep and wail as much as you like. After all, we have all day. But just make sure you stay exactly as you are. Don't you dare to stand up!'

Pauline gasped and screwed her eyes shut as tightly as she could, tears rolling down both cheeks. Oh, mother! He didn't have to warn her to do as she was told! She'd do anything he said. Even if he told her to float through the air and up and out of the window . . .

Oh grief! She'd been branded with a red-hot iron! She'd never be able to sit down in comfort again. Her poor bottom was absolutely ablaze. It pulsed and raged with fire. It was amazing that her little black knickers hadn't burst into flames from the incredible heat. And the pain wasn't getting any less. If anything, it was intensifying and making her weep more profusely than ever.

THWACK!! The ruler had risen and fallen again, along the exact same line. And again Pauline jerked back her head and screamed open-mouthed. A bloodcurdling, heart-rending scream which ensured that her tormentor's already rampant erection stretched a little further towards his chin. Now it was time to be patient, he counselled himself. Now it was time to allow a partial recovery, in order to heighten the suffering to come. He'd wait a few minutes, and then it would be time to remove her knickers and humiliate her some more . . .

Slowly the screams turned to sobs, and in turn these began to abate. Eventually Pauline opened her eyes and blinked. Oh, crumbs! Thank heavens the ruler was bendy and flexible! Otherwise she'd have been damaged for life. Oh! Oh! Oh! Would her rear end ever be the same again?

And then she realised that, behind her back, Mr Davis-Davies was on the prowl again. Carefully he hooked the end of the XT3 under the seat of the tiny black frillies and drew them down, painfully, as far as the tops of her thighs. There he allowed them to repose whilst he gazed at his handiwork. 'My plastic playmate has done well,' he breathed in delight, admiring the fiery red stripe, one and a half inches in width, right across the very centre of each cheek.

Patience, he said to himself. Patience. The longer she was made to wait, the greater would be her eventual torment. The longer she waited for the next cruel kiss of heavy plastic,

154

the louder and longer would she howl and yell in distress when it came. Perhaps he should take a little of his pleasure right now? Just the very minimal amount of pleasure, before returning to the execution of his duty? Perhaps he should lay the ruler down for a minute or so, with the sure and certain knowledge that when it was wielded again its effect would have been enhanced by the delay? Perhaps he should take the merest fraction of his pleasure now, even though his duty was hardly begun . . .?

Pauline heard him undressing behind her. What would be worse, she wondered. The fearful application of the ruler across her behind, or his horrible little Welsh weapon inside her? Surely it was the Devil's alternative . . .?

She looked back over her shoulder and her fears were immediately confirmed. Mr Davis-Davies was naked betwixt waist and ankles, his not-at-all insubstantial penis rearing up and bursting with energy and life. Oh crumbs! For a small man he was quite well endowed. Not in the same league as Mr Harris or Young Harry, of course. But running Mr James a close third. What was it about these legal beagles? Why were they all so handsomely hung? It had been the same in her previous employment. And, come to think of it, in the two firms before that . . .

Mr Davis-Davies saw her staring at his rampant member and swelled with pride. Glancing down at the red hot stripe across the cheeks of her beautiful bare bottom, he gripped her firmly round the waist and carefully measured his aim. Then he thrust forward vilely, piercing her anal passage and forcing himself almost all the way up to the hilt. She screamed at the villainous intrusion. It was only the third time that any man had been in there. Then she screamed again, feeling a really earth-shattering orgasm starting to take hold. As for Mr Davis-Davies, he stood there silent and still, cockily waiting whilst her climax intensified and raged. Not a centimetre would he move until it had abated . . . and then only to hammer himself, very quickly, to ejaculation.

As his fluid dribbled stickily out of her her, Mr Davis-Davies tucked his temporarily flaccid member back into his clothes. Pauline gasped to herself in disbelief. Only three times had she been implanted in there – each time by men she'd hated. Yet the feeling of ecstasy had been beyond her wildest dreams. How could that possibly have been the case? She'd simply have to get Michael to do it to her. She knew how interested he was in her bottom.

Slowly Mr Davis-Davies used the flat of the ruler to caress those sorely upthrust cheeks now carrying the blazing red insignia of the XT3 right across them. Right across the very fleshiest part of her bottom. Then he began tapping her with the end of the ruler, savouring the plumpness of the fat little bottom that pouted up at him in surrender. The fat little bottom he'd just split open and flooded with seed.

Pauline closed her eyes and groaned with shame. It was bad enough having this horrible Welshman standing there staring at her totally bare bottom. But when it was full of his come . . .!

Mr Davis-Davies stood directly behind the perfect full moon of her buttocks, glaring balefully at the tableau he'd taken such care to arrange, yet marvelling at the beauty of those spectacular bare cheeks that were being passed around the office with such generosity on the part of one of his junior partners. Passed from hand to groin, then groin to hand again . . .

Mr Davis-Davies continued to glare at the big, bare, bent-over bottom that was so totally under his control and at his mercy. Not that he was cursed with any of the latter, he was happy to admit. He stared hard at the flame-red stripe he'd planted right across the middle of her otherwise immaculate cheeks. And the harder he stared, the angrier he became. Her buttocks were so infuriatingly perfect, so saucily plump and dimpled, so pearly pink and pert. And so ripe and ready for major abuse!

Mr Davis-Davies scowled darkly as he felt his fury rise. How dare anyone torture and torment him with such blatant disregard? For weeks he'd had to watch these lewd, lightly clad cheeks wiggle and bounce their way around the office, taunting and provoking him as they'd gone, defiantly poking fun at his helpless condition, at his inability to deal with them in the way they so richly deserved. How had she dared to be so bold? How had she dared to parade such breathtaking beauty before his eyes, day after day, so brazenly, yet expect not to pay the price? And he knew that the price was going to be very high indeed. Those juicy ripe cheeks that offended him so mightily would soon receive the full weight of his authority right across them. The due process of the law. In fact, come to think of it, the Rule of Law. They'd broken the rules and now they were about to bend the rule he held in his hand. They were about to bend it again and again and again. They were about to bend it virtually double. Justice was not only going to be done, it was going to be seen to be done. And, in addition, it was most certainly going to be felt to be done. Indeed, it was going to be felt for some considerable time thereafter!

Mr Davis-Davies held the flat of the ruler across the widest part of her bottom. 'These parts have sinned,' he intoned gravely. 'Not only have they sinned against me and my position of authority in this firm, but they have also sinned against your lawful wedded husband. They have failed disgracefully in their duty to keep themselves only unto him.' Purposefully he lifted the ruler above his head. 'But fear not!' he snarled. 'I shall grant them absolution. I shall purify them with fire. I shall purify them with a fire *so* intense that they'll think twice before ever sinning again!'

THWACK!! The XT3 sang viciously through the air and landed noisily across the same fiery-red flesh it had scorched a few minutes earlier, biting her even more painfully than before. As Pauline shrieked open-mouthed at the top of her voice, the ruler rose and fell with deadly accuracy, once again scalding the high point of each cheek. And then again it cracked down across the very same place.

THWACK!! The XT3 colourfully decorated the back of both knees, causing her to yelp in surprise as much as in pain. THWACK!! it painted a searing, brand-new stripe just below and exactly parallel to the area it had initially set alight. THWACK!! A second or so later it painted another, this time immediately above. One stroke followed another, with the result that the screams of pain became one constant cacophony of sound.

Savouring the weeping and wailing and gnashing of teeth, Mr Davis-Davies paused momentarily to adjust his stance, the XT3 balanced carefully in his right hand as he steadied himself to proceed.

'What's that terrible noise?' asked Young Harry with concern.

'What did you say, Harry?' enquired Mr James, without looking up from his file of papers.

'That sort of howling noise. Surely you must have heard it?'

'It's no business of yours, Harry. It's just Mrs Peach, that's all. It's no concern of ours. Just ignore it.'

'But how can I do that? She sounds as if she's in trouble.'

'She is, Harry. But it's nothing fatal, I can assure you of that. It's just Mr Davis-Davies conducting an interview with her on the rather painful subject of office discipline. He's giving her a rather warm reception in an area that holds much appeal to us men.'

'Oh, no! The bastard! I'll break his head in two!'

'Steady, Harry!' advised Mr James, stepping in front of the door and quickly pocketing the key after he'd turned it. 'It's nothing to do with you.'

As her bottom grew redder and redder, Pauline was amazed to discover that her insides were seething in orgasm. Her pussy was wracked with pleasure. It positively gushed with

158

the oil of sexual excitement. The scorching heat of the XT3 had set her off just as effectively as the world's finest fuck. Although she was powerless to stem the sobbing and shrieking, she found that the internal pleasure was now exceeding the external pain. The ruler was making her come as turbulently as ever she'd known. And there was one very definite consolation, she pointed out to herself, as she continued to blubber, climax and bawl. In her present grief-stricken circumstances there was no way that this vile little Welsh pervert would be able to identify what was happening to her inside . . .

At last Mr Davis-Davies decided it was time to rest and take stock of the situation. He stared at the brightly blazing buttocks that he'd roasted alive. Yes, they were done to a turn. He was indeed the master of applying culinary skills to prime young rump. He'd never before encountered such a pleasing shade of red, nor such a handsome crimson where the strokes had overlapped so many times. He was particularly proud of the way he had emphasised the first and unkindest cut of all by laying stroke after stroke after stroke across the very fattest part of each cheek.

Mr Davis-Davies stood directly behind her and continued to stare at the twin peaks of her stricken rear end. No pretty bottom as audaciously perfect as this could complain when someone such as he decided to burn it alive. It warranted nothing less. Those saucy, plump cheeks had no right to exist in any other condition . . .

Pauline took a deep breath and dared to open her eyes for the first time since the spanking had begun in earnest. Was he through with her at last, she wondered. After all, he had laid the ruler down on the table to her right. Surely that must mean something . . .?

Ouch! She was really and truly ablaze! Her poor bottom felt as if someone had poured petrol all over it and then set it alight with a match. She'd never known such a fire. She was sure Mr Davis-Davies could have fried an egg in the middle of each red-hot cheek. Suddenly she felt a welcome hint of coolness. Oh, what a blessed relief! It was a draught from the nearby window. The cool, fresh breeze on her bottom was like a sip of the elixir of life . . .

Heavens, her pussy was hot too! As hot as her poor, sore posterior. It throbbed and burned with lustful desire. It had responded to the ruler in a way she'd never have believed possible. Each fresh slap across her behind had heightened her climax. A good deal of her screaming had, of course, been due to the way Mr Davis-Davies had been searing both cheeks with the ruler. But on the other hand, much had also been due to the intensity of climax induced by that fiendish implement.

Now, as a result, she was so open and oily and moist that she was sure he'd be able to see for himself just how she'd been turned on! But there was nothing she could do about it. She was feeling so exceptionally wanton and wicked . . .

At length Mr Davis-Davies decided that it was proper to consult his personal assistant, the practice manager and head of accounts, Trevor Daniels. After all, Daniels was second in charge of the firm's relations with the female staff. And he was quite a sound fellow, too. It was only proper that he should be involved. This sort of disciplinary action didn't occur very often. Mr Davis-Davies didn't wish to appear greedy over the matter of Mrs Peach and the retribution to be exacted upon her infuriatingly plump, perfect buttocks.

'Stay exactly as you are, Mrs Peach,' he said coolly, walking to the intercom on his desk and pressing a button.

'Yes, sir,' she managed to whisper, her forehead and elbows still resting on the table, her hair still in front of her eyes.

'Ah, Daniels, Davis-Davies here. I know you're a busy man, but I wonder if you could spare me a moment of your valuable time?'

'Yes, of course. I'll be right over.'

Pauline groaned to herself in horror and disbelief. A few seconds later she heard a knock on the door behind her. She closed her eyes and took a deep breath.

'Come in, my dear chap,' Mr Davis-Davies called out affably. 'Thank you for being so prompt.'

'Thank you, Mr Davis-Davies,' replied Mr Daniels, closing the door behind him.

'As you can see,' said Mr Davis-Davies, airily waving a hand in the direction of his mahogany table, chair, and bare-bottomed member of staff, 'Mrs Peach and I have been discussing the rather thorny matter of her continued employment with this firm.'

Mr Daniels gaped open-mouthed across the room at Pauline, her vividly reddened rear end pointing painfully up at the window. 'Yes, I do indeed see,' Mr Daniels gulped, once he'd recovered from his surprise.

'This young lady has cost the firm a great deal of money. Probably in excess of a thousand pounds.'

'That's bad in these difficult times.'

'Indeed it is, Mr Daniels. Very bad indeed. Almost criminal, in fact. We've just been having a rather heated discussion on the topic, as I expect you can tell?'

'Yes, Mr Davis-Davies,' murmured Mr Daniels, admiring the breathtaking view.

Mr Davis-Davies picked the long, heavy ruler up from the table beside Pauline and handed it to Mr Daniels. 'I think, though, that you should discuss this sad affair with her a little more. I think the severity of the matter deserves it.'

Whilst the two men stood directly behind her, Pauline's face was almost as red as her bottom. It had been embarrassing enough when there had only been Mr Davis-Davies standing there, ogling her naked nether regions. But now with two of them, it was more than twice as bad . . .

Mr Davis-Davies glared down at the plumpest part of each cheek, the high points which had suffered the full effect of the ruler, time after time. Slowly he ran a fingertip over that area, making her twitch nervously. 'Here, perhaps,' he said thoughtfully. 'Six of the best, right across here. Right across the tenderest part.

'The backs of her legs are almost untouched,' he continued. 'Apart from the knees, which I'm pleased to see are suitably red and smarting. Would you be so good as to attend to the legs for me too? After you've dealt with this area up here, I mean.'

'Of course,' croaked Mr Daniels, the ruler resting comfortably in his hand as he measured his aim.

'Spare nothing,' urged Mr Davis-Davies. 'This wretched girl has cost the firm dear. Don't be afraid to show her the extent of our authority. Don't feel inclined towards any form of leniency at all.'

'I won't,' Mr Daniels promised sincerely.

The ruler hissed wickedly through the air and delivered the first of the six of the best. As Pauline yelped in agonised outrage, the men gazed with approval at the darkening complexion of those wildly bouncing cheeks.

Yet again the ruler rose and fell, caressing both cheeks with a most satisfying crack. She jerked and howled, whilst the men continued to stare in fascination at her perfectly rounded bottom whilst it reddened under their gaze. Never again would its plumpness and perfection torment them. In the future, whenever they observed it wriggling and bouncing its way lewdly around the office under her mini-skirt, they'd experience nothing but intense satisfaction at the memory of how they'd been able to deal with it in the manner it had so thoroughly deserved. Perhaps, wondered Mr Davis-Davies, from now on she might have some regrets about the way she'd spent the past four weeks flaunting it so teasingly before his eyes . . .?

'Perhaps we should make it nine?' Mr Davis-Davies

murmured thoughtfully, as once again the ruler splattered itself across her. 'Nine of the best, as opposed to six, I mean. What are your views, my dear fellow?'

'I agree with you,' Mr Daniels confirmed at once.

'Good. Nine it shall be then. Nine of the very, very best.'

Young Harry jumped to his feet. 'I'll break his arms as well as his neck!' he cried, as one long howl after another echoed from the adjoining office.

'No you won't,' Mr James replied smoothly, the door key still in his pocket. 'It's no concern of yours. Do you want to lose your job?'

'But it's so grossly unfair, Mr James. She hasn't done anything to deserve that sort of treatment.'

'Life is often unfair, Harry. Take my new armchair, for example. The demonstration model that has now become decidedly lopsided as well as seriously stained, due no doubt to some defect in manufacture. Is it fair that this firm will have to foot the bill, when we know very well that it's hardly been touched at all?'

Harry glanced at the sad-looking object in the corner of the room and decided that it might, after all, be prudent to protest no further.

Mr Davis-Davies stood with his head cocked thoughtfully to one side, scratching his chin as he studied the roasted buttocks and limbs of his errant employee. Then he declared that he was satisfied that justice had finally been done. A view with which Pauline wholeheartedly agreed. The backs of her thighs resembled a freshly boiled lobster, whilst her bottom was a much darker hue, particularly the pouting high points across which the ruler had repeatedly reaped revenge. Years earlier Pauline had learned the penalty that a young girl must pay for being far too pretty in her postern area. A penalty she understood only too well as she stood there, bent over the chair, head low and bottom high, the

163

lower half of her body a blazing inferno. She sighed with relief as the ruler was at long last laid to rest on the table beside her. She was burning alive, but at least no more fuel was to be added to the fire . . . Oh, grief! Now the men were running their hands slowly but thoroughly back and forth over every inch of her bottom. Presumably in order to feel the heat for themselves. How embarrassing!

After a while Mr Davis-Davies turned his head and looked at Mr Daniels. 'Shall we fuck her?' he asked conversationally, his right hand squeezing her ample left buttock.

Mr Daniels tightened his hold on her other cheek. 'Why not?' he only just managed to croak.

Pauline lifted her head and glanced around. Mr Daniels was standing directly behind her, whilst Mr Davis-Davies was on the far side of the table in front of her face. And both men were struggling with their zips. She sighed to herself. Her virtue was under threat on both fronts! Two long, stiff cocks were now waggling at her in evident anticipation, one forward and one aft. There was no doubting how the men intended to proceed. A topping-and-tailing routine . . .

Shameful as it was, she couldn't deny the excitement she felt. She couldn't deny how desperately she was in need. Her overwrought pussy simply craved the comfort and relief of a fully erect penis inside it. It craved the analgesic effect of hard, steaming hot flesh. It wasn't fussed about whose. Any penile presence would do, provided it stayed long enough and probed deep enough to satisfy the demands of a ravenous appetite. Such was the power of the ruler. It had weaved its magic spell in a way she found impossible to understand.

Pauline opened her mouth and squirmed her hips, allowing the men to sink into her from front and rear. As they did so, a reassuring thought crept into her mind. At least Mr Davis-Davies had been right about one thing, she said to herself, as the tip of his erection began to poke down her throat. At least the scalding from the ruler would help to expunge some of the feelings of guilt. She'd been made to suffer for her recent moments of weakness with Jim Browne and all the consequences that had followed. The ruler would help to square her conscience. And in any event, no lasting damage had been done. Sting, bite and burn as the ruler might, she was confident that the worst effects would be gone by the following morning. In the meantime, she'd just have to suffer her bottom having been put to the torch. It was no more than she deserved . . .

The men switched over and then switched again, so that once more she was slurping greedily at Mr Davis-Davies, whilst Mr Daniels slid in and out of her aching quim. It didn't concern her that the man she was sucking was the one who'd caused her such anguish. And she felt exactly the same about Mr Daniels. She wasn't the least bit bothered about who was dicking her, just as long as somebody was. She was quite happy to suck and fuck anyone and accept their lovely hot seed. She didn't even mind the flash of fire every time Mr Daniels pressed into the cheeks of her bottom. In fact, she was starting to enjoy it. She was starting to look forward to each new spark of pain.

Carefully, Pauline built up a synchronisation between the two men she was pleasuring inside her. As Mr Daniels slid in, she swallowed Mr Davis-Davies down to the hilt. And when Mr Daniels withdrew, she pulled back her head at exactly the same pace, matching him stroke for stroke. She couldn't believe the excitement she felt as they glided smoothly back and forth. She could feel how heavily she was lubricating. Whenever Mr Daniels drew back, she could visualise his penis absolutely dripping with oil. The same oil that she could feel trickling warmly down the inside of each leg. She supposed it was a reaction to having this exquisitely satisfying sex so soon after the ruler had flayed her alive and made her feel so feminine and submissive . . .

Mr Daniels gazed in fascination at the sight of his straining erection disappearing and then reappearing between her scalded cheeks. He gasped with appreciation as he pushed forward into her buttocks with slightly more force. Her flesh was so hot that it was burning the skin round the root of his dick. And her insides were just as hot. There was no doubting the extent to which they'd aroused her. It was obvious that she was as horny as hell. And in turn, he was as stretched as ever he'd been. More so, he decided, as he crammed himself hard into the top of her vagina and made her moan. Then, withdrawing himself almost to his full extent, he cupped a hand around each blazing hot cheek and squeezed as hard as he could. Instantly she started to spasm, her vaginal muscles gripping and nipping him with a strength he'd never known.

With her elbows resting on the table, Pauline continued to hold Mr Davis-Davies in both hands and work up and down with her head. Up and down, up and down, up and down, still in time with the way she was being poked from behind. It was the most effective way of producing the result she desired, of bringing both of them off together. Up and down, up and down, up and down, establishing a rhythm between the three of them in the hope that they'd both implant her at the same time. She'd already experienced that wonderful sensation earlier in the day, when Harry and Mr James had been tackling her on the armchair. And she was dying to experience it again. It was just so indescribably satisfying . . .

As the pace of the porking grew quicker, Mr Davis-Davies tore his eyes away from her mouth and looked once again at the scene on the far side of the table. Even when she raised her head at the top of each stroke, the twin peaks of her bottom were still the highest part of her above the floor. In the middle of the cleft between them he could see his colleague's thick round erection appearing and then vanishing from sight. Appearing as he pulled back out of her, then vanishing as he impaled her again. He could hear the gentle sloshing sound it made inside her. And he could see her vaginal juices coating the iron-hard flesh and making it gleam.

Gorged though she was, Pauline couldn't get nearly enough. And the more that ran through her, the more and more she wanted. Fortunately, the men seemed more than willing and able to provide. Length after length slithered in and out, long even strokes filling her two main openings and making her yearn for someone to fill the third. It would be lovely, she groaned to herself. It would be lovely to have another man in her bottom. What a luxury that would be! That tight little passage had always been incredibly sensitive. She really must find a way to talk to Michael about it . . .

Pauline swallowed and wriggled as the topping and tailing continued. But it wasn't only Pauline who was getting double value, for the men were also relishing the spectacle of someone else working inside her whilst they slid in and out themselves. It added both length and girth to their own already overstretched organs. The pace increased as Mr Daniels began to hammer harder and faster into the hot, soaking wet hole between those soundly spanked cheeks. Fascinated, he watched intently whilst Mr Davis-Davies held her head and began pushing in and out of her mouth at exactly the same speed. Mr Daniels could feel himself expanding inside her, stretching her more tightly than ever with every thrust. Pauline could feel both of them gaining in strength and size, and began wriggling her bottom from side to side against each incoming stroke. She was simply loving every moment, every slithery poke and prod. As fast as Mr Daniels thrust into her, Mr Davis-Davies did the same, her head stock still and her mouth open wide to receive him. Now she could feel them starting to tense and stiffen, and was confident that at any moment they'd begin gushing into her together, their boiling hot fluid scalding her throat as well as her womb.

But it was not to be. Just as she thought they were on the point of opening the floodgates, Mr Davis-Davies withdrew from her mouth. 'Time for a change,' he said to Mr Daniels. 'Do you mind fucking her in here for a while?'

Pauline savoured the taste of her own juices in her mouth as Mr Daniels pushed himself into her – all the way down to the hilt. 'Let's have her tits out!' one of them growled. Very uncouthly, she thought. Without further ado her dress was unzipped and the top half yanked unceremoniously down to her waist. Seconds later her bra was snapped open and pulled wide apart. Immediately two men began pawing her breasts. Pawing them and pulling them about rather too enthusiastically for comfort. Not that comfort had ever been very important to Pauline once matters of this nature had got underway. She sighed to herself at the luxury of the situation. Not only had her bottom been spanked until it was raw, but the men were now seeing to her pussy, her boobs and her mouth, all at one and the same time. She could feel the pangs of pleasure racing back and forth between her stiff, overwrought nipples and her equally stiff, overwrought clit. Sharp, hard pangs that stabbed at her insides in a most excruciating way. Now she'd forgotten her earlier yearnings to make them come together. That no longer mattered. She was having too much fun to bother about that. For the time being her whole body was alight with the glorious sensation of having two men shagging her just as they liked . . .

Mr Davis-Davies was thrusting ferociously into her quim. Pauline could tell that his climax was rapidly approaching. She closed her eyes and started to quiver with pleasure, with the anticipation of feeling him start to spout deep inside her. But again it was not to be. Just as he was on the very point of ejaculation, he pulled out and stepped back, watching with delight as his sperm arced through the air and landed on the upturned cheeks of her bottom. Cascade after cascade followed, the glutinous white globules coating both cheeks and splashing stickily into the long deep gap between. More and more sprayed and splattered all over her, clinging thickly and contrasting with the fiery flesh. Mr Davis-Davies gazed in wonder. Never had he encountered such a truly absorbing sight. Pauline, however, groaned with regret. What a waste!

She slurped industriously at the hot, swollen flesh that was being rammed in and out of her mouth. Perhaps Mr Daniels would soon be able to compensate her? He'd been working rather hard, holding her head in his hands and thrusting powerfully back and forth. Perhaps he'd soon provide the satisfaction she sought . . .?

Mr Daniels closed his eyes and started to groan loudly. 'Oh my God!' he gasped, at long last unable to hold back. The first jet slapped hard into the back of her throat, and she sighed with relief. How lovely! He'd done it at last! It had taken a while, then finally come with a rush. He was shooting his thick salty load into her mouth as fast and furiously as she could have wished. Too fast, unfortunately, to enable her to taste every drop. Most of it had to be swallowed unsampled, but she'd savour as much as she could. It would certainly make up for the way that Mr Davis-Davies had denied her a moment ago. And there was still plenty of Mr Daniels to come. He was still very much in mid-flow. And, as with Young Harry a little while earlier, she was enjoying the way that the surplus was starting to run down her chin . . .

Oh! Oow! Ahh! Now Mr Davis-Davies was firmly back inside her again. Even before Mr Daniels was finished! It certainly hadn't taken him long to regain his strength. Perhaps this time he'd have the decency to shed his burden where she'd appreciate it most? Instead of squirting it all over the cheeks of her bottom?

Less than two minutes later, Mr Daniels had been brought back to life through Pauline's expert application of mouth-to-penis resuscitation. Now, as a result, the topping-and-tailing was back underway with a vengeance. Both men were now ready for a long stiff session inside her. Pauline remained bent over the table, great gouts of Mr Daniels and Mr Davis-

Davies dribbling down her face and legs. At Mr Davis-Davies' suggestion, the men changed over once more, enabling her to enjoy the delicious cocktail of flavours yet again. Whilst Mr Daniels gripped her round the waist and beavered away eagerly behind her, Mr Davis-Davies decided to take control of her head once more. He resumed making love to her lovely mouth. Holding her head still with both hands, he started to pump in and out. Mr Daniels stared in awe as time after time the whole of his superior's organ vanished completely between her wide-open jaws. She wasn't giving him head, he was taking it. He was fucking her beautiful face. Yet again she was completely passive, bent over the table, an inactive object on which the men were slaking their lust. She was no more than a vessel for their use. Front and back, she was just an open receptacle.

In and out of her flew both men, plugging and unplugging her at speed, working themselves up to a crescendo as she yawned open for them at top and tail. And there she stood for ages, bare-breasted, bare-bottomed and bent forward over the back of the chair, stock still and letting them pump her as hard as they could, whilst she waited eagerly for more of their seed.

CHAPTER 8

Reflections

Although there was only one other passenger on the bus, Pauline stood near the door, staring out of the window and wincing every time the wheels encountered an irregularity in the road. She'd found it just as impossible to type standing up as it had been to sit down to type. And Mr Davis-Davies had positively refused to grant any sick leave, so she'd been obliged to take half a day of her precious holiday allocation.

'That's a really nasty case of sunburn,' said the young man who sat behind her, gazing at the backs of her thighs.

'Oh, er, yes it is, isn't it?'

'Why don't you perch on the very edge of a seat? Surely that wouldn't be painful?'

'Er, um, well . . . It's a sort of all over sunburn, really,' she stammered, trying not to blush too much.

'Oh, I see. I'm sorry, I didn't mean to embarrass you.'

'That's quite all right.'

'You should try some calamine lotion on it. It's very good. I've got some at home if you'd like to get off at my stop?'

'I think I've got some as well, thanks very much.'

'That's a shame,' the young man said with a grin. 'I was going to offer to help you apply it.'

'I thought you might,' she giggled. 'Ouch!' she gasped, as the bus rolled over a particularly sizeable bump.

Pauline lay on her bed, face down and naked, a large but

171

rapidly melting ice pack in the middle of each scarlet cheek, and two smaller packs spaced along the back of each thigh. She sighed to herself. She'd never been so soundly spanked in her life. She'd had her poor, much-abused bottom assaulted on several occasions, of course. Both in anger and mock anger. But never as comprehensively as this. She was simply ablaze all the way down to the backs of her knees. She just hoped the new ice cubes she'd put in the freezer would be ready by the time the present ones melted. But she was so blisteringly hot that she rather doubted they would be.

Pauline slid a hand under her groin and very lightly ran a finger tip over her lower lips. She was incredibly swollen and sore! It was just as well that she'd escaped from the office when she had. She seriously doubted her ability to entertain any more men. Which was hardly surprising, after the sort of seeing-to she'd undergone during the course of the morning. Mr Davis-Davies and Mr Daniels had shown just as much enthusiasm for her as the three who had gone before . . .

Pauline turned her head and stared at the window. Suppose she was on this bed with someone she really fancied? Someone really nice and hunky like Michael, or Harry? Someone all naked and ever so lovely and hard? Would she really and truly be unable to do it with him? Or would her pussy respond and allow him inside? Would it, in actual fact, get all juicy and sweet once again and welcome yet another new visitor, pounded and poked though it had been? She had to admit that she rather suspected it would open like a flower in the sun and welcome him in . . .

Oh dear! Both the ice packs on her bottom had more or less expired. They were suffering almost total meltdown. That just proved how hot she was. Whatever could she do about Michael? How could she explain herself to him?

There was nothing else for it. She'd just have to fib to him when he came home from work. She hated doing that, but there was no other way. After all, she could hardly tell him the truth! She'd have to say she'd come down with the flu, very suddenly and very unpleasantly. Then she'd spend the night in the spare bedroom, pretending she was ill. How boring that was going to be! By the morning her poor, sore bottom should be back to normal, more or less. And her pussy as well. So she'd be able to announce a sudden dramatic recovery and slip into his bed for a spot of conjugal comfort before it was time to get dressed. Not that she had to go to work tomorrow, of course. She'd arranged days ago with Mr Fennell that she could have Friday off work in order to catch up with her housework. Mr Fennell was ever so good like that. Letting her take the occasional day off without much notice, she meant. So there'd be no hurry for her to get up in the morning. She'd be able to make love to Michael slowly and leisurely and very, very passionately indeed . . .

Oh, Lordy! Thinking about her lovely Michael was making her feel bad all over again. How many times had she committed adultery over the past few days? And with how many people? She'd almost lost count. What a disgraceful state of affairs! And how embarrassing it was going to be at work in the future! Apart from the senior partner, Mr Fennell, and Kevin the office boy, there wasn't a man left who hadn't had her. And all over the course of eighteen hours! Wherever she went in the office she'd be bumping into one of them and knowing he was staring at her bottom or boobs and remembering just how it had been. She always felt so uncomfortable in those circumstances. Of course, she was very used to men staring at her. But there was a world of difference between someone staring at you and wondering what it would be like (which was a bit of a giggle) and someone staring at you and knowing all too well. The latter was really rather disconcerting. You knew that he knew that you knew exactly what he was thinking about. Then you'd recall some very intimate detail of what had happened between you and start to blush like mad at the knowledge that he shared that same private memory. The memory, for example, of how he'd driven you absolutely wild by using his mouth on your pussy . . .

And there was another problem, too. She knew only too well what men were like. They discussed all the gory details between themselves. So everyone at the office would know what she'd been up to with everyone else. Young Harry, for example, would know how Mr Harris had spread her over his table on top of the glossy brochures, and used his gigantic tool to stretch her as far as she'd go. And Mr Harris and all the others would know how she'd sucked and fucked Mr James, Young Harry, Mr Daniels and Mr Davis-Davies . . .

And all of it, all of those men, one after the other, one long hard dick after another, five of them, all in the space of a morning. Oh, what a shocking state of affairs . . .!

Pauline felt a tear trickling down one cheek at the thought of how her wedding vows which she'd meant sincerely had been so grossly breached. And not just recently, but from the very beginning, from the very moment Mark Walker had walked into the honeymoon suite, less than half an hour after the wedding ceremony, and taken her from behind! From the moment when, still dressed in her bridal gown, she'd been bent over the nearest convenient surface and dicked till she'd thought she'd die . . .!

Meanwhile, back at the office, Tracie sat at her desk, enjoying the sensation of knickers still sticky with Kevin's thick young virgin come. She was thinking of Pauline. Of how her mouthwateringly plump bare bottom had so recently been set on fire. Of how Mr Davis-Davies had bent her over the back of a chair, then peeled back her panties and watched those pretty pink cheeks bounce and redden under the weight of his long, heavy ruler . . .

Just as her own cheeks had bounced and reddened six months or so ago, Tracie thought to herself with a sudden shiver. Just as her own poor little, sore little bottom had been so painfully dealt with in this very building and under fairly similar circumstances to those that had overtaken Pauline today. She could remember it clearly. It had been Friday, January 13th. The office had been almost deserted. Most of the partners and staff had been absent because of a flu epidemic. The phones hadn't rung and there'd been hardly a client in sight. But she'd been okay. She'd not gone down with the virus, even though Peter had been sick in bed. Not so sick, mind you, that he hadn't exercised his early-morning conjugal rights, just as vigorously as ever. He might be an ultra-suspicious sort of so and so, but he was also kind of sexy and cute. And he certainly knew how to provide her with the essential diet of dick she needed so much.

She'd walked through the legal aid waiting room, trying to find Young Harry. There'd been a phone call for him from his new girlfriend. She'd sounded very pleasant, Tracie had thought.

There'd come a wolf whistle from the corner and she'd jumped and turned round in surprise. She'd thought the room was empty. It had come from a burly-looking youth, lounging in an armchair in the corner. Probably there to see Jim Browne on a case of GBH, she'd imagined from his general appearance. He'd been about six foot four and eighteen stone of granite muscle. Built like the proverbial, she'd thought. But not her sort at all. He'd been extremely rough-looking, with a skinhead haircut, bare arms and chest and a small tattoo in the middle of his forehead. And his jeans had been very grubby, she'd noticed, as he'd sat there leering at her in a knowing sort of way.

'How about a quick spot of rumpty tumpty?' he'd said with a dirty grin. 'There's no one around.'

Normally she'd have ignored him completely. She didn't go in for the rough types in the least. But some sort of devil had been in her that day. She'd been feeling *so* randy all morning. So extra mega-horny and wet. Probably because of that very fine session she'd had with Jim Browne the previous night. She often found that a lot of a very good thing left her wanting more and more.

Anyway, whatever the reason, her pussy had definitely been ruling her head. Before she'd known or understood what she was doing, she'd flipped her mini-skirt up to her waist and pointed her scantily pantied rear end at the youth in a particularly cheeky manner. 'What are you waiting for, slowcoach?' she'd giggled, leaning forward and planting both hands on the wall in front of her.

But he hadn't been waiting for anything. He'd been on his feet and behind her in a flash, wrestling with his zip and not believing his luck. She'd glanced back over her shoulder and seen about a foot of steaming hot cock being unleashed into the room. This would help her get through the day, she'd sighed to herself in delight. Just what the doctor ordered. Enough brawn to skewer her all the way up to her throat.

A few seconds later her filmy little knickers had been round her knees and the tattooed youth had buried himself inside her from behind.

For the next few minutes everything had been fun and games and she'd really been enjoying herself, even though the youth was more than a bit of a yob and had kept on making remarks about her 'lovely little arse', before breaking the clasp on her bra in his anxiety to handle her bare boobs.

Suddenly the door had opened and in had walked her boss, the very weird, very Welsh Mr Davis-Davies. 'Eeeeek!' she squealed in panic, as he'd glared across the room at her and the tattooed, trouserless youth.

'Mrs Trix!' he'd shrieked. 'What the devil do you think you're doing?' He'd been beetroot red in the face and almost choking with wrath.

'What does it look like, squire?' the youth had asked coolly, still pumping away as hard as he could. 'She's getting herself well and truly fucked, that's what.'

'Come with me this instant!' Mr Davis-Davies had roared, absolutely beside himself with rage.

'You'll have to wait, mush. I haven't finished with her yet.'

Mr Davis-Davies had taken a menacing step forward, but then stopped. He'd looked hard at the fornicating youth and taken on board the fact that he was about a foot taller and eight stone heavier. The youth had continued shafting her happily, as if Mr Davis-Davies hadn't existed.

'Very well,' Mr Davis-Davies had said slowly, after a pause for thought. 'I'll do as you suggest and wait here until you've finished.'

And, to her horror, he'd stood there for a good ten minutes, waiting patiently as the youth had humped and pumped and pounded against her buttocks. He'd stood there watching and listening to the sound of the youth's huge column of cock slithering and squelching up and down the length of her channel. He'd stood there watching and waiting whilst the youth fucked her as fiercely as she'd ever been fucked. Eventually she'd been implanted. Gallons and gallons of the stuff, somewhere in the region of her back teeth, she'd imagined, as she'd wriggled and writhed her bottom and tried desperately not to think about Mr Davis-Davies at her side.

'Okay, mate,' the youth had said, flopping back into his chair and picking up his copy of *Loaded* magazine. 'She's all yours now, if you want.'

Speechless with fury, Mr Davis-Davies had marched her away, almost before she'd time to pull up her knickers. Straight to Mr Daniels' room on the next floor, he'd sped her. So fast that she'd still been pulling down her skirt as he'd whistled her through reception, much to the surprise and delight of a couple of young male clients.

Mr Daniels had then been regaled with every gory detail of her gross misconduct. He'd been just as furious as Mr Davis-Davies. They'd ranted and raved at her fit to bust. 'Bend over!' one of them had yelled. Seconds later she'd been bent forward across Mr Daniels' desk, her bottom bared again and pointing right up in the air. Mr Daniels and Mr Davis-Davies had been standing on either side of her, as angry as hell. She'd almost thought she could see steam come out of their ears as she kept telling them she was very sorry and it wouldn't happen again. But it had all been to no avail. They'd not been prepared to listen . . .

Slap! Mr Daniels had landed his left hand on her right cheek as forcefully as he could, and she'd shrieked. *Slap!* Mr Davis-Davies had landed his right on her left. *Slap!* Mr Daniels had splattered her right. *Slap!* Mr Davis-Davies had splattered her left. *Slap!* Mr Daniels on her right. *Slap!* Mr Davis-Davies on her left. Mr Daniels was left-handed, she'd remembered, as he'd landed another blow across the middle of her right. That was why he was able to make such a joint and equal contribution. *Slap!* Mr Davis-Davies on her left. *Slap!* Mr Daniels on her right.

'Wretched girl!' Mr Davis-Davies had hissed, welting her left buttock with all his might. 'Wretched, wanton girl!' Mr Daniels had snarled, blasting her equally powerfully on her right.

And so on and so on for ages, until her stricken bottom must have been glowing brighter than her flame-red MG Midget. *Slap! Slap! Slap!* 'Wretched, wretched girl!' Mr Davis-Davies had walloped her three times in a row on her left cheek. 'Wretched, wanton hussy!' Mr Daniels had repeated the treatment on her right. On and on and on, their hard male hands relentless and without mercy as one blow after another landed with a crack across her poor, sore cheeks. Tears had poured down her face at the unremitting punishment. In the past, she'd often enjoyed a hard hand spanking from Peter, but this had been way too much. And so embarrassing, too!

At last she'd been released and allowed to scuttle back to her room in disgrace, red in the face, much redder in the bottom, and absolutely brimming over with the tattooed youth's warm, sticky essence of life.

CHAPTER 9

Men Friday

Pauline stretched languidly in bed before slowly opening her eyes. Where was Michael? Why was she sleeping in the spare room? Seconds later the events of the previous day came flooding back to her. Well, at least there was one consolation. At least it was Friday, her day off work to catch up with bits and pieces around the house. At least she wouldn't have to face the men at the office until Monday! It was going to be rather an ordeal when the time came. But she'd try not to think about it over the weekend.

She slid out of bed, wearing nothing but a frown. Had her bottom recovered its normal complexion, or was it still discoloured? She knew that some girls remained bright red for days, but past experience had taught her that her own recovery rate was pretty good.

She turned her back to the full length mirror on the wall, craning her neck to peer over her shoulder at the reflection. She sighed with relief. She was almost back to normal. The fiery red effect of the ruler had all but disappeared. She was just a slightly pinker shade of pink in the plumpest part of her bottom. But it was nothing that Michael would notice if she laid on her back to make love.

She pressed a hand firmly against the middle of each sweetly blushing cheek. Ouch! She was still more than a little tender! But it was only to be expected. After all, Mr Davis-Davies and Mr Daniels had laid the ruler across that particular part many more times than she cared to recall. Small wonder it still hurt! But it was nothing to worry about. She'd be able to sit down without trouble. And the mark was barely discernible, which was the main thing, of course. She could put up with a little discomfort provided there were no visible signs to alert Michael to what had happened. Understanding though he was, he might feel a trifle suspicious about her bottom having been severely spanked at work. Even the most saintlike husband in the world would feel a little aggrieved about that. It was his own prerogative, after all.

Pauline glanced at the clock by the bed. There was plenty of time. Plenty of time to slip into the matrimonial bed and do matrimonial things with her husband. How nice it would be to make love to the rightful person! For a start, there'd be no feelings of guilty conscience when it was over. And there was such a difference, too. Such a difference between the lust of yesterday at work and the love she shared with Michael. Sex for its own sake was great fun, of course. But that was all, just fun. It wasn't the same as sex with someone you loved. The two things were worlds apart. The first meant very little at all. It was just an animalistic pleasure. And when you were happily married, you couldn't help feeling so bad about it afterwards. Even though you knew you weren't totally to blame.

Pauline picked up a bottle of her expensive body oil. Gently but thoroughly she began to massage a liberal quantity into her buttocks, using both hands. It was a job that Michael always enjoyed doing for her, but she didn't want to take any risks, even though the marks had virtually vanished. Again she studied herself in the mirror, running a hand lightly over each gleaming globe in turn. She was happy with what she saw. Carefully she applied more oil to the rest of her body, producing a similar sheen.

Now she was ready for Michael, in every sense of the word. Ready, and ever so willing and able, she giggled to herself. She glanced in the mirror again. Should she slip into a sexy little nightie or stay as she was in the nude? Which would he find more alluring? She really wasn't too sure. Perhaps just stockings and suspenders?

Her gaze happened to settle on the shelf by the window. It was strewn with various odds and ends that Michael had dumped there. Rather untidily, she tutted to herself. Suddenly her eyes alighted on an interesting object. Now there was an idea. That would look rather the ticket. Michael would definitely approve. And she knew exactly what to wear with it.

Thirty seconds later she stood in front of the mirror yet again. But this time she was dressed for the occasion. She was wearing Michael's black bow-tie round her throat and a frothy little suspender belt of the same colour around her waist. But nothing else at all. She approved of the contrast between the blackness of the bow-tie and the profusion of curly blonde hair that enveloped her shoulders. And she also liked the way that the lacy black suspenders emphasised the pinkness of her smoothly shaven groin. She was sure that Michael would feel the same. Mind you, she giggled silently, he'd still have had her in the sack in no seconds flat, even if she'd been wearing one of her Dad's dirty old boiler suits. But that wasn't quite the point. It was nice to take a little time and trouble just to show how much you cared.

She was pleased to see that her nipples were already pointing stiffly upwards and outwards. They were already anticipating the fun and frolics ahead. And she knew that she was well lubricated between her legs. Mind you, that was never a problem. She only had to glimpse something remotely shaped like a phallus, or even think of an object that shape. It had been the same since she'd been eleven or twelve. That delightful state of warm, slippery wetness came so naturally and easily to her, without the slightest effort on her part, with scarcely any prompting whatsoever. And at the moment her mind was filled with the thought of her most favourite part of her husband: long and straight and proud and standing head and shoulders above his navel, the tip round and swollen and absolutely bursting with colour and life.

With this picture in mind Pauline slid a hand between her thighs and then up to the soft, sticky part of her person that now throbbed and yearned for attention. 'Oh, Mikey!' she groaned, gently dipping two fingers inside. 'I love you so much! I'm sorry I've been such an unfaithful wife.'

For two or three minutes she deliberately tormented herself by ignoring the urgent demands of her clitoris and sliding her middle fingers slowly in and out of her tight little channel, right up to the knuckles. She concentrated solely on the image of Michael's rock-hard organ rearing up and waiting to pierce her. Then she began to imagine just how the first moment of entry would feel. The first penetrative prod. The first gentle push of penis into wide-open pussy that always made her suck in her breath and close her eyes. Now he was moving inside her, slowly and deliberately, taking his time and kissing her sweetly, his hands cupping the cheeks of her bottom. Now he was pushing faster and faster and squeezing her until she gasped.

In her mind she could see his bloated erection working backwards and forwards inside her, forcing its way through the soft, unresisting flesh of her quim and making her wriggle and squeal. At last she could wait no longer. The image was just too real. She slipped her fingers forward through the warm, gooey syrup and squeezed at the plumpness of her own, relatively minor, erection. 'Oh Mikey!' she moaned. 'Oh, Mikey, Mikey, Mikey!'

One hour later the conjugalities were complete. Pauline heard Michael bang the front door behind him as she lay back, swathed in satin sheets. She yawned and stretched luxuriously and decided to stay where she was for a while. She was enjoying that extra warm glow that always followed a really passionate bonk. She was savouring his fluid inside her, wallowing in the sense of contentment it produced. She could still feel his hands exploring every intimate part of her person. She could still feel the sweetness of his body against hers, and the length and girth of his member as it stretched her so nicely. For the second time that morning she cupped a hand round her groin, now far wetter than before, and began to stimulate herself. Michael had made her come so many times. But, even so, she'd still like to come a few more. She'd just lie here and think about him, whilst her fingers took over his role. If only it had been a Saturday or Sunday, she could have continued for hours with the real thing. No wonder the housework was always so sadly neglected!

For another half hour Pauline wriggled and gasped and groaned and thought about Michael and the way he used his weapon on her so wonderfully well. Briefly she remembered Mr Harris and Young Harry and allowed her fingers to continue working their spell. Then she returned her mind to her husband and came again, almost at once. Inside her head she caught a quick glimpse of Mr Davis-Davies' huge ruler, and that had the same effect. Then she was able to overcome any other outside influences and concentrate on her spouse. It was almost as if he was right there on top of her as her hand continued to provide. She recalled the way in which he regularly drove her crazy by kneeling above her on all fours and tickling her overwrought nipples with the hairs of his chest, at the same time refusing her any other form of contact whatsoever. This he did until she became so worked up that she simply had to roll him onto his back, straddle his legs, and then desperately impale herself on him as hard as she could. Then he'd just lie there, absolutely dead still, letting her do all the work. She'd come time and again, but it would be ages before she could finally make him spurt. And even when that was happening to him, he still wouldn't move. He'd just smile up into her eyes, his hands exploring her bottom, and tell her she was the most beautiful creature on God's earth.

At the memory of this particular piece of loveplay, her fingers worked harder and harder and her orgasm became stronger and virtually constant. She thrust up with her hips and down with her hand and groaned loudly enough to be heard in the hall. She remembered how satisfying it was to force him to shoot entirely through her own efforts, without any assistance from him. Doing that with her pussy was just as nice as using her mouth to produce the same result. Sometimes, she recalled, still orgasming violently, she'd do it to him as they lay on their sides like spoons, her bottom pressing backwards and forwards into his stomach and groin. That was usually the quickest way to bring him off without his active participation. He just couldn't stand up to the combination of silky bare buttocks and hot wet pussy.

'Oh, Mikey!' she cried, as a particularly violent eruption took hold and began to overwhelm her. Now she was pumping herself up and down against her hand as fast as she could, her face brightly flushed and perspiration trickling down her forehead. 'Mikey!' She squealed loudly, as her dripping wet quim suddenly demanded attention. 'Mikey, I need you to love me again!'

But Mikey was already at work and behind his desk, tapping away at his computer, unable to alleviate her plight. Yet her quim was absolutely insistent. It simply had to have him, it told her. It wouldn't take 'no' for an answer. It must be assuaged this instant. Otherwise it would cause her such anguish she'd never be the same person again. 'Get me fucked now!' it hollered and howled. 'Get me fucked, or you'll never live long enough to regret it!'

She rolled onto her side, eyes wide and staring, and grabbed the clothesbrush that lay on the table beside the bed. The large, old-fashioned clothesbrush she'd had since she was a child. The one with the round wooden handle that so closely resembled a rampant male organ. It was all she could do. She couldn't ignore such an urgent ultimatum.

184

'Ohhh! Ohhh! Ohhh!' she shrieked wildly, as the long, thick handle served its purpose once more.

She'd lost count of the times it had served her well in the past. Particularly in those early years of yearning when boyfriends had been virtually non-existent. Now she lay almost still, slowly and rhythmically squeezing her insides around the stout wooden handle, and sighing happily to herself. She knew she really shouldn't let her pussy boss her about in that way. But sometimes she just couldn't help it. Neither could she help the bad language it so often used.

She'd once told Nick Blowers about her favourite clothesbrush, she suddenly remembered. About the use to which it had often been put. She'd forgotten how or why she'd told him, but she could clearly recall his reaction. 'Do it for me!' he'd breathed hotly. 'While I sit here and watch. Go on! Do it for me right now!'

Highly embarrassed, she'd eventually agreed, because he'd been so incredibly keen. She'd stretched back on her parents' comfortable settee and slipped a hand under the hem of her mini-skirt, red-faced and studiously avoiding his eyes. Taking a deep breath, she'd started to stroke herself inside her little white knickers. Strangely enough, his presence had proved no hindrance at all. Rather the opposite in fact. She'd found herself in the mood the second she'd touched herself with her fingertips and gasped. Her pussy had started to boil at the thought of him sitting there, studying her closely. Then, just like today, she'd slowly worked herself up to the point where she'd had no option but to gain the relief of being filled to the brim. Panting wildly, she'd picked up the clothesbrush and slid it deep into the softness and moistness within. For the next five minutes she'd rolled from side to side, groaning with pleasure as she'd pumped the handle in and out. Then she'd discovered Nick Blowers standing over her, naked from the waist down, rampant from the groin up. He'd found her solo performance absolutely electrifying – as witness the incredible dicking that had followed, during which he'd insisted on shafting her in a different position in every part of the house.

Fortunately her parents had been late returning home from their dinner dance. Mind you, her identical twin sister, Pennie, had arrived back just as she and Nick had been doing it doggy fashion at the top of the stairs. 'It's only me!' Pennie had sung out as she'd opened the front door. (They both used to shout something like that when they came home to a parentless house, she remembered. In order not to spoil any fun and games the other might be having indoors.)

Pennie had thought it a wonderful giggle as she'd stepped carefully over the copulating couple, half on and half off the landing. She'd thought it even more of a laugh twenty minutes later when Nick had insisted on finishing off across the foot of her bed, with Pennie lying there reading a book. 'Couldn't you lend him to me for half an hour?' Pennie had asked eagerly, when he'd finally done. 'He seems so full of energy and enthusiasm.' So Pauline had agreed. After all, Pennie had done the same for her on a couple of previous occasions. And Nick had only been a fairly casual boyfriend. And anyway, she'd been quite glad of a rest.

Pauline's mind came back to the present. She squeezed herself harder against the clothesbrush and moaned. Goodness, it seemed she was getting sexier by the day! Her pussy just wouldn't leave her alone for a moment. It made all sorts of wild demands. Was that the result of being happily married? She supposed it must be something like that . . .

Oh, rats! Someone was ringing the front doorbell. What a pity! She was feeling so snug and sexy wrapped up warmly in these sheets, making love to an old friend and climaxing almost all the time. Whoever could it be? Had Michael forgotten something? But then, he'd let himself in with his key. Unless he'd forgotten that as well.

Carefully she withdrew the sopping wet handle of the clothesbrush and then swung her legs off the bed. She'd better get a move on. It might be something important. Oh dear! She couldn't exactly answer the door like this. She wasn't wearing a stitch of clothing. Not even Michael's bow-tie. Michael had made a big play of removing that, and her suspender belt, using his mouth so cleverly on her boobs and then her pussy as he'd done so. Now where on earth was her housecoat?

Quickly she slipped into the short, snug-fitting garment, pulling the zip up to her chin as she hurried down the stairs. Really, she ought to be wearing knickers, she thought. But it would be okay, provided she remembered to stand perfectly straight. Her bare essentials would be covered like that. Just about.

'Hello, my dear,' said her boss, Mr Fennell, as she opened the door. 'Can I come in for a moment?'

'Oh! Hello, Mr Fennell. Crikey, I didn't expect to see you here. Yes, of course. Come inside.'

Pauline groaned inwardly. It was already well into the morning and Mr Fennell would easily be able to see that she hadn't made a start on the housework. It would be obvious to him that she'd been lazing away in bed. How embarrassing!

'Would you like a cup of coffee?' she asked.

'That would be nice, Pauline. I'll follow you through to the kitchen, shall I?'

'This way, Mr Fennell. Oh dear! Michael has left it in a bit of a state, I'm afraid.' She crossed her fingers as the little white lie tripped easily off her tongue.

'Don't worry, my dear. I'm used to that. You should see my own kitchen since my wife left home. Mind you, she's back now. Unfortunately.'

'Mr Fennell! You shouldn't say things like that.'

'I was only joking. Mainly. Yes, milk but no sugar, that's fine.'

Standing directly behind her, Mr Fennell tried gallantly but failed to avert his gaze as she bent forward to collect the tray from the table. Her plump little bottom was every bit as pretty as he'd always imagined it would be. The housecoat slid back into position as she straightened up, ready to carry the tray through to the lounge.

Pauline perched demurely on the edge of a chair, her cup and saucer balanced in the middle of her lap and her legs pressed together and tucked as far underneath her as they'd go. She trusted that in this way her knickerless condition would not be apparent, unaware that the very brief glimpse of very, very bare bottom had already given the game away.

'Is anything wrong, Mr Fennell?' she asked, tugging at the hem of her coat.

'I'm afraid there is, my dear.'

'What is it?' she enquired nervously.

'It could be rather serious.'

'Oh, crumbs!'

'It's about Mr Franks and his photographs of you.'

'Oh, no!' she squealed in dismay.

'He showed them to me this morning.'

Pauline covered her eyes in shame. 'Oh! How awful! How could he? Oh, how horribly, horribly embarrassing!'

'Don't be embarrassed, Pauline, my dear. I've seen quite a lot of the world, you know. There's no need to feel bad on my behalf.'

'I shall just die! You mean you've actually seen them?'

'Come now, my dear. Don't be upset. As I said, I've seen a lot of strange things in my time. This is nothing at all compared to some of the seamier aspects of life that I've witnessed. Nothing at all.'

'Oh, Mr Fennell! I feel so terrible!'

'Just sit quietly and sip your coffee, Pauline. And then I'll tell you what's going on.'

Pauline closed her eyes and groaned. She felt so bad she could hardly sit still. She must be the colour of a beetroot. To think that Mr Fennell, of all people, should have looked at those dreadful photographs! She'd always got on so well with him. He was ever so sweet to her . . . And she was very fond of him, in a daughterly sort of way. Not that he was all that old, of course. Only about forty or so. No age at all, really.

'I'm okay now, Mr Fennell,' she said softly, staring down at her bare feet. She'd been in such a rush to open the door that she'd forgotten about slippers, as well as knickers.

'I've come to warn you, Pauline. About Mr Franks and the use he intends to make of those photographs.'

'Go on.'

'Yes, I'm afraid it's not at all good, my dear.'

'He promised he'd give them to me.'

'I don't think he has any intention of doing that. Much the opposite, in fact. He intends to keep them and use them for his own benefit.'

'Oh, Lordy!' she whispered.

'He came to see me this morning and offered me a deal. He suggested that I might like to take advantage of the photos. Or rather, to take advantage of you by making use of the photos.'

'The rotten so-and-so! How could he!'

'Very easily, it seems, my dear. I think I must have been rather naïve about Mr Franks in the past. He's not a very nice man at all.'

'You can say that again, Mr Fennell.'

'His terms were very simple. I was to agree to give him a full equity partnership in the firm, and in return I could blackmail you over the photographs whenever I liked.'

'The rotten, cheating sod!'

'Yes, it's utterly despicable. Of course, I didn't tell him so, because I wanted to warn you about what was happening. I just said I needed time to think about it, and that I was quite interested in his proposition.'

'I see. Thank you very much, Mr Fennell. But what can I do? How can I get them from him?'

'I'm afraid I'm not going to be much help to you there, Pauline. I've wracked my brain, such as it is, but I can't come up with anything. There must be a way, but for the moment it escapes me.'

'I know. It's very difficult. I'd rather guessed he might try something like this with you. I spent ages last night trying to think of a way out, but I haven't come up with anything very positive. It's really rotten of him.'

'All I can say to you is this. Well, two things really. In the first place, if there's anything else I can do to help you, please let me know. Anything at all. Just ask and I'll do whatever I can. Secondly, if and when you do manage to get them from him, he's out of a job. He'll be on his way to the dole queue before he knows what's hit him. And serve him right, too.' Mr Fennell stood up ready to leave. 'In the meantime we'll just have to play a waiting game.'

'Oh, Mr Fennell!' she cried, jumping to her feet and throwing her arms around him. 'Thank you so much! How very kind you are!'

She hugged him as tightly as she could, finding him extremely cuddly. In fact, her embrace became so enthusiastic that the zip of her housecoat shot right down to her navel, freeing her boobs. At the same time the hem rose several inches, leaving Mr Fennell patting acres of extremely bare bottom.

'Thank you, Pauline,' he breathed, when she'd finally released him. 'I think you'd better do that zip up as fast as you can. Otherwise I might be very tempted to change my mind and take Mr Franks up on his offer . . . I'm only joking,' he added quickly.

'There's many a true word spoken in jest.'

'Yes. I shouldn't have said it.'

'Don't worry about it, Mr Fennell,' she said with a dazzling smile, suddenly pulling the zip all the way down, not up, and then tossing the garment over the back of an armchair. 'Sometimes it's good to give in to temptation. Just very, very occasionally. When you know it's with the right person.' Once again she embraced him, much more tenderly than before.

Mr Fennell sank back into his chair, but this time with Pauline spreadeagled naked on top of him. Carefully she undid his shirt, tie and trousers, kissing him with her tongue as she did so. Then she shifted slightly to one side, thus enabling herself to expose him from his neck all the way down to his knee-caps. 'Mr Fennell!' she giggled naughtily, when it was done. 'Something big has suddenly come up!'

'Not so suddenly,' he breathed. 'It's been like that since I first saw you in that rather undersized housecoat.'

'How presumptuous!'

'Not at all. I was fully expecting to have to return to the office suffering from the same problem.'

She stroked him slowly with both hands, starting at his chest and then venturing as far as his groin. 'As part of my secretarial duties, I think I ought to deal with it straightaway. Your problem, I mean, of course. I'll just use my own initiative.'

'I'd be very much obliged if you would, Mrs Peach,' he murmured faintly, as she took a two-handed hold on the hottest, stiffest part of his person and then started to pamper and pet.

'You're beautifully hung!' she whispered, taking his tightly packed testicles in her right hand and slowly stroking his long, smoothly stretched penis with her left. All feelings of daughterly affection had now been replaced by an urgent desire to take him all the way up to the top of her wildly throbbing quim.

She wriggled until she was lying on top of him again, her feet on the floor and her legs straddling his lap. Purposefully, she arched her back. Then, judging matters to perfection, she carefully lowered her hips and, at the first attempt, snared the tip of his eagerly waiting erection. She paused and smiled into his eyes. Then with one smooth downward push he was entirely taken in, surrounded by warm, willing flesh that seemed to suck at him in welcome. 'I don't think this should be one of those rushed jobs,' she murmured, kissing the side of his neck. 'It's a very fine legal point, after all.' She wriggled her hips appreciatively. 'A very fine one indeed. It will take time to resolve it properly.'

'I hope so,' he sighed with a smile.

Slowly she began to ride him, to ride up and down on the stout, stiff stalk she'd first brought to life and then captured and imprisoned inside her. Slowly she rose up and slid down, crushing her clitoris against his rigidity as she did so, and groaning with the intensity of the pleasure this produced.

Suddenly it occurred to her that she was still very wet from Michael. She opened her eyes and glanced at Mr Fennell. Clearly he was quite happy with everything, so she decided not to worry – to concentrate on the matter in hand, and enjoy herself some more.

'Oh Mr Fennell!' she gasped. 'You feel so good in there!'

'A man's only as good as his secretary,' he murmured. 'At least, that's what they told us at law school.'

'In that case, I shouldn't believe all you were told.'

He closed his eyes and relaxed, savouring the feel of diamond hard nipples pressing into his chest as her snug little sex slithered up and down from the tip to the root of his erection, squeezing and sucking at him as it went. She kissed him warmly and he opened his mouth to receive her tongue, at the same time marvelling at the vibrant lubricity of her buttocks as he ran his hands back and forth. Dreams were made of such matters, he said reverently to himself. In the future, he'd be able to recall the sweetness of their touch whenever he caught a glimpse of them swelling the seat of her skirt. Her delightful little bottom was so slippery smooth that the flesh simply slid out of his fingers when he squeezed.

Suddenly her vagina tightened sharply around him and he felt her starting to come. Not violently, but very slowly and softly to begin with, then gradually increasing in force. 'This happens quite a lot,' she giggled. 'You'll get used to it after a while.'

'It's very gratifying,' he managed to gulp.

* * *

Ten minutes later, Jack the window cleaner walked back down Pauline's path towards the road, deep in thought. The windows he'd left untouched. What does a chap do? he asked himself. What does a decent chap do when he's about to plonk his wet cloth on the lounge window and then catches sight of something fascinating inside? Something truly fascinating, like the exquisitely shaped bare bum of the young lady of the house rising and falling smoothly over the person of a person who was definitely not the gentleman of that house?

Well, thought Jack, if you were a pleb like his partner, Wally, you stayed very still and watched the entire performance with pleasure. Then, when the couple were done and the gentleman was wiping his dick on a cushion, you burst into a round of noisy applause. You'd get a customer for life like that, Wally had once explained to him. After all, how was the pretty young housewife going to explain matters to her husband if you ever chose to be indiscreet?

That was Wally's way, at least. But not his own. Oh no. Jack prided himself on being a bit of a sport. He'd just take a good long gander at the way the beautiful young woman was dicking herself on her illicit partner. Then he'd steal away, just as he was doing now, and do a couple of other houses. Later he'd return to this one and start on a window that didn't have a view of the scene of the crime. As noisily as he could. And, if he got half a chance, he'd chat up the young lass something wicked, in the hope that it might pay off in the future. After all, he'd always found that a young lady who entertained a gentleman who wasn't her husband, was often prepared to entertain other gents as well. Provided you had the right line of approach, of course.

So he'd just drive his van round the block to Mrs Reynolds' house. Not that Mrs Reynolds was a likely candidate for a spot of the other. But he could do her windows, and then Mr Loftus' next door. Then he'd come back to see if the pretty young maid with the sweetest little rump in the world was still face down on that armchair, spiking herself on her visitor.

Mr Fennell held out extremely well, but eventually his outstanding problem was resolved. Pauline squealed with delight as she felt the first rush of scalding hot seed burning its way into her womb. Immediately her own climax was renewed, as was almost always the case when her partner came.

She thrust hard down with her bottom, wanting him to implant her as deeply and as thoroughly as possible. One long, fierce squirt followed another, whilst she groaned and squirmed her hips from side to side. 'Oh, Mr Fennell!' she gasped, burying her face in the side of his neck. 'Oh, that feels so nice!'

At length he was through, and Pauline made some more coffee. She decided to postpone a visit to the bathroom for as long as possible. She was enjoying the feel of his seed inside her, mingling warmly with Michael's. Then it was time for him to get back to the office for his appointments. She followed him to the front door, still not having bothered to regain her housecoat, or indeed anything else. They embraced and then he was gone, having first turned her round and planted one farewell smack of gratitude right across the middle of her pouting bare bottom.

'Oow! Mr Fennell!' she'd giggled, as he'd stared hard at the bouncing pink cheeks.

He'd store that memory up for the future, as well, he decided, closing the gate behind him. The picture of those big, shapely buttocks, he meant. He'd store up that picture, as well as their satin-like feel. He'd retain the sight and the feel of those buttocks in his memory for as long as he drew breath. Those pert, saucily dimpled buttocks which her husband undoubtedly worshipped and regarded as belonging solely to him.

* * *

194

Pauline wandered upstairs to the bedroom to dress, deciding that there was still no real need to visit the bathroom. It was very wicked, she knew, but she just loved the feel of the fluid inside her. The fluid of her two favourite men. The two men she respected most in the world. What she'd just done had been wrong, of course. But it was too late now to reverse it. So she might as well enjoy the naughty but nice sensation in her quim.

She stood in front of her open wardrobe, stark naked, debating whether to wear jeans or a mini-skirt. She certainly wasn't going to wear *that* skirt, she told herself firmly. It held too many bad memories. It was the one she'd been wearing on Wednesday when Jim Browne had accosted her so blatantly in the copying room at work. The same one that he'd hoisted above her waist whilst she'd been bent over the photocopier. The same one that had then been hoisted again, by that awful George Franks, such a short while later.

Perhaps an old pair of blue jeans was the answer? She'd got four or five of those. But on the other hand, she wasn't at all sure which was the fatal pair she'd sworn never to wear again. The pair that she'd worn to that barbecue in Majorca on honeymoon, when she'd got separated from Michael and, through a series of ghastly coincidences, had ended up fast asleep in the right-numbered room in the wrong hotel . . . with the wrong man climbing stealthily into bed beside her. By the time she'd fully awakened it had all been far too late. By the time she'd come back to her senses and realised that it wasn't Michael bonking her in her sleep, the damage had already been done. Mind you, it had been very greedy of Keith to insist on inflicting it all over again!

She'd meant to throw the jeans away, just in case they were jinxed or cursed or something. But now she'd muddled them up with her other pairs. And she couldn't throw all of them out, could she? After all, she always spent a fortune on buying really well-cut jeans that fitted tightly round the hips and thighs. It would be such a waste to dump all of them in the dustbin.

Oh dear! There was that bouncy grey micro-mini-skirt that Mighty Malcolm had so admired. Mighty Malcolm from her previous employment with Mr Robinson. She definitely couldn't wear that! Not after that drinking spree at the office last November to celebrate Malcolm passing his exams. How had she ended up on his knee in front of half a dozen people from work, all of them swigging volumes of red wine straight from the bottle? How on earth had she come to let him do what she did let him do? In public as well! She supposed it must have been the drink. She'd taken rather too much on board at the pub, let alone all the wine she'd consumed when they'd got back to the office. If she'd been sober, she'd never have contemplated snuggling up on his lap and letting him masturbate her to orgasm through her knickers! How embarrassed she'd felt when it was over! All those girls, red-faced and giggling! Not to mention Tim and Tony staring at her that way.

And now that she thought about it carefully, it was the very same skirt in which she'd almost got herself into trouble a few weeks later, at Christmas, with that cheeky Andrew Huxley, whilst she'd been stretched out in Mr Robinson's own office armchair. If they hadn't heard Mr Robinson's footsteps, it would have been a *fait accompli* a few seconds later. Heavens, she'd never reacted so fast! Skirt, knickers, bra and blouse had never been so hastily rearranged. And Andrew had vanished back into his trousers like a video of the Indian Rope Trick in very fast reverse. Then he'd sidled out of the door unseen, grinning knowingly at her as Mr Robinson had knelt on the floor beside her and started plucking at the buttons she'd only just done up.

Oh crumbs! The more she looked along her wardrobe, the more disreputable memories came flooding back to haunt her. But she couldn't just junk everything she owned. That would be silly. She'd simply have to learn to live with the unsavoury episodes from the past. She'd have to ignore the memories evoked by that frothy black suspender belt, those filmy pink knickers, that smart blue trouser suit, that cocktail dress she'd worn to the lifeboat ball, that navy mini-skirt that—

'Oh, sorry!' cried Jack the window cleaner, from the window behind her, not looking too sorry at all.

'Eeek!' she squealed in panic, plonking her bottom down on the bed and using her hands as best she could to cover her boobs and pubes.

'I thought you were downstairs,' explained Jack, making no move to withdraw from the scene.

'I was. I just came up to get dressed.'

'Well,' he laughed kindly. 'If you will walk round the house in the buff, you must expect the window-cleaner to collect the occasional eyeful.'

'I know. It's my fault entirely.'

'I'm too quiet on the job, that's the trouble. I'm always getting this problem.'

'I'm surprised you've got any customers left,' she giggled.

'Oh, a lot of them do it deliberately, you know. They enjoy flaunting themselves.'

'I hope you don't think the same about me?'

'Of course not. It was just an accident, I know. I can tell what a nice sort of person you are.'

'How kind.'

'Look, shall I cover my eyes with my hands while you slip into some clothes?'

'That's a good idea. Thank you.'

Through the gaps between his fingers Jack studied her closely as she wriggled into minuscule pink knickers and matching bra. Still being in a quandary as to which clothes to wear, she decided that she was sufficiently respectable for the moment. After all, he was a really charming young man. And these knickers might be small, but they definitely weren't at all see through. She'd be wearing just as much as

197

she normally did on the beach.

She picked up a bottle of nail varnish and moved over to the window, turning her back to it as she studied each nail in turn. 'Excuse me a moment,' she murmured, deep in concentration.

'Ping!' went the elastic in the seat of her knickers.

'Oh!' she squeaked in surprise.

'I'm sorry,' he chuckled. 'I just couldn't resist it.'

'I didn't know the lower half of the window was open,' she giggled again, moving out of his reach and readjusting her knickers.

'That's a very smart bra and panty set,' he said with feeling.

'Oh, er, thanks. Perhaps I'd better slip into something else as well?'

'Don't bother on my account, Missus. I like you just as you are.'

'Actually, I think I'll take a bath,' she said thoughtfully, squeezing her thighs together and feeling the sperm that was oozing out of her. 'You'll be through here by the time I've finished.'

'I suppose so,' he replied reluctantly. 'But I really won't be offended if you want to stay in your undies,' he urged. 'I'm used to that sort of thing. I see it all the time.'

'I'm sure you do. But I really do fancy a nice hot bath. Cheerio.'

Jack watched the tiny pink panties wiggle their way out of the room, and sighed. This was undoubtedly the best bit of goods on his round. The best by a long, long way. In fact, the best he'd ever encountered. And she was so friendly and pleasant too. If only he'd been the lucky so-and-so in the armchair downstairs! He wouldn't have let her go so soon. He'd have still had her there, writhing and jiving on top of him. He'd have kept her there for another half hour at least. He'd have still had his hands clamped round that lovely pert little bottom as it rode endlessly up and down on a shaft so hard and unmoving that it might have been cast in iron.

Pauline started to run the bath and then slipped out of the sexy little skimpies she'd only just donned. She really did need a bath, she told herself. Michael and Mr Fennell were both very present indeed. They'd soaked the knickers already, and were now dribbling down both thighs. It would be a pity to wash them away, but she simply couldn't spend the rest of the day like this.

She realised she shouldn't have done what she'd done with Mr Fennell. It was wrong when she loved Michael so much. She'd just over-reacted to his kindness. To his offer of help. Until then she'd felt so all alone in the matter of George Franks and the way he was blackmailing her out of her knickers so unspeakably. She'd just over-reacted to Mr Fennell's kindness and consideration, and before she'd really thought about what she was doing it had already been too late. It was going to be more than a trifle embarrassing when she saw him on Monday. But he was such a nice man she was sure he'd make every effort to put her at ease. Nevertheless, she was going to feel a bit uncomfortable in future. Perhaps she should pretend that it had simply never happened? That might help, might it not? And she could tell him about what she was doing. He was bound to understand her feelings. He was bound to appreciate her embarrassment at what they'd just done downstairs. Yes, she'd just pretend to herself that it had never happened, and ask him if he'd mind doing the same.

But that, of course, wasn't until Monday. In the meantime there couldn't really be any harm in thinking about it. There couldn't be any harm in remembering how right it had felt to have him inside her, despite the fact that she'd known full well it was wrong. In the meantime there couldn't be any real harm in reliving the way they'd made love so tenderly and so beautifully, just as she and Michael had done a little while earlier in bed.

* * *

Pauline stretched back in the bath, luxuriating in the steaming hot water. No part of her was visible except for her head and the very tips of her upthrust breasts. The effect of the bath was so soothing as she gently swished and swirled the water around. She saw that her nipples were very erect and pointed, but that was no surprise. That always happened when she was enjoying a really long lazy bath. It also affected her in a similar way below the belt. Below the suspender belt, she giggled to herself. Her pussy always felt so nice and ready when it was full of warm soapy water. Well, she supposed, actually, that it felt that way almost all the time. But particularly when she was lying back in the bath.

Goodness, that window cleaner had a really cheeky grin! And also a really cheeky way about him. He was just the sort she might have fallen for in her single days. A bit like Clive Calver, she supposed. Yes, a bit like Michael's close friend, Clive.

Heavens, her hand had just strayed between the tops of her legs without her even realising! But it had nothing to do with the thought of Clive Calver or the cheeky window cleaner, she was sure. That would have been a positive disgrace for a respectably married young lady.

Pauline removed the offending hand, but a few seconds later she was surprised to find that both hands had alighted on her nipples. She sighed and placed them on the side of the bath. She seemed to be feeling extra sexy today. She really ought to try to think about something else, like cleaning the oven and dusting the lounge and bedrooms, and—

Suddenly there was a tap on the bathroom window and she jumped with surprise. 'Excuse me,' called the window cleaner. 'But I need a good wash before I can have my lunch.'

'You can use the sink in the kitchen,' shouted Pauline. 'The front door isn't locked.'

'I can't really. I saw through the window that it's crammed with dirty plates and dishes. Your good hubby hasn't been doing his duty. Not that sort of duty, at least.'

'All right,' she told him, covering her boobs with her hands. 'You can come in here if you want.'

A few seconds later she heard heavy footsteps on the stairs and then the bathroom door flew open. 'I was hoping you might say that!' cried Jack, marching through the door wearing nothing but a massive erection. The old vertical smile. 'Budge up a bit, love. I'm in need of a really good wash, and there's plenty of room for two.'

In utter amazement and panic, she opened her mouth to protest. But not the slightest sound escaped. 'Now then, lady,' he chortled, climbing straight into the bath without waiting and kneeling down between her outstretched legs. 'Here's a favourite topic of mine. Let's talk about the place of extra-marital sex, and non-ferrous bathtubs like this, in a caring, hygiene-conscious, but permissive society.'

'What are you doing?' she finally managed to shriek. But his reply was quite inaudible, due to the fact that he appeared to have swallowed her pouting left nipple almost halfway down his throat. At about the same time that she took that fact on board, she realised in alarm that the nice feeling she'd had in her quim a few minutes earlier was getting much, much nicer all the time. Due, mainly, to the fact that she was being penetrated with consummate ease.

Fifteen minutes later Pauline stood in the bathroom staring at the seriously flooded floor in angry disbelief. She glanced at her watch, but realised that she wasn't wearing it. In fact, she wasn't wearing anything else either. She collected some bath towels from the airing cupboard and began mopping up the water. Really, she tutted to herself, she could have expected the window cleaner to have given her a hand. A hand with the mopping up, she meant. After all, his hands had been everywhere and done just about everything else! Helping her with the flood was really the least he could have done in the circumstances. But he hadn't hung around at all. He'd been dry and back in his clothes within seconds

201

of finishing her off. Then there'd been just a cheerful wave and a 'bye-bye' and he'd been away to attend to his round, leaving her sprawled out in what little water had remained inside the bath. It really wouldn't have been asking too much for him to have helped her a bit, bearing in mind that it had all been his fault in the first place. Grief, what a terrible sauce that young man possessed! Fancy him just clambering into her bath without so much as a by-your-leave or anything . . . and then clambering into her in very much the same way, before she'd even had half a chance to realise what was happening, let alone take evasive action. He'd simply been in the bath and then in her in less time than it took to recall.

Pauline sighed. Of course what she should have done, with the benefit of hindsight, was to have pulled out the plug right away. That would have saved this awful mess on the floor. But it just hadn't occurred to her. She'd been far too busy trying to wriggle herself free from the window cleaner. Of course that had proved quite impossible once he'd wedged his feet against the tap end of the bath. So there she'd been stuck. There she'd been well and truly nailed for the next ten minutes or so, whilst he'd humped and pumped and then swamped her with seed. Well, she supposed that at least there was one consolation. It must have been just about the cleanest act of adultery that anyone could possibly commit . . .

Having mopped up most of the flood, Pauline started to clean the bath. How nice of Mr Fennell, she mused to herself. How sweet of him to offer his assistance. Now she had another incentive to free herself from George. If she managed to do that, Mr Fennell would sling him out on his ear. Which was really no more than he deserved. She supposed, when the time came, she'd be silly and feel sorry for him. She was that sort of a person. But there was really no justification for feeling that way. George Franks had asked for all he might get, and more. Mind you, as yet she still had to find a way out . . .

The bath was sparkling clean. So Pauline was now finished with her immediate chores and could apply more of her body oil. She reached for the bottle she kept in the bathroom and began to massage it into all parts of her person, experiencing the usual pleasure it gave her the second she reached her boobs. Now then, she told herself sharply, she mustn't start all that up again! There was washing and ironing to be done. And piles and piles of dirty dishes. And a hundred and one other things as well. The problem was that she and Michael spent so long making love that there just wasn't enough time to see to her other wifely duties. Not that she'd want it any other way, of course. It was lovely having a really passionate husband who was always upending you in every corner of the house. And, just occasionally, in the back garden as well.

Pauline giggled aloud. It had been ever so funny that time last week when Michael had insisted on sorting her out in the tiny utility room! There was so little space that the only way they'd been able to do it had been for her to stand on tip toes and lean the top half of her body right out of the window, whilst he'd taken her from behind. Everything had got nicely underway and she'd been huffing and puffing and panting, when the next door neighbour had popped his head over the fence and tried to engage her in a conversation about pruning roses. Fortunately, Michael had been out of his line of sight, but the neighbour must have been somewhat perturbed at her inability to string more than three short words together, interspersed with much gasping and groaning with delight. Unsurprisingly, he'd gone out of his way to avoid her since then.

Pauline took a fresh bath towel out of the airing cupboard, leaving the two wet towels hanging over the side of the bath. Oh, crikey! That incredibly cheeky window cleaner! She'd never known anyone to possess such exceptional sauce! Next time she took a bath during the day, she'd have to make sure the bathroom door was locked. And the front door, as well. And if she was ever alone in the house when he appeared, she'd lock herself away in the broom cupboard until he was done. That would be the only safe way of ensuring that she kept her virtue intact.

Bother! Someone was ringing the doorbell again. If it was that window cleaner she'd really give him a piece of her mind. Fancy leaving her with all that clearing up to do on her own! Oh, dear! She had nothing to wear apart from this bath towel. It would just have to do. At least it would cover the necessaries, even if there was only a couple of centimetres to spare top and bottom. It was unfortunate that she couldn't slip into her little pink undies, but they'd been soaked in the flood. Still, the towel was more or less okay.

Pauline opened the front door. 'Hello there, Pauline,' Young Harry Hotspur sang out breezily.

'Hi, Pauline,' said Kevin the office boy.

'Oh, hello you two. What on earth are you doing here?'

'I like the towel,' Harry said with a grin.

'I was just finishing a bath,' she murmured, plucking anxiously at the towel to make sure it was entirely secure.

'Can we come in?' asked Harry, stepping forward over the threshold as he spoke.

'Do you mind?' asked Kevin, closing the door behind them.

'No, that's all right,' she said cheerfully. 'I can't really stand in the doorway like this, anyway.'

'It is a bit on the small side,' observed Harry, flicking the front of the towel with a fingertip.

'Be careful!' she said, folding her arms round the top of the towel to avoid a potential mishap.

'I think you look great in it!' breathed Kevin, his eyes darting up and down from her cleavage to the tops of her thighs.

'Er, thank you, Kevin.'

'I don't think it's too small at all. I think it's exactly right.'

'Well, I'm not too sure about that. But anyway, what can I do for you two? I hope there's nothing wrong?'

Kevin reddened and gazed studiously down at the carpet. Harry shuffled his feet awkwardly and looked more than a trifle uncomfortable. 'What's the problem?' Pauline asked with a sense of foreboding.

'Mr Franks sent us,' mumbled Harry, avoiding her eyes.

'Mr Franks?' she asked nervously. 'What for?'

Harry thrust his hands in his pockets and stared at his feet. 'He asked us to speak to your husband.'

'My husband?' she stammered.

'Yes, that's right,' Harry continued. 'Mr Franks wants us to give him this envelope.' He pulled a large brown envelope from his jacket pocket and held it out to her view. She could see at once that it was exactly the right shape and size to contain a set of photographs.

'What's in it, Harry?'

'I'm not really sure. It's very securely sealed.'

'Well, Michael's at work.'

'That's rather unfortunate.'

'But I can give it to him,' she offered hopefully. 'I'll give it to him when he comes back tonight. That'll be okay, won't it?'

'I'm afraid not, Pauline,' replied Harry, absentmindedly flicking the front of her bath towel again. This time she was too preoccupied to object.

'I'm afraid it won't really be okay at all,' confirmed Kevin, stepping across the hall so that he was standing behind her.

'Why not? What's the problem?'

'We're not allowed to,' explained Harry, staring at the pattern on the bath towel. 'Sorry, Pauline.'

'Yes, we're very sorry,' murmured Kevin, sharing Harry's close interest in the towel.

'What do you mean?' she asked, trying not to panic.

'Mr Franks told us we were only to give it to Mr Peach,'

said Harry, as he ran a fingertip lightly over the prettiest part of the pattern.

'He was very definite about that,' Kevin agreed from behind her back. Gingerly he reached out and tapped his fingers against that part of the pattern that stretched across the fullest part of her hips. He stared down at the spectacular swell of her buttocks under the bath towel, and swallowed hard. 'Our instructions were very clear,' he said in a croak.

'But surely . . .'

Harry took a deep breath. 'We're very sorry, Pauline. But what can we do? Mr Franks was very emphatic.'

'But couldn't you stretch a point for me?' she urged. 'Just a bit? Just for my sake? Just for the sake of my marriage? I'm sure you can guess what's in that envelope. Couldn't you please stretch a point for me?'

'What do you think, Kevin?' Harry asked with a frown.

'I think I could,' he replied slowly.

'I think I could too,' Harry nodded after a pause.

'Oh, thank you, boys! How kind!'

Harry took another deep breath. 'In fact, I already have,' he declared, gently tugging down the top of the bath towel from in front and exposing bare boobs. 'Stretched it rather a long way, to be honest.' He gestured down at the very prominent bulge in the front of his trousers.

'And so have I,' confirmed Kevin, gently tugging up the bottom of the bath towel from behind and then gaping in awe at the acres of bare, honey-smooth cheeks he'd revealed. 'As far as it's ever been stretched in its life.'

'Oh, no!' she gasped in dismay, trying unsuccessfully to reposition the towel around her. 'Surely you can't mean *that*! Surely you don't expect *that*?'

But, alas, it seemed that they did. The marathon stretching of one point after another was just about to begin. Purely for the sake of Pauline and the stability of her marriage, of course.

* * *

Within seconds the bath towel was discarded in the hall where she stood, leaving her totally naked once more. 'Oh, mother!' she sighed heavily, staring down at the towel by her feet. 'Not again.' Gently but firmly she was turned round and guided upstairs between them, Harry's right hand clamped firmly round her dimpled left buttock, Kevin's left round her right.

'Listen, boys,' she began as they approached the top of the stairs. 'I really ought to be getting on with some housework. That's why I've taken today off work.'

Instinctively they tightened their hold on the plumpest part of each cheek. 'Surely a young housewife's first duty lies in the bedroom?' Harry pointed out wisely.

'Well, yes,' she murmured. 'With her husband.'

'Think of this as just a spot of practice.'

'I'm not really sure I'm in need of any practice.'

'But we are!' growled Harry, gripping her bottom so forcefully that he feared the satin-smooth flesh might slip right out of his fingers. 'We need just as much as we can get!'

'Oh, well,' she sighed again, realising there was no way out of her unhappy situation. 'Perhaps you could give me a hand with the dishes afterwards?'

'I'm sure we can,' Harry replied at once. 'And I'm a dab hand with the vacuum cleaner as well.'

'I often do the cleaning for my Mum,' Kevin chimed in eagerly.

'That would be a great help,' she said over her shoulder as she opened the bedroom door, their hands still gripping her rear end as if they feared it might try to escape what lay in store for it.

Inside the room she turned to face them, making Kevin gasp in disbelief. Downstairs in the hall he'd assumed that nothing could compare with the breathtaking curves of her lovely bare bottom. But he'd been wrong, he realised, his mouth hanging open as he goggled in wonder at the front of

her body – at the slimness of her waist and the graceful swell
of hips and breasts, at the long, smooth thighs and, finally,
at the totally shaven pubic mound below which the lips of
her vagina were delightfully just on display. Despite himself,
he was so fascinated that he was quite unable to drag his
eyes away from the gorgeous pink plumpness that nestled
between the tops of her legs. Pauline blushed at the blatancy
of his stare, but at the same time experienced a familiar
pang of excitement in the pit of her stomach. A very familiar
pang.

'Come on, Kevin!' Harry sang out brightly, kicking off
his shoes as he spoke. 'Stop gawping and look after the lady
while I get out of my kit. Try not to let her get bored.'

The spell was broken. Kevin looked nervously at Pauline,
unsure as to how to proceed. So she decided to lend a hand.
With a smile of encouragement she stepped up to him and
helped him fold his arms round her warm, silky smooth body.
Then she snuggled herself against him, using a hand to turn
his face to meet her lips and tongue. He responded to her
kiss at once. Very hungrily indeed. He was terribly young,
she thought to herself. But he seemed to be mastering the
general idea quite quickly. And there was certainly nothing
timid or shy about the use to which he was now putting his
right hand. The saucy little devil! She supposed she really
ought to respond in kind. It wouldn't take her two shakes to
have him out of his knickers. And she could tell that there
was something very worthwhile inside. She could feel it
jammed against her stomach as they embraced. She could
feel it twitching violently, as if it had a life of its own.

'You're *so* beautiful!' Kevin croaked breathlessly, between
kisses, unable to believe his extraordinary luck.

Five minutes later Pauline lay on her back in the middle of
her jumbo-sized bed, an untidy array of male clothing heaped
in the far corner of the room. Harry was lying on his side to
her left, administering a long, lingering kiss, whilst Kevin

208

was on her other side, fingering her slowly and easily. Harry slid his left hand up to the junction of her thighs. Now both men were exploring inside her, gently but deeply, causing her to spread her legs a little wider in order to accommodate them. She sighed at the luxury of the situation, and continued to squeeze rhythmically at the two overstretched penises she was nursing, one in each hand. All three of them savoured the sensation of her making love to both men at the same time.

Slowly she wriggled her hips in time with their fingers, feeling the warm waves of pleasure fanning out from her groin. Kevin raised his head and gazed down at the glorious sight of wet, wide open pussy being delicately but extensively probed. His fingers were coated with oil, as was the palm and the back of his hand. Smooth, slippery oil that he could see oozing slowly out of her and trickling over their hands. As if by mutual agreement, he and Harry worked their fingers a little harder, producing even greater quantities and making her moan softly and sweetly. She was so hot, he gasped to himself. So really, incredibly hot. Her insides were on fire as he slid his fingers back and forth. Surely his prick would burst in her hand!

Now all three of them were nicely in rhythm. As her groin rose and fell in time with their fingers, she rubbed their bulging penises up and down at an identical pace. In and out, in and out slid the fingers, up and down she rubbed their dicks. Slowly and evenly moved the fingers, slowly and evenly moved her hips. Up she moved to meet the fingers, down she moved as they withdrew. Slowly down she drew their foreskins, up she pulled them once again.

The men adjusted their positions and then both slipped a hand underneath her bottom, so that they were cupping one cheek each. Much to her approval, as she wriggled smoothly up and down. Then the more experienced Harry began using a fingertip to tease the hole of her bottom – again with her approval. Now she was able to lift her hips to

209

meet their fingers and then sink down to spike her bottom gently on Harry. Up and down she wriggled, filling her pussy with fingers, then pricking her bottom again. Slowly and sweetly she moved, loving every gentle poke and prod. Her pussy, her bottom, her pussy, her bottom, one and then the other, causing her the most delicious sensations, making her feel she was floating on air.

With Harry's tongue still in her mouth, she felt Kevin's lips on her breasts and sighed again with delight. She was really being spoilt, she said to herself happily. Her pussy, her bottom, her boobs and her mouth, all were being attended to so sweetly by these two young lads. And on top of that, her hands were full of their lovely smooth young weapons. What more could any girl ask? And they were being so gentle with her. Lads of this age were so often exactly the opposite. So often they were only interested in ramming their fingers in and out as hard as they could, or squeezing or sucking or prodding for all they were worth. But these two boys were really giving her a treat. They were really making her feel so wonderfully special. And the alternative piercing of pussy and bottom was simply something else! It was making her even more lubricated than ever. She could feel her juices running down the cheeks of her bottom and into the upturned palms of their hands. And – very cleverly – Harry was using it to lubricate the finger that was poking into her bottom, with the result that she was now able to press down hard and push it almost all the way home. It was giving her the most gorgeous sensation, particularly now that Kevin had slightly adjusted his hold on her crotch, enabling her to rub her clit against the heel of his palm each time she lifted her hips.

As Kevin leant over her, his mouth on her breasts and his hands round her bottom and groin, he could feel Harry's finger inside her anal passage. Tentatively, he moved the middle finger of his left hand until it was side by side with Harry's. 'Oh, yes!' gasped Pauline, greedily forcing both

210

fingers into her bottom as she bore down. Then she returned her mouth to Harry's and started to orgasm very gently. Now both of them were fingering both of her nice little openings, whilst Kevin was sucking each overstretched nipple in turn.

She was simply dying of pleasure, she groaned to herself. She was simply drifting away towards Heaven on a cloud of her own. And it was largely due to the way that the boys were stretching her poor little bott. Or rather, the way she was stretching it on them. The discomfort was definitely a stimulant. The harder she spiked it on them, the sexier she felt. Just like she'd done at her engagement party. Her very wild engagement party, during which that awful Tim Reynolds had trapped her in the bathroom in the middle of that 'Knickers-and-Nothing Else' game of hide and seek, and somehow managed to force almost all of his tool into that poor little hole. The pain had been so delightful that she'd not been able to believe it was true. She'd been sore for ages afterwards. Wonderfully, beautifully sore. And she just couldn't begin to describe how it had felt when he'd started to shoot!

The two lads could feel her climax growing stronger and stronger. Eventually she had to break the kiss with Harry, because she needed to fight for breath. Then the rhythm of the lovemaking suddenly changed and she began to beat up and down with her hips, hammering their fingers into her bottom and then forcing their other fingers hard into her quim. 'Ohhhh!' she groaned, thrusting up and down as fast as she could. 'Oh, I'm going to die!'

But eventually it was over and she lay peacefully on her back, waiting to regain her strength, their hands still all over the lower half of her body, their fingers unmoving but still inside. Pauline drew a long, happy breath and opened her eyes. 'Who's going to go first?' she asked dreamily, squeezing their cocks in her hands.

'Perhaps I should,' murmured Harry, slowly licking one

sharply pointed nipple, whilst Kevin nibbled the other. 'Kevin could watch and take notes. He's only done it once before.'

'You needn't have let on about that!' complained Kevin, slightly miffed that his lack of experience should have been divulged so unnecessarily.

'That doesn't matter, Kevin,' she said kindly. 'That isn't important at all. At least you've done it once. That's always the really big one, isn't it? Everyone has to begin somewhere.' She smiled, and by way of comfort and reassurance, gave an extra special tweak to that very stiff part of his person still cradled in her right hand. 'I'm sure you'll manage just fine.'

'And you'll have gained a lot more experience after today,' Harry laughed good-naturedly, carefully rolling on top of Pauline and obliging Kevin to remove his hand, somewhat reluctantly, from the piping-hot delight of her quim.

'That's true, Kevin,' she breathed, closing her eyes as she felt Kevin's middle fingers being replaced by something even more substantial. She gave him a final good-bye squeeze and then wrapped both arms round Harry, leaving Kevin's long, deserted dick pointing dejectedly up at the headboard, full of self-pity at having been abandoned to its own devices.

Harry proceeded to set a fine example, giving his usual expert performance. He started to pole her slowly and steadily, to the accompaniment of gentle sighs and moans. Gradually he picked up speed, the long powerful strokes turning the sighs to sobs and the moans to groans of delight. Faster and faster he shafted her until it seemed she'd be unable to stand any more. Then, having reached a crescendo, he began to vary tactics and pace in order to achieve the maximum effect. Kevin watched in fascination as each thrust from Harry caused a fresh wave of orgasm to race through her. He wondered anxiously whether she'd react in the same way when his time finally came. Would his own cock make her wriggle and squeal in that way?

'Oh, Harry!' she gasped, thrashing her head wildly from

side to side on the pillow. 'Oh, Harry! You're making me come so hard!'

At last Harry was spent and he rolled slowly onto his back, stretching luxuriously as his long, wet tool began to subside. Pauline leant over him and reached for the large box of Kleenex she'd had the foresight to place on the bedside table. 'Is it my turn now?' Kevin asked eagerly, when she was done.

'Of course it is,' she whispered, reaching out to welcome him with both arms, as well as spectacularly upthrust breasts.

He eased himself on top of her, unsurely, concerned not to cause any discomfort through some act of clumsiness on his part. 'I never thought this moment would arrive!' he gasped. 'I never dreamt I'd get the chance to do this to *you*! I still can't believe it's real.'

'You're a lovely young lad,' she cooed softly, slowly running her fingers through the long hair on the back of his neck. 'You've got nothing to be timid about. Any girl would be happy to have you.'

'This is unbelievable!' he groaned, as he settled himself between sweetly smooth thighs and prepared to push forward with his throbbing erection. The thought of exactly whose honeypot was lying there, eagerly awaiting his pleasure, seemed to fill his whole being. Rapidly it became overwhelming. He was just about to fuck her, he gasped to himself. He was just about to fuck the most beautiful girl in the world. He was just about to poke his plonker into her warm, willing quim. It was utterly incredible. Totally beyond his wildest dreams. He was just about to fuck Pauline Peach! She was actually lying underneath him, stark naked, pussy open, waiting and wanting him to fuck her all the way up to the top of her hot little cunt.

Kevin lifted his head a fraction and began to push forward with his groin – to push forward towards achieving the unthinkable. 'I never once imagined that— *oh my God!*' he wailed in despair, suddenly aghast at finding himself spraying

213

great thick streaks of white-hot semen all over the upper half of her body. Stream after stream he vented, almost up to her chin.

'Oh, Jesus! Oh, Mary!' he sobbed, staring in horror at the premature produce of his loins. 'What have I done?'

'It's nothing to worry about,' she said soothingly. 'It happens quite often, Kevin. Really it does. You needn't be ashamed. And it feels lovely all over my boobs.'

But Kevin was distraught. Far beyond consolation. 'I knew it was too good to be true!' he moaned hopelessly. 'I knew I'd make a prat of myself somehow! What a terrible thing to have happened! I just knew deep down that I'd never really manage it with you.' He slid off her and lay on his side, in tears. 'I knew something awful would happen.'

Tenderly she cupped the whole of his over-enthusiastic tackle in her hands. 'Of course you'll manage it, Kevin. Just give me half a mo. Look, he's getting bigger already. Bigger and bigger and bigger. Now he's fully grown again! Already! Goodness, that was incredibly quick!'

'Yes,' he groaned despondently. 'But I'll never be able to get it inside you. You're just far too beautiful. The same thing will simply happen again. I know it will. I'll never be able to get it in!'

'Yes you will, silly boy!' she whispered, ruffling his hair affectionately and then kissing the tip of his nose. 'Just listen to me. Years ago I had a boyfriend with a similar problem. So I know all about it. If you do exactly as I tell you, everything will be just fine.'

'I don't think so.'

'Be quiet and pay attention,' she giggled, playfully slapping him on the rump. 'The trouble is that you get over-excited.'

'I know.'

'So we have to take things one step at a time. Very slowly and gently.'

'How will that help?'

'You'll soon see. Now, first of all you must roll back on

top of me. Just that and nothing else. Don't try to put it in. Just get used to lying on top of me, that's all. And don't even think about what happens next. Just get used to my boobs pressing into you . . . and your thingy pressing into my stomach.'

Carefully he did as he was told, holding his breath and praying not to shoot his load. He tried to ignore the hot, pointed nipples that seemed to bore deep into his chest. He also tried to forget all about the proximity of his sexual organ to hers.

'Think of something unpleasant,' she advised him. 'Like smelly old socks, or girls with pimply bottoms, or Mr Davis-Davies.'

Kevin concentrated on recalling the time when he'd been very young and had been playing, contrary to strict instructions, with his father's angling equipment. Somehow he'd succeeded in getting a size sixteen hook caught in his foreskin. Fortunately, the hook had been one of the barbless variety. But even so, the experience had been considerably less than happy.

'How are you feeling?' she asked after a while. 'Not too excited by the feel of my boobs?'

'They're very nice,' he gulped. 'But I think I'm getting used to them. What do we do next?'

'Just lie there a little bit longer and think about having to clean your bike.'

'I hate having to mend a puncture. It really pisses me off.'

'Kevin! How crude!'

'Sorry, Pauline,' he murmured, trying hard to ignore the way in which his penis was throbbing so violently. 'I mean it's a real pain in the . . . neck.'

'That's much better. Nice language doesn't cost anyone anything. You're judged by how you talk, you know, Kevin.'

'You sound just like my Mum.'

'I'm glad to hear it.'

'Mind you, you don't look like her. And I've certainly

never tried to do this to her, either.'

'Kevin! Keep your mind on other things. You're not trying to do anything to me. You're just lying on top of me, getting used to me, that's all. And if there's any more dirty language, you won't be doing anything more. And that's absolutely flat!'

'You're really lovely when you get cross, Pauline. Has anyone ever told you that before?'

'Well, yes, I suppose they have . . .'

'It makes me want to fuck the hell out of you!'

'I've heard that one as well,' she sighed.

'I'm not surprised. I've never seen anything so stalky as you when you're a little bit angry.'

'We'd better talk about something else. Otherwise you'll be gone again before we get started.'

'I don't think so, Pauline. I'm feeling quite strong, really I am. I think I'll be okay this time.'

'Don't think about it at all, Kevin. Remember what I said. Concentrate on something else entirely.'

'It's a bit difficult to do that . . . lying here like this.'

'Perhaps it's time to move on to phase two,' she wondered aloud. 'Are you sure you feel in control?'

'I think so, Pauline. I really think I do.'

'You don't find me too much of a novelty? My nipples and pubes and so on?'

'No. I just want to get to use them, that's all.'

'All right, Kevin. We'll take the next step. But make sure you leave it all to me. Think about something that turns you off. Think about anything you like, except what I'm going to do.'

'What are you going to do?'

'You're going to lie there and pretend that I'm nowhere in sight. Count your eight times table, or something like that. Meanwhile, I'm going to slip you inside. But don't try and do anything yourself. Don't push or press or do anything like that. Leave it all to me. And try to imagine that none of this is happening. After that, simply get used to being inside me. But don't move about at all. Just get used to the feel of my pussy all around you. It's a perfectly natural thing, Kevin. Men and women are at it all the time. It's as normal as going to work to earn a living. More fun, perhaps. But just as ordinary and everyday.'

'I'm not so sure about that,' he gulped, as Pauline wriggled herself up the bed underneath him, until her pubic area was well past his navel. Then she engaged the tip of his burning hot erection between her thighs, so that it was touching the sweetly opened lips that nestled nearby.

'What are nine eights?' she asked, gently sliding her groin back towards the foot of the bed.

'Sixty-four . . . No, seventy-two, I think.'

'I haven't a clue,' she giggled as she felt the first two or three inches gliding smoothly into her welcoming hole. 'I'm hopeless at tables since I started using a calculator. Have you got one of those? A pocket calculator, I mean?'

'Yes, but I try not to use it,' he croaked, closing his eyes whilst Pauline wriggled and eased him deeper and deeper inside. At last there was no more of him left to accommodate. With Kevin jammed tightly all the way to the top of her vagina, she glanced to her left and was glad to see that Harry was watching intently, his penis fully erect.

'There you are, Kevin,' she whispered, kissing him tenderly on the lips. 'I told you I could get you inside me. Oh ye of little faith!'

'You feel fantastic!' he breathed.

'So do you, Kevin. I'm so full of you that you're starting to make me come! Lie still until I'm finished. Think about something else.'

'I don't think I need to anymore, Pauline. I feel pretty strong within myself.'

'Oh, Kevin!' she gasped, grabbing hold of his buttocks and trying to force him even further inside. 'You're making me come so beautifully! And you're not even moving about!

217

You're so hard and hot . . . And almost up to my throat! Oh, Kevin! Oh, that's so unbelievably good!'

The climax subsided and she kissed him, rubbing her nipples into his chest and stroking him slowly with both hands. Stroking him from the nape of his neck down to the backs of his knees, and lingering on hard young haunches that made her feel sexier than ever.

She decided it was time to test him further. Cleverly she began to manipulate her vaginal muscles, without moving her body, so that it felt to him that he was being squeezed and teased by some sort of internal hand. 'I didn't know girls could do that!' he whispered hoarsely.

'I don't think all girls can. It's just a sort of a knack. I can do it harder, if you like.'

'Yes, please,' he breathed, closing his eyes and relishing the sweetness of the sensation.

'It's easy to do it to you,' she explained. 'Because you're big enough to fill me right up to the brim.'

Kevin withstood the treatment well, remaining intact and crammed deep inside her throughout. He found he no longer needed to concentrate on other matters. He felt in no danger of repeating his earlier lapse. As the seconds ticked by, his natural masculine aggression began to increase. He was going to give it to her good and proper, he told himself fiercely. He was going to dish it out even better than Harry had done. He was really going to fuck her like fury. He was going to make her squirm and squeal and scream. He was going to make her cry buckets as he stretched that tight little pussy as far as it could possibly go.

'Right, then, Mrs Peach!' he grunted at length, transferring his weight to elbows and knees as he spoke. 'I really think you've done the trick. I said you made me want to fuck the hell out of you. Well, that's exactly what I'm going to do now. Except ten times more than you've ever imagined possible.'

'I've got a very fertile imagination!' she giggled naughtily.

'So I only hope that you're right.'

For the next fifteen minutes Kevin lived up to his word, shagging her with an unparalleled level of effort. He didn't possess quite the same style and finesse as Harry, but what he lacked in that respect he made up in sheer enthusiasm. Even Harry was impressed by the show. And there was no doubting how Pauline felt. Harry gazed at the long, gleaming wet cock as it flew in and out of her pussy at pace. 'That's it, Kevin,' he breathed with approval. 'Give her as much as you can!'

For the next few minutes Kevin did just that. Then he stopped. 'Is anything wrong?' she asked.

'No, nothing. It's still my turn, but I'd like to watch you on top of Harry for a couple of minutes.'

Sixty seconds later Pauline was spread out on Harry, her toes almost touching his, due to her height. In absolute fascination, Kevin watched the smooth rise and fall of her bottom as she impaled herself on Harry at a very leisurely pace. In addition to that spectacular sight, he was surprised to find himself intrigued by the thought of Harry's dick crammed tightly into the hot little opening he himself had only just vacated. But the vision of her sweetly undulating bare bottom was the real delight. He reached out and ran a palm back and forth across each pouting, highly polished cheek. They were so pert and perfect that he experienced a physical pang in the pit of his stomach.

'It's strange,' he gulped innocently, gently squeezing her bottom as it continued to undulate up and down. 'I've no idea why, but you're so pretty down here it makes me want to smack your cheeks really hard.'

'Join the club!' chortled Harry.

'I just can't explain it,' mumbled Kevin, shaking his head in bewilderment.

'You don't have to,' replied Harry. 'We understand exactly what you mean. Don't we, Pauline?'

'I don't know what it is with you men,' she sighed through

a faceful of hair. 'I can't think why all of you feel that way about a girl's defenceless rear end.'

'But we do, don't we?' growled Harry, squeezing her himself. 'About a prize specimen like this, at least.'

'Well, I certainly do,' Kevin agreed slowly, still puzzled and perplexed. 'It's really very odd.'

Pauline lay still on Harry, his penis wedged solidly inside. She turned her head and looked at Kevin. 'You can do it to me if you must,' she said softly. 'It won't be the first time, exactly.'

'Oh, no!' he replied quickly. 'I wouldn't dream of hurting you. I like you far too much for that.'

'How sweet!' she said.

Harry lifted his hand in the air. 'I will,' he said eagerly.

'No, you won't!' snapped Kevin. 'She's been much too kind.'

'But she likes it,' laughed Harry. 'Even if you do it hard. Isn't that right, Pauline?'

'Oh, er . . .'

'I thought so,' grinned Harry, raising his hand even higher.

'Don't you dare!' snarled Kevin, placing a protective hand over each gleaming, upturned globe.

'Keep your hair on, Kevin,' Harry said in an appeasing tone.

'I don't mind if you want to do it, Kevin, she whispered. 'As Harry says, it can feel rather warm and sexy.'

'It just wouldn't be right,' he sighed. 'Much as I'd like to. Anyway, your bottom seems to be blushing quite a bit as it is.'

'It must be embarrassed by all this talk about spanking,' she giggled.

At Kevin's request, Pauline carefully disengaged herself from Harry and lay face down on the bed. 'A backscuttle!' Harry murmured with approval, as Kevin mounted her back, his legs straddling hers, and his overheated member buried in the very ample cleft between her buttocks. Savouring the feel of firm, silky-smooth flesh pressing warmly into his stomach and groin, he began to slide his penis up and down the long deep valley that divided those gorgeous cheeks.

'This is almost like being inside you,' he whispered, before biting her gently on the nape of her neck. 'Have you done it like this before?'

Pauline pushed upwards so that the thick stem of his erection was rubbing back and forth over the entrance to her anal passage. The sudden surge of pleasure made her struggle for breath. 'Yes,' she was able to wheeze. 'It's nice, isn't it? For a change.'

She thrust up even harder against him, increasing the delicious effect as she jammed the hole of her bottom against his rigidity. Kevin sensed how she was responding and began to move faster, making her puff and pant. Eventually the friction of penis against anus was simply too much for her to bear. 'Ohhh!' she squawked loudly, as her insides began to spasm in a most unusual way.

They lay still for at least sixty seconds, Kevin still wedged hotly into the gap between her buttocks. 'That was fun!' she said breathlessly. 'I've never come like that before.'

Kevin drew back and took his weight on his knees so that he was ready for a more conventional form of lovemaking. Yet again he glanced down at the plump pink cheeks that waited for him just beyond his out-thrust shaft, and groaned at the exceptionally sharp pang of desire that suddenly shot right through him. He adjusted his position slightly and then sank back down on top of her, pushing the tip of his penis forward between the very tops of her thighs.

'Kevin!' she sighed happily, feeling him slither and slide all the way to the top of her vagina. Powerfully he started to shaft her, wallowing once more in the comfort of her superb posterior as he dug his groin deep into the bounciness of her buttocks at the end of each forward stroke. 'Kevin!' she squealed again, his long, hard horn of

221

plenty opening her as wide as she'd comfortably go. 'You don't know how good that feels!'

'The boy's not as daft as he looks,' Harry told himself pensively. 'I'll definitely do her that way myself.'

With Kevin set securely in the saddle of her buttocks, Pauline buried her face in the pillow and groaned at the intensity of yet another orgasm. He really was a fast learner, she told herself, as she squirmed her hips from side to side. Like all beginners, he'd started off by banging away as fast and as hard as he could. Not that she'd objected to that, of course. It had made her come time and again. But then he'd learned the art of variation, and that had been even better. And now he'd discovered another little trick of the trade. In fact, he'd discovered it rather too well. Her insides were simply melting away.

As Pauline continued to wriggle and moan, Kevin proceeded to torment her with his new technique. He'd raised himself a few inches on elbows and knees and was now frigging the knobbly end of his erection in and out, causing her to seethe with frustration, as well as a longing to be impaled to the full. As he did this, he gazed down and admired the sight. And still he worked just the tip back and forth, teasing the lips of her sex. Lips that screamed out for something much more substantial than just the end of his end. Lips that longed, in fact, to be crushed hard against the girth of its root. And Kevin had perfected the process. Every twenty seconds or so, without prior warning, he'd suddenly provide Pauline with what she wanted. He'd suddenly plunge himself right up to the balls, making her shriek with the pleasure of being properly penetrated at last. Then he'd withdraw all the way back to her entrance, and start tantalising her all over again.

Pauline gasped with frustration. This latest bout of tortuous end-frigging was lasting a really long time. Whenever was he going to pierce her with his full length? It seemed ages since he'd last done so. The anticipation was driving her mad. All she craved was the relief of being stuffed until she felt she was going to burst. But still he hadn't obliged. Still he was only slipping the tip in and out, making her poor pussy sizzle and seethe with desire. And it was impossible to help herself to him. She'd tried several times, but every time she'd pushed up with her bottom, he'd simply pulled back and denied her even so much as a centimetre of additional brawn.

Pauline made one final effort. She thrust violently upwards and felt several inches slip nicely inside. But almost at once he was gone. He drew back and continued to frig.

At last she twisted her head and looked up at him as, once again, he plucked the swollen head out of her aching quim. 'Kevin!' she gasped anxiously. 'Kevin, I really do need you now. All of you.'

And now he was pleased to provide, spearing her with all his force and sending her into squeals of ecstasy as she thrashed her bottom from side to side and groaned with relief. He withdrew and then speared her again. Almost at once she realised that he'd come to the end of his tether. For the second time that morning he'd begun spurting forth the hot fresh seed of his loins. But this time it was gushing into her, rather than splashing and splattering her torso. Suddenly he was struck by an idea. He pulled out of her completely and then, with one powerful thrust, forced the head of his ejaculating penis two or three inches into her bottom. 'Oh my God!' she shrieked at the top of her voice, as she felt the next scalding hot burst burning her anal passage.

'I love you, Pauline!' he cried, forcing himself all the way home.

'*Oh my God!!*' she screamed in delight.

'I love you!' he repeated, pumping sperm into her bottom with a force she could scarcely believe.

* * *

223

Kevin rolled off her, reluctantly, staring up at the ceiling as he fought to regain his breath. Pauline lay stock still and exhausted, but enjoying the feel of his seed as it started to trickle slowly out of both of her lower openings. Never had she been doubly implanted in that way. How very clever of him.

For several seconds she lay there, relishing the sensation, relishing the steady dribble from pussy and bottom. Then she turned her head to the right and looked at Harry. How prettily he was shaped in the region of his groin! How perfectly proportioned! Long and as straight as a die. For some reason she always appreciated that in a man. The straightness, she meant. It just looked so much more attractive.

Harry raised his eyebrows questioningly, and she smiled a watery smile. 'Can you give me another minute?' she said weakly, by way of reply.

As she lay there, gathering her strength, a rather unnerving thought flitted unexpectedly across her mind. With the advent of Kevin, the card trick was now complete. The circle had been drawn. There wasn't a single male left at the office who had yet to possess her. From the highest to the lowest, all of them had run all the way through her with ease. From senior partner to office boy, there wasn't a soul who'd failed to infiltrate her. She'd been had by every man there. And all in the space of a hectic thirty-six hours! From now on life at work was going to be somewhat awkward and embarrassing for one respectably married young lady. Wherever she went there'd be someone, or several someones, running an eye over her and recalling exactly how she'd been had and used by him and everyone else. Had and used just about as extensively as anyone could possibly have been.

Pauline sighed to herself at the thought of how comprehensively George Franks had gained his revenge. His revenge for a totally imaginary sight. Would it end after today? After she'd been obliged to accommodate the whole of the office? After today, would she be allowed to stay faithful to her absolute *angel* of a husband? She supposed she could only wait to find out. In the meantime there was Young Harry to think about. No doubt he was absolutely itching to get underway . . .

Pauline was quite right. Harry was gazing down at her recently shagged bottom, so big and inviting as it lay there, smiling up at him. There was no way he wasn't going to fuck her in there, he promised himself. She was already perfectly lubricated for him. Kevin had seen to that. He was going to fuck that beautiful bottom himself. Right now, in fact. She'd had plenty of time to recover. So he'd just carry on from where Kevin had left off . . .

'Oh, yes!' gasped Pauline, as Harry began to ease himself into the tight little hole that Kevin had flooded such a short time before. She lay still, not daring to move a muscle, consumed with excitement and awaiting the unique combination of pleasure and pain she'd experienced only four times in her life.

Pauline groaned again, feeling him pushing further and further inside. She could feel him so exactly – every single contour of his dick. She could even feel his pulse beat as he plugged her bottom deeper and deeper. Oh, this was simply heaven.

Kevin lay back happily on his side of the bed, his hands cupped under his head, watching Pauline receiving Harry in her rear end. He was extremely proud of the job he'd just completed. What a stroke of genius it had been, finishing her off in there! Hadn't she really loved that! Hadn't that really driven her wild! And it had put him one up on Harry, even though Harry was doing the same thing to her now. It had been his idea and he'd executed it to perfection, leaving her as satisfied as she could possibly be.

Christ, how she'd squawked when he'd stuck it in! He

supposed it had been the surprise, as much as the pleasure. And then she'd been delighted by how much he'd been able to shoot. And so had he, as a matter of fact.

Pauline opened her eyes and caught Kevin staring at her intently. She smiled sexily, bright-eyed and flushed in the face. She thought she could half read his thoughts. He was as pleased as Punch, she reckoned. As pleased as Punch at the way he'd just performed on her. She gazed deeply into his eyes. There was something really erotic about doing that. About looking into one man's face, whilst being dicked by another. Particularly when she was getting it in her bottom. It was lovely that Kevin could see, not only what Harry was doing, but the precise effect it was having on her. It was lovely that he could watch as Harry started to make her come.

Oh! Ouch! Her poor little bott was going to be incredibly sore inside. Harry was now beating against her buttocks every bit as hard as that awful Tim Reynolds had done.

Some minutes later, still plugged deep in her bottom. Harry turned himself and Pauline on their sides, so that they were both facing Kevin. 'There's all this glorious wet pussy going spare,' he said to Kevin, using a hand to part her legs and show it to him. 'It seems a waste that no-one's using it.'

'Oh, mother!' she gasped in excitement, as Kevin slid eagerly across the sheets towards her.

Pauline lay on her side, sandwiched between the men. Sandwiched externally and internally. She lay stock still, groaning in disbelief as they thrust forcefully in and out. She'd never even imagined such an experience. She was beyond orgasm, in the sense that her whole being seemed in a state of constant, continuous spasm. All she could do was lie there, eyes tightly shut, and absorb the totally unique sensation of being taken from both front and back.

Cleverly, the men varied the routine. To begin with, both of them pushed into her at the same time, filling her to an impossible degree. Then they pushed alternately, filling pussy and bottom in turn. Then they reverted to their original technique, simultaneously stretching both of her nice little holes and making her scream.

On and on they shafted, now filling her together, now filling her in turn. She felt as if she was floating. As if she was floating right away. She was weightless. Her body had ceased to exist, apart from the two tight little passages into which the men were hammering with glee. This was the end of her, she gasped to herself. There was no way she was going to survive this. As soon as they started to implant her, she just knew she was going to die. There was no way that anyone on earth would be able to live through the sort of pleasure she was going to get when she felt them starting to spurt. Particularly when she felt Young Harry's liquid fire burning its way into her poor, sorely abused bum . . .

For the next two hours the men kept her fully occupied, in every sense of the word. Sometimes both of them were inside her together, sometimes one was resting whilst the other was fitted snugly somewhere within. Whatever the combination, throughout the whole of that time some part of her internal anatomy was being vigorously poked and prodded and then flooded with yet more seed. There was always someone to continue, or take over, as soon as the other was done. It was as if all of their lives depended upon her being fucked somewhere by someone, such was the enthusiasm displayed by all three.

But all good things must come to an end. And surely enough, at long last, the men were finally spent. Not a twitch could be raised by either of them. Not so much as a millimetre of cock could be stirred. 'I'm shagged!' groaned Harry, lying on his back and staring down at his lifeless equipment.

Pauline lay face down between them, feeling herself leaking like a sieve. 'What do you think I am, then?' she scarcely managed to croak.

'You could still shag, if one of us could shag you,' wheezed Harry, stating one of the age-old truths.

CHAPTER 10

Men Friday Continued

When Pauline returned from the bathroom the men were fully dressed, although sprawled wearily across the bed once more. 'Oh dear! I suppose I'd better put some clothes on.' she murmured, turning towards the wardrobe.

'Before we get any more ideas,' laughed Harry.

'I'd have thought that unlikely,' she replied. 'I'd have thought you'd have used them all up by now.'

'We've used up quite a lot of things,' sighed Kevin, stretching his arms in a yawn. 'As well as ideas, I mean.'

Pauline stepped into a pair of tiny black kickers and began to ease them into position. 'I don't feel at all sorry for you,' she said, wriggling herself into the skimpy little undies. 'At least you've both had some time to rest and recuperate. Think what I've had to go through! Hardly a moment's respite during the last three hours!'

Kevin thought hard. 'There was that time you asked Harry to hang on until you were ready.'

'Goodness!' she squealed indignantly. 'It was all of twenty or thirty seconds! That's as long as he could wait to get into my poor little bottom.'

'Better than no break at all,' said Harry, leaning forward and playfully whipping the seat of the kickers down to her knees the very second she'd finished adjusting them.

Kevin gazed at her perfect, bare-again bottom and sighed. 'It doesn't do a thing for me now,' he muttered tiredly. 'Mind you,' he suddenly brightened up, 'give me another quarter of an hour or so.'

Pauline giggled and grabbed a white mini-skirt from a clotheshanger. 'In that case I'm getting dressed in sixty seconds flat!' As indeed she did, scrambling hurriedly into skirt, T-shirt, and high heels and then daintily repositioning the displaced panties. The skirt was so short that it scarcely reached the tops of her thighs.

Harry scratched his chin thoughtfully. 'Short white skirts and little black knickers turn me on,' he said slowly. 'They always make me horny.'

'I know what you mean,' murmured Kevin, displaying a moderate degree of interest at the way the black panties peeped out just a fraction from below the hem of her skirt. Her crotch was just above his eye level, due to his horizontal position on the bed.

'Come on, you two!' cried Pauline, quickly ushering them off the devastated bed and out of the room. 'It's time for you to get back to the office. You've had more than enough hanky-panky for one day. Harry! Take your hand away from there!'

They followed her downstairs, lagging behind the brisk pace that she set. 'We never got round to helping you with the housework,' Harry said from the foot of the stairs.

'Don't worry,' she called back to them. 'I'll get through it this afternoon.'

'We could stay and help you now,' suggested Kevin, feeling a sudden twinge of life inside his underpants as she bent, straight legged, to retrieve the bath towel they'd earlier abandoned in the hall.

'That's not a bad idea,' Harry agreed readily, having experienced much the same thing himself. 'It doesn't matter if we're late getting back to work. Mr Franks will cover for us.'

But Pauline was only too well aware of what they had in mind. Any further delay in their departure was fraught with danger, she warned herself wisely. Another ten minutes convalescence and they'd have her flat on her back once again. Or her side, or her front, or slaving away on top.

Quickly she opened the front door. 'There's no need for that,' she smiled sweetly, stepping outside into the garden. 'But thanks very much for the offer. It's very kind of you both.'

Kevin's eyes settled on the spectacular swell of her breasts, clearly discernible through the tight white T-shirt she'd pulled on a couple of minutes beforehand. 'You're sure you don't want us to do the drying up?' he asked hopefully, whilst at the same time recalling the fact that she hadn't bothered to slip into a bra.

Harry stared at the magnificently filled seat of her skirt. Kevin's kind enquiry had suddenly transfixed him with the mental image of Pauline bending over the kitchen sink, her hands in the washing up bowl . . .

She's wearing nothing but one of those sexy little aprons you sometimes see in adult-only cartoons. Harry is standing directly behind her, both hands wrapped round the best erection he's ever experienced in his life. He moves forward stealthily, guiding his tip to a point between and just below the plump cheeks of her lovely bare bottom. He gives one firm, fierce push and is several inches inside her quim. He feels her wriggle and writhe in delight. He sinks all the way in with a sigh and then cups a hand round each pendulous breast, biting her gently on the back of the neck as he does so. He's so rigid and rampant that she can only move up and down on him. All lateral movement is denied her, due to his incredible penile power. He starts to shaft her, slowly and deliberately, making her scream with pleasure. He feels so huge that he fears he'll do her a mischief. Then . . .

'Sorry!' gasped Harry, vigorously shaking his head. 'What was that you said, Pauline?'

'Your scooter,' she repeated, fully clothed and back in her front garden once more.

'What about it?' he asked absentmindedly, trying but failing to return to his shattered daydream.

231

She pointed to the customised red-and-white scooter he'd parked on her drive. 'It's a Lambretta GP200, isn't it?'

'Yes, that's right. How do you know that?'

'I had a boyfriend who was heavily into scooters. Particularly Lambrettas. He spent all his spare time building them up, or stripping them down, or travelling hundreds of miles to the rallies.'

'I've been to most of the rallies in the UK,' said Harry. 'But not to the ones on the continent.'

'I went to a few with my boyfriend. Camping, not bed and breakfast. But he was so jealous of all the attention I got that I decided it was best to stay behind.'

'I can imagine you were popular on the campsite,' grinned Harry. 'You don't get that many girls around. Just two or three thousand blokes.'

'The other lads kept getting him blind drunk,' she giggled. 'So that they could try to take advantage of me.'

'I hope they failed!' Harry said with feeling.

'I'm not going to say anything about that.'

'I'll take you to the next one, if you like. It's at the end of the month.'

'If I wasn't married, I'd love to. Michael's very understanding, but I don't think that even he would be too keen on me spending a weekend with you and thousands of other men.'

'That's a shame. Couldn't you make some sort of excuse?'

'I don't think it would be right, Harry. Do you?'

'I suppose not,' he muttered, unconvinced.

'It's an Italian one, isn't it?' she asked, peering closely at the gleaming scooter.

'Yes. They're far better than the Indian models. Far more reliable. Do you fancy going for a ride?'

'What, now?'

'Yes, why not? Kevin can always get a bus back to the office, can't you Kevin, old sport?'

'I guess so,' he replied reluctantly.

232

'Do you mind doing that, Kevin?' she asked with evident concern. 'I'd quite like to have a ride on Harry's Lambretta. It will bring back old memories. But only if you're sure you don't mind?'

Kevin shuffled his feet. He would dearly have loved to have spent some more time with her himself. But he had nothing to offer, apart from his company. It was all a bit of a pisser, he thought. 'It's okay, Pauline,' he said slowly. 'I'll find my own way back . . .'

'You're sweet!' she smiled, planting a kiss on the tip of his nose. 'Kevin!' she squawked, suddenly jumping backwards as he repaid the compliment by slipping his hand under the front of her skirt and patting her warmly between the legs. 'Not out here in front of the neighbours!'

'That felt nice,' he mumbled to himself, suddenly finding he was fully erect once again.

Harry kicked the scooter into life. It roared throatily as he twisted the throttle back and forth. Kevin kicked morosely at a stone and decided to have his say, even though it was unlikely to achieve the desired result. 'I want to fuck you again!' he yelled above the noise of the engine, much to the interest of the next-door neighbour who was busily tending his roses.

Harry laughed goodhumouredly. 'You'd better jump on board,' he advised her, patting the seat of his machine. 'And quickly, too. I think he means he wants to do it now.'

As Harry reached the end of her road, Pauline tapped him urgently on the shoulder. 'What is it?' he called back to her.

'I think you'd better find a nice quiet country road. Without any traffic or people.'

'Oh? That sounds promising?'

'Don't go through the town,' she yelled into his ear.

'Why not?'

'It's my skirt. It's so short and tight that I've had to pull it right up to my waist in order to sit down.'

233

The Lambretta wobbled wildly as he twisted round to glance behind. 'Careful!' she screeched at him.

'I see what you mean. Very fetching indeed. Not to say unbelievably stalky.'

'Keep your mind on your driving!' she shouted.

He swung down a side road that led away from the town centre. Two male pedestrians turned to stare in admiration at the sight of long blonde hair streaming back in the wind, coupled with a tiny pair of lacy black knickers hiding virtually nothing from view. 'Wasn't that Michael's wife?' asked one.

'Must have been,' replied his companion. 'There's only one bum like that in the world.'

'What the hell's it doing on the back of some bugger's scooter?'

'I'm sure Michael would like to know. On the other hand . . .'

Half an hour later the much-admired rear end was in even greater evidence. The Lambretta was parked in a cornfield, some eight miles out of town, a white T-shirt dangling from one handlebar, minuscule black panties from the other. Young Harry was on the seat of the machine, but facing the back. Pauline sat on his lap, facing him, her legs on either side of his. Slowly and rhythmically she rocked back and forth with her hips, causing almost the full length of his erection to slide gently in and out of her well-oiled quim.

She arched her back as far as she could, so that the whole of his dripping wet member was now exposed to the relative cool of the day. His hands were still locked round the cheeks of her bottom, and he was tempted to exert sufficient pressure to return her to her former position around and about his dick. But this was her fuck, he reminded himself. This was entirely her show. She'd asked for that privilege when they'd started. 'Let me do it to *you* this once.' That's what she'd said, as she'd been unzipping his flies. 'You and Kevin have spent hours and hours doing me. Doing me every

234

which way but loose. Just for a change, let me have my wicked way with you!'

It wasn't entirely true, Harry pointed out to himself. It wasn't entirely true that they'd spent all the time dishing it out to her. There had been that spell of about twenty minutes when they'd lain on their backs, side by side, and she'd moved from one to the other every couple of minutes or so. It had been a competition to see who could last out against her the longest. It had been quite good fun, he remembered. In a frustrating sort of a way. The short wait between bouts had considerably enhanced the effect each time she'd returned to tuck him back into her tight little opening. Which was exactly where he'd like to be right now . . .

Pauline kissed him slowly and sweetly, still maintaining her distance, still making him wait for the soothing syrup of her quim. Then, after what had seemed an eternity, she started to re-impale herself on him, slowly and steadily, breathing deeply as yet another climax began. The smooth, gentle sort of climax that usually marked the latter stages of a prolonged period of lovemaking.

She felt so hot, he gasped to himself. So steamy hot within. He supposed it was more noticeable because his dick had been exposed to the outside air temperature for so long. Nevertheless, it was impossible to imagine that any other girl possessed the same degree of internal combustion. Feeling his erection probing all the way into that fiery furnace was the most delightful experience in the world.

Little by little she removed her tongue from his mouth, her eyes sparkling happily into his. Tenderly she placed a hand on each side of his face. 'Supper time' she whispered guiding him down into acre upon acre of cleavage. Her boobs were fantastic, he reflected. So smooth and firm. So upthrust, perky and proud. And with nipples that had a will of their own. Long, pointed nipples that sprang instantly to attention at the slightest provocation, at the merest accidental touch.

He turned his head slightly to the side and took one nipple

between his lips, tickling and teasing it with the tip of his tongue. The other poked warmly against his ear as he sucked. She responded by pushing forward with her groin. Again he felt her starting to come, easily and gently, just as before, displaying none of the violent urgency that had seized her when they'd first coupled together in bed.

'How can you possibly make it so often?' he asked her, as she wriggled and sighed with enjoyment.

'I don't know,' she croaked. 'It's just how I'm made, I suppose. It's always been that way. I hope it doesn't put you off?'

'It's wonderful,' he enthused. 'So incredibly rewarding. I really do love you, Pauline . . .'

'Don't you mean you fancy me a lot?' She wasn't speaking unkindly.

'No, I think it's more than that. I feel that I'd do anything for you. Anything at all.'

She unbuttoned his shirt and slipped it down his arms and cast it away. 'What else do you feel?' she asked.

He took a deep breath and seemed uncertain whether or not to speak. 'Come on!' she whispered. 'Tell me if there's anything else.'

'I feel it's wrong of me to take advantage of Mr Frank's photographs,' he muttered at last. 'I love you too much to do that again. I won't force you to have me against your will again . . .'

'Oh, Harry!' she sighed deeply, a tear starting to roll down her cheek.

'I'll help you get the better of him if I can. I'll do anything I possibly can to help you kick his arse.'

She ruffled his hair and kissed him lightly on the forehead. 'You're lovely!' she replied. 'I'll take you up on that offer if I ever get the chance.'

'Do you want me to stop?' he asked uncertainly, glancing down at his glistening penis, half way in and half way out.

She moved forward and quickly engulfed him. 'We've

started, so we'll finish,' she giggled softly. 'But I do appreciate what you said, Harry. Really I do. I think it's very noble of you. And I believe you mean it, too.'

'I do. I won't take advantage of you again . . . Unless you want me to, of course . . .'

'How many times have you come inside me today?' she whispered in his ear.

'Four,' he said at once.

'Well, then, I'm going to make it five . . . but in a rather different way.'

'How's that?'

'I'm going to make you shoot with both of us sitting absolutely still. No-one is to move about at all. Here, let me show you what I mean. First of all, push into me as far as you can. Then sit still and concentrate on me.'

'I can think of worse things to do . . .'

'Ooh!' she breathed, as he penetrated her to his absolute limit.

She pressed her boobs lightly against his bare chest, folding her arms around his neck and nuzzling his head against the side of her face. Then, slowly but surely, she began to massage him with her vaginal muscles, squeezing and teasing the penis that was buried so nicely within. 'Yesterday Mr Davis-Davies spanked me with a ruler,' she whispered in a caress, feeling him twitch inside her. 'He made me bend over the back of a chair so that my bottom was sticking right up in the air.' There came an even more pronounced twitch. In fact, more of a jerk than a twitch. 'He had this huge, whippy ruler. It was three feet long and very heavy.' Now she detected a very definite jerk. 'First of all he used it to lift my dress right up my back and then remove my knickers.' Another jerk, and then another. And then another two after that. She pressed her thighs together, squeezing him with her quim as hard as she could. Gently she rubbed the very tips of her nipples against his. She smiled as his hands tightened their hold on her buttocks and his body began to stiffen. 'He stood behind me for ages, just holding this wicked looking ruler in his hand and staring at my bare behind.' There was more jerking inside her. 'Then he hit me with it as hard as he could. Right across the middle of my bottom. Time after time. It made me feel incredibly sexy . . . It made me think about *you*!'

The jerking inside her became a series of powerful palpitations, and he began to puff and pant. She ran her fingers through his hair and pressed his face back into her breasts. 'When I got home I looked in the mirror. My rear end and the backs of my legs were bright red. But my pussy felt even hotter.' She took his head in her hands and tenderly kissed his forehead, eyelids and face. 'Harry, my sweet,' she cooed in a whisper, massaging his penis for all she was worth. 'Just think how lovely it would have been if *you'd* been the one laying that ruler across me. Just imagine how lovely it would have been for both of us if *you'd* been the one welting my poor little bum!'

She felt him suddenly tense up inside her, and knew that she'd succeeded. Three very violent jerks were followed by a series of even more violent spurts. The effect on Pauline was instantaneous. Her own orgasm was triggered by the pleasure and satisfaction of feeling him start to gush.

'That was unbelievable!' gasped Harry as they were slipping back into their clothes.

'You're the unbelievable one,' she replied in admiration. 'To come like that for the fifth time, without moving about inside me, or anything like that. I never really expected you to manage it.'

'I feel a bit drained now.'

'I'm not surprised!' she laughed. 'Look, you've absolutely flooded me yet again! It's pouring down my legs! I can't imagine where it all comes from.'

'It depends on the girl– the prettier she is, the better you screw her, and the more you squirt. I bet you've never had any problems getting yourself topped right up to the brim?'

'No, I suppose I haven't . . .'

'I'd better get you home,' he muttered, carefully zipping himself up. 'You've got all that work to do.'

'Crumbs! Don't remind me. Still, I'll have a couple of hours or more before Michael gets back.'

'It'll only take ten minutes to run you home. Come on, Pauline. Tuck those fabulous boobs away and we'll be off.'

Some considerable while later Pauline paused on the pavement, thirty yards from her gate, and sighed wearily. She looked down at her skirt and tried to smooth it with both hands. Oh dear! It was more like a concertina than a skirt, due to the fact that it had spent all afternoon rolled up round her waist. She glanced at her watch. Crikey, it was ever so late! Michael would soon be home – if he wasn't home already. Where on earth had the afternoon gone? Well . . . she supposed she knew the answer to that. She supposed she could hardly deny how the time had been spent.

Two hours earlier Harry had been driving her home. They'd just stopped at a red light on the outskirts of town when these three huge motor bikes had pulled up, one on either side of the scooter and the other behind. Five large, greasy-looking bikers in black leather gear had started to leer and letch at her as she'd sat there in her knickers. She'd prayed, but the lights had stayed red. Then suddenly the pillion passenger to her right had jumped off his seat and grabbed her round the waist. In a trice he'd lifted her up and planted her on the back of the singly occupied bike to her left. 'Vroom! Vroom!' The bike had shot off with her clinging to the driver for dear life. The other bikes had followed close behind, even though the lights had still been on red. Of course, Harry had given chase. But the motor bikes had been far too powerful. Great big 1000 cc jobs. Huge, evil-looking black and chrome beasties that travelled at the speed of light. So the bikers had been able to lose poor Harry after taking two or three sudden turns, leaving her alone, and very much at their mercy.

She closed the front door behind her and dropped the latch. It had been unlocked all afternoon, she realised. It was lucky she'd got back before Michael. He was always telling her off for forgetting about that sort of thing. There'd be time for a quick shower before he came home, if she was lucky. She was certainly in need.

She walked into the kitchen and stopped in her tracks. Lordy! The washing up had been done in her absence. Michael must have been home during the afternoon. Oh, dear! What a mess she'd left for him to sort out! Whatever would he think of her? Crumbs, it was lucky he hadn't paid her an unexpected visit during the morning!

'Hello, Pauline,' Kevin said rather shyly, having come through the door behind her.

'Kevin! What on earth are you still doing here?'

'I've been helping with the housework. I've done the washing up and changed the bed. I've also hung out the washing and hoovered the carpets for you.'

She hugged him warmly. 'How kind of you Kevin! What a sweetheart you are!'

'I was really waiting to see you again,' he confessed, dropping his gaze to he floor.

'I guessed that,' she giggled. 'But it was very nice of you to do all that work for me while you waited.'

'Pauline,' he started uncertainly, shuffling his feet awkwardly as he spoke.

'Yes, what is it?'

'I need to have you again,' he mumbled.

'Oh dear! There really isn't time. Michael will be back any minute.'

'I expect you've been doing it with Harry . . .'

'Well . . . just the once.'

'Only the once in all this time?'

'Yes, only once with Harry . . .'

'Please, Pauline! I'm desperate. Really desperate. Look, my trousers are bursting at the seams!'

'Yes, I can see what you mean,' she said sympathetically. 'But what can I do? Michael's overdue already.' She looked up at the clock on the kitchen wall for confirmation. 'He's usually back by now.'

'It won't take long,' he urged her. 'You'll be amazed how quick I'll be. I'll hardly take any time at all.'

She looked around the room. 'I suppose we could do it in here,' she said slowly. 'By the back door. Then you could nip out that way when you've finished. I suppose that would be okay.'

'Thank God for that!' he gasped, almost sobbing with relief.

She turned away from him to face the wall beside the kitchen door, wriggling and jiggling her mini skirt up into the position it had occupied for all but a few minutes since she'd first slipped it on. Then she reached down and slid the black panties as far as her knees, before placing her hands on the wall and tipping her buttocks up towards him when it was done. 'All yours,' she giggled wickedly, giving him a provocative wiggle as she spoke.

Kevin fought with his zip, cursing under his breath as it refused to budge over the enormous bulge in his trousers. 'Please, God!' he implored. 'Don't let this happen to me!' A split second later it gave way and his throbbing, plum-coloured member shot out like a human cannon ball and stood there, pointing excitedly in the direction of her saucily bared rear end. Eagerly he leant forward and clapped a hand round each sweetly dimpled cheek. 'I've been longing to get my hands on you here,' he panted, squeezing the ample portions of firm, silky smooth flesh rather more roughly than he should. 'I couldn't bear the thought of Harry having all this to himself.'

'Come on, Kevin!' she hissed anxiously over her shoulder, deciding there was neither time nor reason to disillusion him. 'There isn't a moment to lose!'

He released his two-handed grip on her bottom and quickly adjusted his stance so that he was lined up and on the point of effecting re-entry from behind her back. Suddenly there was the crunch of tyres on gravel from the driveway beyond the front door. 'Oh, dear!' she sighed. 'It's Michael. I'm afraid you're too late. You'll have to leave it till another time.'

'I said I'd be quick,' he grunted, lunging forward powerfully and spearing her right up to the hilt in less time than it takes to tell.

'Kevin!' she began to protest in a squeal. Then she stopped, realising that he was already ejaculating fiercely. With his first and only stroke.

'Crumbs!' she gasped, as he continued to unburden himself deep inside her. 'You really were worked up, weren't you?'

'I love you, Pauline!' he moaned. 'I wish I was your husband.'

She screwed her eyes tightly shut and started to shudder and shake. The boiling hot jetstream pouring into her from behind had caused her to climax as well, as was nearly always the case.

'Oh, Sweet Mother!' Kevin groaned. 'This is just so good! I've spent three hours longing for this.'

They heard a key turn in the front door. 'Quickly!' she cried, sliding herself free from him, with some difficulty, and frantically wrenching the kitchen door open. As she did so, she felt a final plume of sperm land wetly and warmly across the middle of her bottom. 'Run as fast as you can!' she urged.

But Kevin needed no bidding. He fled down the concrete path that led towards the back gate, his trousers flapping round his thighs, his hot sticky tonker in hand. 'Evening,' said the next door rose-grower, glancing up as he hurtled by.

Pauline shut the back door with a bang as Michael did the same with the front. 'Where are you, Sugarpie?' he shouted loudly from the hall.

'In the kitchen,' she called back, crossing her fingers. 'Just finishing the washing up.' She glanced down at herself and dived to retrieve her knickers from the region of her knees.

Crumbs, she'd completely forgotten about her state of undress! She tugged her short skirt down as far as it would go, which was about half an inch above the tops of her legs. It would just have to do, she thought. It was so crumpled that it wouldn't pull down any further.

'Well, get up to the bedroom,' yelled Michael. 'I've been day-dreaming about your fat little bum all afternoon. I want a very generous slice of it right now!'

'Oh, golly!' she gulped, casting around vainly for a packet of tissues. 'I won't be a minute,' she called out aloud.

'A minute will be too late,' he shouted. 'If you're not upstairs by the time I've counted to ten, I'll take you wherever you are.'

'It wouldn't be the first time,' she laughed breathlessly, dodging his outstretched hands by a whisker and sprinting athletically up the stairs. Michael stood at the foot, gazing up with husbandly approval at her lightly knickered behind as it bounced from side to side under the hem of her skirt.

She flew into the bedroom and groaned. Oh mother! The box of Kleenex was nowhere in sight. Kevin must have tidied it away. She'd just have to hope that Michael was so pent up and in such a hurry that he wouldn't notice her lamentable condition. Otherwise she'd just have to tell him the truth. Perhaps he'd understand? Perhaps he'd understand if she explained that it was only a case of some very young lad from the office being *so* desperate that she'd simply felt compelled to lend him the use of her buttocks and pussy for a mere twenty seconds or so? To grant him a very temporary loan of her facilities so he could gain much needed relief? She needn't say anything about it having made her come too. Nor of the fact that she'd spent at least eight and a half out of the last nine hours stuffed full of one ramrod-stiff object after another . . .

EPILOGUE

Later that Friday evening Michael went to the pub with his lifelong friend, Clive Calver, leaving Pauline in front of the television, staring blankly at the screen as she wrestled with her thoughts. Thank heavens Michael hadn't noticed that anything was amiss! Three hours earlier, on his return from work, she meant. She'd whipped off her spunk-soaked knickers as he'd pounded up the stairs towards her. Then she'd kicked them out of sight under the bed. Within a matter of seconds she'd been flat on her back, legs wide apart, mentally crossing her fingers as Michael plunged lustily into the soaking-wet privacy of her person. The soaking-wet privacy of her much abused, over-used person. 'You're beautifully oiled!' he'd breathed appreciatively, wasting no time at all in starting to bounce her bottom up and down on the bed. She'd blushed, and groaned inwardly with shame. 'And you feel harder than ever,' she'd whispered, closing her eyes so that he couldn't read what she'd known was written all over her face.

Poor Michael, she said to herself, as she used the remote control to flick from one channel to the next. How could she be so unfaithful to someone she loved so much? Well, she supposed she knew the answer only too well. It had all started last Monday evening when she'd been so wretchedly weak with Jim Browne . . .

The telephone started to shrill and she got to her feet,

245

still deep in thought. 'Hello,' she said down the line.

'Hello, Mrs Peach,' George Franks said with more than a hint of sardonic humour. 'I hope you've had an incident-packed day?'

'What do *you* want!' she gasped in dismay.

'That's not very nice,' he laughed. 'Not after I've gone to such trouble to enrich your sex life.'

'What do you want?' she repeated coldly.

'One final favour.'

'Final?' she asked doubtfully, tugging at the hem of her skirt.

'Yes, final. Final as in finality. As in the end of the road. As in one last request.'

'Then you'll give me the photos? All of them? And the negatives?'

'Yes, that's right.'

'How do I know I can trust you?'

'You don't, of course. But I can't see that you have any alternative. Now then, listen to me very carefully. I shall be a most unhappy man unless everything goes exactly to plan . . .'